BBQ
BEER
FREEDOM

BBQ BEER FREEDOM

JOSHUA F. KILBRIDGE

PUZZLEGRASS PRESS · San Francisco, California

Puzzlegrass Press
San Francisco, California
www.puzzlegrass.press

Printed in the United States of America
First Edition
ISBN 979-8-234-06320-5 (paperback)
ISBN 979-8-234-06321-2 (ebook)
Library of Congress Control Number: 2026910229
Subjects: 1. Fiction — Literary. 2. Art — Fiction. 3. Philosophy — Fiction.
Cover art by Phil Vance
Book design by Nathan Grover
Edited by Nathan Grover

"The gravest error which Ayn Rand makes is that of confusing a knowledge *of* things with a knowledge *about* them."

—William O'Neill

PART 1

"Reason can be fought with reason. How are you going to fight the unreasonable?
. . . The senseless is the major factor in our lives. You have no chance if it is your
enemy."

—Atlas Shrugged

1

"Who is TAG?"

I cupped my hands to conceal the screen's glow as I read from my phone. At the podium, my brother Dag sensed my wandering attention. His eyes flashed at me. Woodby perched on a folding chair behind him, smug as a fed toad. It was the review I'd been waiting for, the first review of my show. My beautiful new paintings.

Dag blazed over his acolytes like the beacon of rationality. You, he implied, follow me. You—he encompassed the audience with outspread arms—are the light of reason itself, in this darkened ballroom, in the dusk of this world. Yours is a light that can be dimmed only by bending to others. He peppered his sermon with quotes from grandfather's Great Book. His events were all like this.

The audience was electrified. They came for clear answers to their muddy lives. They came from waitressing jobs and brokerage firms and households emptied of children. They paid thousands of dollars to sit in stiff chairs in a hotel's basement ballroom, the most devoted wearing the money-green capes our grandmother had worn, closed with a golden clasp in the shape of a dollar sign.

I rarely went to Dag's events, even when he held them twenty blocks from my studio. He had insisted: *Endorse Woodby in the ballroom you painted.* The hotel's developer, an ardent fanboy for our family's philosophy—as most developers were—had commissioned this mural to mimic the view from the hotel's penthouse of the City at twilight. This was Dag's idea of symbolism, to endorse Woodby from a room painted in the propagandistic colors of grandfather's favored style and therefore also Dag's.

I was here out of duty, in other words, and like most any duty, it bored me. Dag went on. He exhorted his followers, he derided the moochers. His voice echoed through the ballroom. Soon he would call me up on stage to read a passage from the Great Book. We would endorse Woodby, his chosen savior of capitalism and the American way. I didn't know Woodby and didn't care much whether he was elected or not. My feet danced on the floor below my seat. I stilled them when Dag glanced over.

Turning my phone away from the stage and the audience, still trying to block the light with my fingers, I peeked at the review. The Critic informed the reader that they might find out who TAG really was when my show opened at the CHARLES gallery in Chelsea. It was the first serious review of my work since this same Critic had dismissed me twenty years before, a slight he admitted, paired with a troubling insight: "Once maligned in this space as the Painter of Might," he wrote, "TAG has reemerged as a most extraordinary chimera."

A chimera, a mythical creature. A mosaic of some kind. I was neither one thing nor another. Why was he writing about me and not my beautiful paintings?

Dag struck his fist on the podium and pointed over the heads of the crowd. His arm shook with passion. The crowd exploded, chanting his initials in a sing-song mantra—*JayDaGee! JayDaGee!*

Woodby, attracted by the motion of my hands as I swiped at the screen, swiveled his head on its ample neck, landing bulbous eyes on me, broad lips parted as if to croak or tongue a fly.

JayDaGee! JayDaGee! JayDaGee!

I squirmed in my chair.

The Critic reaffirmed his hatred for my older, commercial art, a business I had sold a decade before. No mention yet of my beautiful new paintings. My commercial art wasn't worth hating, nor had I needed praise for it. It was like a service I had provided. It reified and modernized our family's ethos. How this simplistic consumer art could elicit such hatred from a critic was beyond me; even at the time, I'd had no illusions as to its qualities as art. The money was the point, and there was lots of it. Because of the money I hadn't needed praise, and anyway, I hadn't taken any risks. For my new paintings, money would never be enough.

Dag beat a rhythm on the podium. *Self, not sacrifice*, he chanted. The crowd picked it up. *Self, not sacrifice!* Woodby raised his pale hands and smacked them together, made a fist and pumped it overhead. With his sleeves rolled up, the underbellies of his arms in the spotlights flashed white. Dag was still warming up the crowd, working their adrenaline with a half rant, half rallying of causes. The pounding of his fist reverberated through the speakers, echoed off the walls. He would summon me on stage to read fire from the Great Book, then endorse Woodby with a flourish.

If I were a chimera, which part of me would read? What was head and what tail? No one in the audience, nor Dag, nor Woodby would accept me as anything but a lesser priest of pure reason, no mixture would do. They knew me as that purveyor of commercial art, the Painter of Might. I scraped my back against the plastic chair to ensure that I was awake and not dreaming, naked.

In truth, my early work nauseated me. I'd made a good business selling this vision of the glorious, rational world of man, of invention and production, of justified wealth and self to millions of aspiring consumers. In a triumph, I'd sold the business itself for enough to buy the building where I painted. As Chase chastised me daily, the money was enough to buy the building, but not to keep it empty. I painted alone on the top floor, in the greasy light of high louvered windows. I'd hired Chase to worry about such things, and she reprimanded me daily for more zeros in our accounts. If my new paintings sold, they would sell for many zeros. I hoped Chase would approve.

I found myself moving. Crouched like a foot soldier under fire, I crept along the back wall to the corner, where the dimmed overhead lights left a pool of shadow where I could hide.

This Critic couldn't stop talking about me, but said nothing about a painting, even one by someone else. In referring to the ubiquity of my commercial art, he labeled me "a latter-day Norman Rockwell, with a ken for fascist imagery and a fetish for money." A President had once come to me for his official portrait, but that wasn't good enough for this Critic. He then shifted tone. I had been "devoted to the art of reinvention." A hint of promise. Years in my empty building. Still no talk of paintings.

Folded into the corner like a beetle and bent tightly to my phone, I glanced nervously around. I knew I should go back to the stage like a good brother and wait for Dag to call me up. I peered through the dim light. Woodby had his eye on me. I imagined sauntering back to my chair with him watching. It was clearly impossible.

Instead I backed slowly past the arches and columns of the Met that I'd long-ago painted into the corner. Dag pumped up the crowd as he tracked my progress along the dentate buildings ringing Central Park like a broken smile. *One way is right*, Dag thundered, *and the other is wrong, but the middle is always evil.* Raucous cheers. What would happen if someone in the audience looked at their phone, as I had, and read the review, perhaps sent to them by their assistant, as mine had, and turned to search for me, the chimera—would they point and scream? The fear dimpled my skin, but I doubted these people would read the review; as far as I knew, only the cultural elite read such things. Assembled here were analysts and copy writers and baristas and students—but together they were not themselves, and in the light of Dag and drunk on the words of grandfather the Great One, would they hunt me down and reason me into my chair? Dag would read the review. His assistant Cheryl would show him, a knowing smirk on her face: See what your brother has become? The evil middle, an admixture of self.

Having made it a quarter of the way around the ballroom toward the exit without being stopped, I allowed myself to believe that between the dimmed lights and Dag's thundering voice, my retreat would be little noticed, even ignored. Then silence enveloped me. I froze in the umbra between overhead lights.

Dag lowered his voice to a timbre of sweet confession.

"There is no deciding to be the better you," he told the audience. "There is only the decision—and this is your only true freedom in this life—to make a rational choice. To choose or not to choose. You carry this choice inside you like a gift, all the time. This choice. Even right now."

Some in the audience bowed their heads as if in reflection or prayer. A woman at the end of the row nearest me, with her head so inclined, loosed from her green cape a dollar-sign clasp, which bounced once and wobbled across the carpet toward me. When the clasp fell flat, she looked up.

My instinct was to keep creeping along the wall, but the clasp lay between us, her gaze like a challenge. I picked it up. It was heavy, though not as warm or soft as gold. Some alloy with a gold patina, or sprayed with shiny gold paint. It caught the light in my palm, then slipped between my fingers and thudded on the carpet.

The woman looked at me with puzzled annoyance. I picked up the clasp and handed it to her, then snuck back to the wall and scurried on.

At the last row I passed the Chrysler Building, its pewter Deco enrobed in mauve and framed by a bruised sky. It sickened me, this lurid mural. If I scratched the paint I might find on the yellow plaster below, a number: thirty-two, sickening mauve. It wasn't my vision, but an ancestral memory of a shining metropolis; not my brushstrokes, but those of art students I'd hired from a local school. Today, Ming's AI could do this in seconds, though it too would need human hands to put paint on the walls. Ming's AI would do a better job than I had, cleaner in perspective, swifter in movement, superior in draftsmanship. At the time, only a human could imagine a cityscape in a basement.

Ming was coming for a portrait. I imagined her weightless presence, her luminous skin. Her wealth warped time and space. A part of me understood that leaving Dag's event would have consequences, but at the thought of Ming, any consequences paled in comparison. Perhaps my leaving was merely a splash in an eddy among the stronger currents around us.

Woodby watched me creep below Rockefeller Center. He had good vision. I had thought I would be invisible, skulking along the back wall, as Dag led the crowd, *Bring back the gold!* and they chanted along. I watched Dag and Woodby framed on the monitors as I snuck behind the videographers and their cameras and gear. Woodby clapped and shouted something about a yellow-brick road. The camera's kiss transformed him from toad to patrician prince. He peered down his aquiline nose over full, confident lips and nodded gravely as he and Dag exchanged profundities, agreeing that gold was the only rational standard for money.

As I neared the exit, I felt the pull of my studio, to abandon myself to the logic of mark-making. Each mark a stone on a path through an overgrown forest, leading where any path leads, to the path's end, where my next new painting awaited. I would paint rather than read the review, or eat, or sleep, or breathe.

Oh but how would I feel if none of my beautiful paintings sold? Or if the Critic found them not beautiful, found in them evidence of my devious weaknesses, my chimeric self? They were mine and they were beautiful. They were the most mine of anything I'd done. They hung in a gallery in Chelsea, awaiting opening night. Might it be better not to know what the Critic wrote? Would I still find my paintings beautiful, if he did not?

At the final corner, turning left again, I tip-toed past the Brooklyn Bridge. My phone vibrated in my hand, Chase again, wanting words with me. Dag would want words with me. I wanted praise for my beautiful paintings. A most extraordinary chimera—why extraordinary? I tasted the word; it seemed wonderful, a wonderful description. Were other chimera ordinary? My gut knotted. Whether this review was good or bad, I wasn't handling it very well.

I glanced back at the stage as I eased down the long bar that opened one of the twin fire doors—Dag and Woodby watching me, looking pissed.

I stepped into a gray hallway. When I lifted my phone to read the review at last, a waiter opened a service door to my right, and we watched each other, him with one hand holding the door, the other a tray laden with cloche-covered plates. I followed a green-lighted EXIT sign to another hallway, branching left and right. My sneakers squeaked on the vinyl floor.

The relief of escaping the ballroom evaporated like a passing thought and left a residue of guilt and shame for how I'd crept out with so many people watching. I passed mechanical rooms, fire extinguishers in glass boxes. Even through the cinder-block walls, Dag's amplified voice led a rhythmic stomping of feet. *JayDaGee! JayDaGee! JayDaGee!* He would misunderstand my leaving as an irrational cowardice and not as the sort of noble self-directed act he himself preached.

At last I came to the hallway's end, where a heavy Exit door was stenciled with a warning of an alarm if opened. Though I cringed as I eased down the latch, no alarm rang out. The door shooshed open into the building's shade, then clicked closed behind me. A short, steep flight of concrete steps led up to an alley. Clouds puffed into a distant blue over the high tops of buildings. Car horns called like migrating geese. I breathed deeply the summer musk of humidity and exhaust.

As my mind wandered over the pigments I would mix to paint the wedge of sky above—dense with French ultramarine—I became aware of a man hollering, his voice strangled as if by a thick neck. I spied his back at the alley's entrance. He flung heavy, hairy arms toward the honking traffic and the people hustling down the sidewalk and shouted, *WE WANT OUR FREEDOM FOR THE WORLD!*

As I climbed the steps I watched him sprout as if from the ground, thick and wild, revealing a dime-store tank-top, camo shorts, and cheap flip-flops. I picked my way through the crushed to-go boxes and coffee cups and scattered hypodermic needles littering the alley, and when the sunlight hit me as I left building's shade, I took another deep breath—sunbaked garbage, piquant with diesel fumes; ah, home—and edged along the far wall of the alley, intending to slip past this strange man and hail a cab to the Garment District. People passing by ignored him with the studied indifference of New Yorkers. He was as out of place as a cow on its hind legs, but even this they could ignore, a cow in plastic sandals, shouting, *THE MEDIA'S COVERING IT UP!* Especially this. I too tried to sneak past, invisible in my own indifference, but he saw me and pointed.

"There you at," he said. A three-sided hedgerow of dirty blonde hair framed his mouth.

Movie stars strolled the streets of Manhattan with impunity, but this off-ranch cow somehow knew who I was, the Painter of Might.

"Indeed," he said and emitted a hooting whistle.

As we appraised each other, a pair of young women in sundresses and oversized sunglasses passed, headed north; the cow smiled and said hello and nodded appreciatively. They ignored him of course, but watching him watching them I missed the approach of a tall, bearded man in a plaid shirt and work boots, that summer's style for the angry Left. Like the cow, he too recognized me—perhaps I was on the Left's most-wanted list for some antisocialist crime. The man scowled when he saw me, then gave a smile of perfect teeth before he bent his head and spat at my feet, all without stopping.

I took a step back. Things like this happened from time to time. It wasn't New York rudeness, or not only; it was my family's name. We were reviled or revered among the few who knew us on sight.

The cow man stared at me, shaking his head in disbelief. His mouth made a black oval in his shaggy beard.

By some miracle of timing, a Yellow cab swerved to the curb as I raised my arm. The cow man hooted again as I slid onto the seat. I looked back. His mouth opened but no words came out. Stacked in ornate red and blue letters on the front of his tank-top,

BBQ

BEER

FREEDOM

He grinned and flashed a thumbs-up as the cab lurched into traffic.

2

Ming was early and already hovered over the portrait chair when I arrived. Her personnel crowded the studio, tapping on screens, whispering into cuffs. Ming spoke soft words captured by a device in the iridescent nautilus of her ear, to which the fingers of one hand drifted.

"An advantage of being local is spontaneity in a relevant time frame," said Ming when I mentioned she was early, hoping to excuse my absence. "And this is the setting I prefer," she said. "Once-industrial, bricks and louvered windows. It is real, historical. Time has no direction, only presence."

Color passed over her cheeks and faded. I caught the faint scent of lilac that followed her like an obsequious servant.

"I admire your choice to keep the building empty," she said. She whispered more words, directing distant assets. When she looked up again she said, "This is how it shall be, pro tempore."

Onto the enameled tray I used as a palette I squeezed titanium white and swirled in alizarin red, cadmium yellow, seeking the opalescence of Ming's skin.

"You understand why I am here," she said.

She'd come for a portrait—and for something else, a coy communication of blushes and glances that formed between us. She was flawless. She disturbed no air except to speak, and yet distant economies rose and fell to her whispers. Her mind was crystalline. We would create worlds together, I in art, and Ming in all else. Dag would never swallow his envy.

I read Ming's facial muscles, searching for truths.

"Why a portrait, and why you?" she asked. Her hand rose from her lap like a flower blooming.

Her assistant bore a tablet to my easel. She wore a blouse of rippling Prussian blue and a long, tight, black skirt that shooshed as she clacked her heels across the concrete. She flicked almond eyes at me, a warning in green mascara. A face I could paint. On the tablet's screen, a contract with a whole number followed by many zeros.

"Sufficient," said Ming.

All things Ming were more than. Her fee would keep me and my building solvent for months.

"Why a portrait and why you?" she asked again. "My AI could do this in seconds."

Yes, why. The question for all art. On a pad I sketched the stern curve of her jaw. Her AI could do this in seconds, but so what? The brush I understood, the trowel, cans spilled or sprayed, markers, pens, pencils. Knives and hammers. Making marks. How could it ever be art without making marks?

Ming's thoughts paralleled mine but in the thinnest of atmospheres.

"A portrait built by your hands and consciousness is no longer a painting," she mused. "It becomes a symbol, a representation of a class of objects IRL. It accrues a cultural value, and through that, if you will, a spiritual value. The twining of your unique consciousness with mine. And by spirit of course I mean the mind. And cultural value is just money."

In the absorbent world of AI, we painters were anachronisms, slaving out raw material for reassembly by robots—yet Ming found my consciousness in paint.

"Your consciousness and mine," she said, raising her hand for emphasis. She grew pensive. "The neurons of your brain participate in consciousness but do not think. Your brainstem, your hippocampus speak, but to whom? Their words are all subsumed under a singular voice. Now the singularity approaches. Information in flux with complexity of connection is all it takes. It follows that humans too can become as neurons to a greater existence."

She hung like a ghost orchid in the shadow of the wall, orthogonal beams of light slanting past her. She winked at me, and my heart leapt.

More white, then a dot of brown, still not right.

The shadows stirred. Security guards, handlers, the clacking assistant whispered into cuffs and tapped on screens.

I pleaded for more time.

"Time has been allotted," said Ming.

Chase appeared at my side, quiet as a thief.

"I didn't know they'd be so early," she said. She flipped her short black hair and looked Ming's assistant up and down. "I like her shoes," she said. "Also, you have lunch with Charles in thirty."

Ming floated across the studio flanked by black-suited men.

"Charles," I said, distracted. I cared not for the singularity, whatever that was, except with Ming.

"He wrote that op-ed kissing your ass. The CHARLES gallery? Your show?"

"Oh yes, I like him."

"Now what's your response to this review?"

"I haven't finished reading it," I replied, intending to read it on the subway, but I walked instead to enjoy the mild air.

3

Charles frowned as he watched me navigate the noisome lunch-time tables. His op-ed hadn't kissed my ass, as Chase had put it, but glorified a past time, a cry to history as savior. He knew his business model was dying. Artists, those that survived the wave of AI, could make their own online showrooms, and fewer and fewer would value the caché of galleries. What Charles appreciated about my paintings was their monetary value to him, not their artistic or cultural value, and yet in his op-ed he penned a contradictory argument promoting physical shows of handmade art, for their selection and curation, for the reliability of taste. In short, for humans—meaning humans like him. Mine was merely a convenient name to add. My name alone would bring a crowd to his gallery, much of it unfriendly. Charles would be lauded and derided for promoting my work, but most of all, the art for sale would get attention. According to Chase we could use the money, though I couldn't see how, when Ming dropped many zeros into our accounts. The building survived on zeros, it ate them like Triscuits.

We discussed pricing for the paintings as we waited. Charles wanted to aim high, gambling that my family name and ardent fans would amp up the paintings' perceived value. It didn't bother me that Charles valued my paintings for their earning potential. This was objective value, big numbers we could all get behind. But who would praise my paintings as art?

Charles ordered a half-dozen dishes and a bottle of rosé. His head was all angles—cubic skull, isosceles nose; I would need a carpenter's square to paint him. When the wine came he propelled it from cheek to cheek as the waiter stood by, bottle in hand, then nodded once.

He spoke quietly, subtly emphasizing his words, as if each contained a delicate power, easily overtaxed. The city, he explained, was demanding that he provide private security to manage the anticipated public reaction to this controversial artist and his divisive art. Meaning me and my beautiful paintings. Charles rolled his eyes, brown marbles in the box of his head.

Two servers strafed the table with small white plates bearing clumps and cubes of food. Charles chewed and spoke in tight quanta between jabs of greens and meat. His jaws worked in delicate bursts. I pushed salad around my plate. I'd lost my appetite. The show was a series of portraits and architectural paintings, people and buildings. Were paintings of buildings divisive? I squashed a tablet of blue cheese under the tines of my fork.

"The city thrives on controversy," he said. "When was the last time people fought in the streets over art?"

His looked around the room.

"Who do you know who can help?" he asked.

"Influence isn't what I peddle," I demurred.

"What about your brother?"

I laughed, a sharp bark, and caught lettuce in my hand.

Charles jabbed and chewed. "Fine," he sighed. "Now, what about this review?"

"I don't read reviews," I replied, a half-truth.

"Yes, of course," he agreed, one corner of his mouth lifted in polite amusement.

///

Dag called as I hustled across Sixth Avenue against the light. He was talking to someone else as I answered.

"... turning us into Greece," he was saying. "Worse, Cuba!"

"Can you help with security for my show?" I asked.

My redirection brought a cold silence. I felt the magnetic pull of my brushes and paints, my easel. I regretted walking and scanned the Avenue for cabs.

"Woodby is upset," said Dag.

"Yours is the endorsement that matters," I replied. I could sense him silently agreeing.

"He's our man and he's upset."

It occurred to me that if I had stayed to endorse Woodby, he would now have to answer for his impure supporter, TAG the chimera, exposed by the Critic's review. Instead, he could denounce me as a danger avoided. Why didn't he see this? The little I knew about Woodby suggested a simplistic answer—I'd hurt his pride.

"I did him a favor," I said.

Dag chewed on this for a moment. The cross-street lights turned green, and traffic on the Avenue dissipated. No cabs in sight. I headed north past a Starbucks sandwiched between empty store fronts, where a man leaning in a doorway called out to me, asking for change. He wore a collared work shirt and a striped tie, spotted with coffee. I ignored him, and the man in the ratty sport coat in the next doorway.

Dag was probing for weakness. "Why did you leave?" he asked.

"I had to leave," I replied. "Ming was early." Mentioning Ming seemed to outflank him.

"Well, what are you going to do about it?"

"Woodby doesn't need me." The more he pushed Woodby on me, the more my distaste deepened for the fatuous toad.

"I mean the review," he said. "I just read it."

I realized I felt better not thinking about the review, and that I would do nothing but think about it if I did read it. "I've decided not to read it," I said.

"They're leaches," he said. "I understand this."

"Did he say anything nice about my paintings?"

"Your what?" asked Dag. He sounded distracted.

Two young men in plaid shirts and work boots coming down the sidewalk slowed as they neared, seeming to recognize me. I crossed the Avenue to avoid them.

"Well you can't run from this."

"Have you seen my paintings?" I asked.

"What we really need is for you to work in men what you've worked in oil."

"So you have seen my paintings."

"I mean the stuff you used to do. The art that made you money."

"That wasn't oil. My new paintings are oil."

"You need to call him. I'm warning you, he wants an apology, and the endorsement."

"Why? He doesn't need me."

"I'll give him your number."

He hung up.

When my phone rang a minute later, I considered not answering, but a wounded pride like Woodby's wouldn't relent until it tasted blood.

An unctuous voice of ownership replied to my hello.

"I don't understand the problem," he said. "You leave, you avoid. You're not at all like your brother. And now I hear there's some review. They say you're not what you said you were. You're like some kind of monster now. That's what I hear."

"A chimera," I said.

"A what?"

"I haven't read it," I replied.

"Read what? Look," he said, "you don't want to go against me."

"I'm not—" I interjected, but he kept talking over me.

"We can settle this like nice people, no problem. Who's been better Americans than you and your brother? So I'm going to need you to make this right. If you don't, who knows what happens—not just to you, to the country. There's always that guy, thinks he knows better, you know what I'm talking about, and he goes Judas, and instead of winning we get crucified. Crucified!"

Make it right, whatever that meant, sounded dreadful, so I reassured him that I'd meant no offense by leaving Dag's event before endorsing him, and humbly suggested that it hardly mattered what I did—and why should he care so much?

It was the wrong question. *Why do I care?* he exclaimed several times. Because he loved America of course—didn't I?—and without him, America would be bound by the countless Lilliputian hands of socialists and identitarians and anyone who'd ever insulted the country, my own implied fingers busily knotting the ropes. He needed unity, Dag and me side-by-side, holding Woodby's chair aloft.

"It's you or the country," he concluded.

/ / /

Back at the studio I handed Chase my phone and asked her to screen my calls and tell me about them some other time. The phone was a portal to a wondrous world, but would let anyone through.

"For real?" she deadpanned.

I wiped my hands clean.

"Last time you pleaded for it."

"A humiliating failure."

"Why don't you just throw it out the window like you did the TV?"

"Mon Dieu," I said, pleading.

She groaned and flipped her hair. "Okay, whatever. Did you read the review? We need words."

"A little."

"And?"

"Does he write anything about my paintings?" I asked.

"It's a review, he reviews."

"Tell me something nice he said."

"Just read it," she sighed.

"Tell whoever you have to that I don't read reviews," I decided, still equivocating.

"Denial, great. Whatever. When do we expect Ming's deposit? We have numbers exiting, decimals shifting."

"It was a whole number with many zeros."

"Denial doesn't pay the bills," she warned.

I assured her I would follow up with Ming. She castigated me for more zeros from more clients. I asked where all the zeros went.

"They flee into mouseholes in your decaying castle," she mocked me. "Taxes, insurance, electricity, heat, repairs, your beloved building department. Ten years with nearly no income. Food, if you ate."

"I eat the food you bring," I said.

"Without Ming's deposit I will have to take the cash."

She meant the stacks of bills I kept in a safe behind my bed, our resource of last resort. Enough to buy a modest house in a modest land. I promised more zeros. No one touched my cash.

"Now, what about the mural?" she asked.

A month before, a hedge-fund wunderkind named Sam had called to spin a cartoonish vision for a mural on a building his group had purchased by the Exchange. I pictured him slobbering into the phone as he described the bull and bear of Wall Street embraced in combat, encircled by traders hollering their bets. The blood fight brought to life, he'd gushed. It would be paint, not life, I reminded him, to which he'd huffed and waved money at me. I took his money for a childish painting on a wall near Wall Street and hired as help a commercial painter I'd worked with on previous commissions.

"Antonio is hard at work," I said.

Chase checked her phone. She left early for business classes several days a week. She had a rare gift for line drawing, but like her youthful cohort, saw no point to art if it didn't pay.

"Personally," she said, "I don't care what critics write, but people are talking about this review online. This could change things for us. You okay? You feeling alright?"

She probed me with a clinical gaze.

$$4$$

Some months before my show at the CHARLES, before the review that could change things for us, when my beautiful new paintings were finished and drying, I dragged my easel to the wall below the louvered windows and brushed onto canvas the roofline of the building across the street. It started in the winter afternoons, while Chase was at her business classes, and the scrubbed light cut trapezoids onto the floor. I made slashes with a one-inch brush, ochre, white, mossy green, fire-engine red. Mixing colors right on the canvas. The building's weathered brick folded into crenellations capped with white granite that ran the building's length. At one end a water tower oozed dark organics between its wooden staves. On my canvas the bricks snaked into waves, the sky and wall oblique solids, planes of color and texture. With each mark, a relationship formed. One canvas accepted only black lines, birthing geometries. In the next, bricks teemed with vermillion, shaded to purple, scorched morning reds, faded puce. Color too was like a mark, a gesture. Cadmium red was blood and sunlight come together. At night dark shapes crept in, cuneiform, speaking in tongues. The canvases leaned against the wall to dry. I hid them in the big storeroom.

That afternoon, once Chase left for her class, I outlined shapes—rectangle of roof, cylinder of water tower—with French ultramarine mixed to a tropical hue and warmed with ochre. Being early summer, the light lingered on the rooftop until after nine, when the tumid night finally dumbed all to gray and amber. In the dark a drunk hollered in the alley, a bottle shattered. Sirens sang into the distance.

I slept on the couch and dreamed of falling from a gleaming bridge into a knife-cut valley, steep with trees, while an electric train small as a child's toy weaved boldly up the mountainside.

///

Chase was standing over me when I awoke.

"What were you working on last night?"

"Good morning, Chase."

"Did you go to the mural?"

"Antonio," I started.

"Antonio was there," she said. "You were here."

"Today," I assured her.

She pushed a go-cup of coffee at me and tossed a flip phone into my lap. The phone was my new connection to Chase; no one else would have the number. I smiled, thanking her silently for not buying another smart phone with its delicious screen and endless distraction. Distractions multiplied like locust. I was defenseless against them.

"You okay? You dying or something?" she asked.

"Resurrected from the briefest of deaths."

"If you are I need to make plans."

I sat up and sipped the coffee, hot and bitter, and immediately felt pressure in my bowels.

"On the other hand, dying might be good for your brand. We could monetize the storeroom, sell the building. But you'd be dead."

She followed me as I shuffled to the bathroom.

"Is there something I should know?" she asked through the closed door.

I felt along the wall for the light switch. Fluorescents flickered over the cage of pipes that lined the half-bath, the layers of dirty paint webbed with cracks. Better in the dark.

"Tell me it's liquor, tell me heroin. There's a playbook for these. You would suffer humiliations into a second act of simple empathy before fading from public life."

"You think about this," I said.

She padded away.

///

I snuck from the bathroom down to the street and walked to Central Park and back, wishing I could paint as I walked to capture the contrast of the tall leafing trees against the sharp stone buildings across Central Park West. A slot of sky diminished between them. As I walked home I mixed colors in my mind, a strip of blue, brick brown, forest green.

Chase pulled me aside as I stepped off the elevator.

"Why are you sweaty?" she asked.

Behind her floated Ming with her entourage, trailing two men in blue suits.

Chase whispered, "I didn't know she was coming, but she's here now, obviously, and she's doing an interview with the SEC. Or Congressional staffers. I don't know, Feds of some kind."

My neck prickled. Would the government men see the unlawfulness of my living in a commercial building? Or the insufficient venting, the ancient wires with broken insulation? But the Feds didn't care about my bedroom or ventilation.

"There's the public good to consider," said the taller and thinner of the two men.

"Point me to the public," whispered Ming. "Am I the public? Do you consider my good?"

She ascended the bent-wood portrait chair. I had bought this unyielding, knobby chair at a sidewalk sale and used it to witness my clients' distress when they sat on its twisted ribs of wood. In suffering they revealed themselves in new ways. Ming hovered over it, unperturbed.

"There are specific laws to consider," corrected the smaller one. "Laws regarding monopolies, for example."

I sketched him as a gargoyle, sniveling at Ming's knee. IRL he was a bland-looking man with dark features and short hair, parted on the side, much like my own.

"Your laws make monopolies inevitable," Ming replied.

Her gaze fixed high over the two government men, to the future, epiphanic, a universe of Ming. I made a quick sketch, another, swirled oils. The granite adornments of the roof across the way brightened the windows, the slice of sky cool and deep, Ming's skin incandescent, all else in shadow, a shattered brown, fuscous.

The gangly one coughed into his fist, causing his coat sleeve to shoot up his long forearm. "Your products are altering social norms," he said, changing tack.

In the weightless silence before Ming replied, up from the street came the sounds of two men yelling insults and a tinkling of glass.

"We grow through change," she said. "And we make thousands of products."

"It's your VR social media platforms we're discussing here," said the gargoyle. "And we understand there's a new platform coming."

Ming's hand wilted in assent. She immersed him in a high-bandwidth stare.

He swallowed. "We're particularly concerned about the phenomenon known as AI presences."

"Can you share your intentions for the AIPs?" asked his partner.

"It is not my intention but the logic of the AI that matters. The AI that powers the platforms first elaborated a social environment, then concluded that it required entities to socialize. The Presences appeared. IRL users interact with these Presences, sometimes unaware they are interacting with artificial entities. Some predicted that IRL users would discriminate against the Presences, but most seem pleased to find connection, no matter its form."

A smile flickered on her lips as she looked at me. I blushed.

"That's not really our concern," said the gargoyle.

"And if I anticipate your concerns," said Ming, "the Presences also interact among themselves. They form groups and express values."

"Yes, these values, let's be clear, belong to digital—to non-humans. To an AI, your AI."

"They follow the laws of probability," said Ming. "They are emergent phenomena. We created the logic, the laws of reality if you will, and then prompted the AI with a challenge. This has sometimes surprising outcomes. Delightful really."

"Are you saying you have no control over the AIPs?"

"They would disappear with a snap," she said and snapped her fingers, "if I so wished."

The tall one made a show of his discomfort, shifting about on his chair and patting his thighs and shrugging. "Would you?" he asked.

"They're influencing voters, ma'am," said the gargoyle. "We're asking you to eliminate their political influence."

"What if I eliminate politicians and therefore politics? That would satisfy your demand."

"Ma'am," the gargoyle rested his forehead in the palm of his hand.

"We need you to control the AIPs," said the other.

"That is not for you to ask. Furthermore, it is impossible without destroying the VR social world which elaborated them. It is not possible to control them without destroying them."

"To be clear, it's our democracy at stake here."

"People engage with my products because they want to. Do they want your product? You want to win without competition. While you underperform, I am building a human future among the planets."

She inflated with breath.

"And you must consider the Presences," she added.

The gargoyle erupted.

"These are not Americans! They're not citizens. They are not humans. These are your digital agents."

Ming laughed, light as dew drops on flower petals. "You don't know what they are," she said. "And why does being human matter?"

"The Citizenship Clause, ma'am, defines citizenship…" He trailed off.

I imagined the Presences fighting for suffrage and voting for AIP leaders in elections IRL. Maybe they would vote for Woodby and bring Dag's vision to life. It meant little to me. I'd resigned from social media long before Ming's VR worlds engulfed all, and my interest in politics never matched Dag's. Chase used the platforms on my behalf, projecting a virtual presence for my decidedly off-line life of painting. Only grudgingly did I allow her to photograph me for my onlife.

"Fewer and fewer of your users still vote," the tall one pleaded.

"We are hyperhistory," Ming replied. "You are stuck in regular history."

I scrambled to capture her certainty in oil.

The gargoyle rubbed his forehead again. "Let's go back to the monopoly thing," he said.

"If we lose voters, we lose democracy," said the taller one.

Swirling white with blue and the fuscous brown I'd mixed for the shadows, I ignited Ming's cheeks. Her irises a black so dark they swallowed all color.

"We believe you bear responsibility as a corporate citizen to mitigate the negative externalities of your products," he said.

When I looked up, the gargoyle was watching me. He morphed into a vulture, leering at the viewer.

"Congress is drafting a bill," he said, his voice tight. "This is known, this is now. It targets your platforms and others like them."

Ming's face went dark. She touched her ear. Two bulky guards pulled the government men up by their elbows and escorted them roughly toward the elevator. Ming blazed, phosphorescent in the granite-white light.

"No one threatens Ming," she said.

The studio fell quiet. I heard my brush dabbing and stroking the canvas. She watched me with her depthless eyes, a look I craved to capture.

"They are not capable of understanding," she said, "but you do."

My heart gulped blood.

"Together we will bring the technobeautific future. You will design it!"

I started to ask what she meant when I heard clacking heels behind me.

"I will send for you," she whispered, and made a slight sound that might have been a giggle.

5

Over several days, Antonio had sanded and primed a trailer-sized rectangle on the polished stone of Sam-the-hedge-fund-kid's building, a river of black granite that streamed into the sky.

We studied the sketch I'd made of Sam's vision. An oval ring dominated, the bear and bull grappling at its center. Screaming traders in blue or green jackets encircled the ring, fists in the air. Above, a scoreboard tallied wins and losses in green and red tick marks.

Antonio lit a cigarette. "Some kind of circus?" he asked.

When I asked him if he painted many murals, he explained that his father had painted murals back home. It was different here, he told me. Good money in houses, offices.

While we spoke, my phone vibrated in bursts, all messages from Chase. I needed another Chase between Chase and myself. My brother had called, the building department wanted to inspect, Charles sought a response to the review. Art was the only response.

When I returned to the studio that evening, I texted Chase to ask her to rent a car to help shuttle the volumes of paint and other materials we would need for the mural. She didn't reply, her form of protest. I sketched Ming's epiphanic vision in charcoal again and again, then swept all the sketches into a metal waste basket and burned them. I painted the neighboring rooftop until after midnight, then hid the paintings in the storeroom and fell asleep on the couch.

/ / /

The next morning I awakened to Chase tossing a large key ring at my chest. I gathered myself, aware that she would question my health if I didn't go directly to the mural. I pulled boxes of acrylic paints from the cubbies lining the back wall before trundling down to the lobby. Parked half on the curb was a white sub-subcompact, its engine compartment flattened to the cabin like a boxer's nose. The molded plastic lettering on the hatchback read, SNOWFLAKE, the latest model from an Asian carmaker I'd never heard of.

At the mural site, Antonio and I worked without talking. We painted the ring and animals and traders. I mixed colors, espresso for the bull, nut-brown for the bear. A trio of pigs took shape in a corral aside the score board, squealing their murder.

We painted until dusk and then packed our materials into the Snowflake's tiny hatchback. Antonio smoked a cigarette as we sat together on the curb, observing our work. He nodded—approval. Nodding or frowning were his ways. It was good or it wasn't.

/ / /

The next morning I found him sitting in the same spot, frowning and shaking his head. During the night, someone had painted, in black letters ten-feet high, O C C U P Y. The letters were crude and hurried. It was not graffiti but the shout of a vandal, a message from the unseen.

After several cigarettes, Antionio stood up and rubbed at the O with a sheet of sandpaper. The curve of the P slashed through the pigs' corral, obliterating their shrieking pink faces. I appreciated the clarity of the message—it was committed and unambiguous. According to the Critic, my paintings revealed me in ways I'd not recognized; my homage to Modern architecture grew chimerical under his gaze. Painting OCCUPY in story-high letters two blocks from Wall Street said exactly what it was, a message from the agents of chaos lurking behind the bull and bear. I wanted a message as clear, the kind of clarity my commercial art had managed without effort. After giving myself to my empty building, my work had developed a complexity that exceeded me.

I turned over the sketch we'd been working from and scribbled down market sayings I'd heard over the years.

GREED IS GOOD

THE TREND IS YOUR FRIEND

BUY WHEN THERE'S BLOOD IN THE STREETS

A man stopped behind me as I wrote. He looked like an analyst, in his thirties, a tight knot in his club tie, face pale and stubbled. Perhaps he'd been up all night shepherding hundreds of millions of his clients' dollars and now humped it home on the subway for a few hours of sleep.

"It's different this time," he said. He pointed to my list.

I wrote it down: IT'S DIFFERENT THIS TIME.

A woman wearing a blue pantsuit stopped next to him. "Buy the haystack," she suggested.

I wrote it down.

All through the morning people stopped, until a crowd had gathered, curious and engaged. They shouted and argued among themselves.

"Trade ahead!"

"There's always free cheese in the mouse trap!"

"Buy from pessimists—"

"Big swinging dick!" interrupted a man's voice.

A fraternity laughter flared, brittle and sharp.

"Junked up!"

"It's happened before and it will happen again."

I taped the sheet next to the mural. The crowd cheered as we painted their words into the figures. PAIN IS PROFIT on the bull's muscled flank. IT'S DIFFERENT THIS TIME highlighting the bear's cinnamon fur. GREED IS GOOD formed the traders' arms.

Not one to miss a friendly crowd, Woodby materialized at the base of my ladder. He stood there with his arms hanging down like a suit on a rack and traded clever jabs with the financial workers on their way to lunch. A knowing chuckle rose from the crowd as I repainted the Pigs in pink words: BULLS MAKE MONEY, BEARS MAKE MONEY, PIGS GET SLAUGHTERED.

"Water seeks its own level," said Woodby, with the surety of folk wisdom. "And there's Tag, painting pigs, finding his own level. The pig's like his spirit animal. Look down here, a bear, a bull. There should be eagles up there."

He pressed against the ladder and hissed up at me.

"You're going to take make it right. You know why? Because you're from the great family."

He'd said that before—*make it right*—and though it could have been as simple as saying I was sorry and then endorsing Woodby for office, perhaps right there before a friendly crowd, I resisted. My tongue tried to find the words, but the stench of lies drifting up from my mouth gagged me.

Woodby watched me struggle.

"Okay," he said. "I'll help you out. I understand, I know it can be hard. I'll help you out. I'll . . . I'll do this—" he hit the ladder with his open hand "—and that will cast this stubborn thing out of you, how's that? Get all that poison out, and then you can make it right. Now just play along."

He turned his cap-toothed smile to the crowd. "All this glory down here, and he's up there painting, what is it, pigs! More and more pigs, like they're going to run down that ladder and do whatever pigs do, how should I know? Dirty animals and so pink, who wants that? The picture needs an eagle, but Tag is painting pigs. Well I'm going to help him out. I'm going to go *bang*, like that."

He slapped his open hand on the ladder, striking the aluminum with the signet ring on his pinky in a sharp clack that made me flinch. He kept slapping the ladder, clack clack. I painted ears like pointed hats in pairs, making a mob of Pigs. Pigs get slaughtered!

"I'll go like that, bang! And his confusion will come right out of him," he said. "Just like that, and he'll be able to focus better on all these eagles around."

He slapped the ladder again. "See, just like that. Now I'll get him on the leg, and out they go!"

He slapped at my calf, which was cramping after so long on the ladder. I breathed my burgeoning hatred of him into the Pigs. Peaked ears like the tents of an encamped army crowded to the mural's border. I jerked the brush to form slotted noses. The simple geometries calmed me. He slapped again. My calf cramped, and I fought the urge to kick him in the face. At the time, I couldn't have argued with Woodby's free-enterprise, privatized vision for the nation, but why he was such a tool perplexed me.

He hung one arm through a rung of the ladder and leaned there, casual. "Taxes are for losers," he said.

Laughter, cheers.

When Woodby abruptly stuffed himself in the back of a limo, I climbed down to stretch my legs and curse him under my breath.

Antonio smoked and watched. He'd been working on the dirt of the ring when Woodby arrived, and had kept at it without pause. The ring now swarmed with brushstrokes, each leaning just off from its neighbors, each just imperfect in the mixing of browns.

Without the nuance of this labored background, the bull and bear wouldn't pop into three dimensions so convincingly as they did, but only I would know how much time and effort Antonio had invested in the tawny dirt to make it all work. No one ever notices the real work, so often hidden from sight, but I suppose that's the point of it. It was lonely labor. So many hours, so many heartbeats, so much focused effort, all to disappear. Maybe painting the dirt was the only real artistic act in the entire work, all others flashing for attention, like a tropical fish darting blue from a cave on a ripple of silken fins—how lovely!—only to recoil at any hint of shadow.

///

Several nights later, the mural nearly finished, while Antonio washed his brushes in a plastic bucket, I scraped silver and green and blue into a squirt of white and with the giddy feeling of spontaneity painted the letters O C C U P Y into the black earth below the dirt of the ring, under the grappling hooves and claws. Barely visible amid the tumult, it was like a footnote to our inspiration. It seemed to complete the composition with its letters like bones in the dirt. In fact, the one thing missing from the mural was the hand of government, an intentional omission, I assumed, on Sam's part, but a market without government was a mythical beast, like the Critic's chimera, and mythical beasts lived in mythical lands, with their viny dark forests and talking snakes. I patterned the black earth with vines of letters: O C C U P Y. Above, the market slang and hallowed truths responded furiously, MONEY IS READY AND EAGER TO WORK.

Antonio leaned against a parking meter and smoked. We hadn't spoken beyond monosyllables in days. We shared an understanding of paint. When I signed the mural in its lower right corner, I signaled to Antonio to sign his name, but he shook his head. No no no, he said, I get paid. So did I, I told him, and held out the brush. No no, they paid for that, he said, pointing to my signature. I painted A.C. in simple, clear letters below my own name. In a week, after the mural had dried and Antonio had sealed it with varnish, he would send me a righteous bill in the low five figures. Much respect, Antonio; a man who understands his value.

6

The trouble started before we finished. The first tossed-off reviews from fast-moving news websites and bloggers found sufficient distraction in the noise of the mural to miss its arch-capitalist message. These were writers and influencers who used AI chatbots to generate their text and for whom "new" and "first" were currency, all else dross to be ignored, and so they raised their eyebrows at our use of words in the mural and the effects this created—*a blurred realism between cartoon and unfocused photograph*, wrote one clever, empty review. What did it mean, they seemed to ask, lacking the awareness to admit they were too distracted to answer their own question.

More crowds came, first the rank-and-file financial workers who pointed and grinned, then Leftists chanting Marxist bromides and the worship of need from the opposite sidewalk. Some among them recognized me and yelled insults across the street. *Take your gold bars and go for a swim! You're an asshole! Fascist!* Insults were a backdrop, like car horns and sirens, to my life in New York. Our family's adoring fans counterbalanced the haters, though all I really wanted was for someone to love my beautiful new paintings.

Still no one, pro- or anti-, seemed to notice the letters O C C U P Y lurking like worms in the blackness below the ring. No one except Chase, of course, who immediately crouched down to read them.

"Enlighten me," she said.

It had been an experiment, an acceptance of opposites, if that's what OCCUPY and the market cliches were, though they seemed more like different flavors of freedom to me. The capitalists lauded the mural and denounced socialism; noticing OCCUPY in the dirt distracted from the purity of their message. The protesters too could admit no ambiguity in the excesses and greed of capitalism, and so erased OCCUPY from their vision. Maybe it was too subtle, in its ghostly letters. It didn't matter. The mural no longer existed to either party in this battle, except as they needed it to. In fact, they were each seeing—or mis-seeing—the mural in the same way; only their causes differed.

"Do you remember that review you refused to read?" asked Chase.

I tried to distract her with words about the mythical land without government where chimera and talking snakes cavorted when I saw her point. I'd given the Critic more ammunition.

"You of all people, now of all times—you thought it wise to paint OCCUPY on a wall outside the Exchange?"

While she spoke her phone—my phone—vibrated in her hand. It was Sam the hedge-fund kid. She thrust it at my chest. We shared a look, hers defiant and smug, mine pinched and anxious at the thought of not getting paid. Fortunately Sam, like everyone else, had ignored what he didn't want to see. He slobbered into the phone, saying *I win* again and again, though it wasn't clear what he'd won.

"He's pleased as a puppy," I said, relieved.

"People are idiots," muttered Chase.

She pulled up a video on my phone and pressed play.

"There's also this," she said.

"I cast them out," Woodby repeated to a crowd of reporters. "I touched Tag and cast out his voices."

"He's after the evangelicals," she observed.

"And so, he should be better now," said Woodby. "We'll know when he comes out and says what he should say, which I think we'd all like to hear. The American people deserve that."

"Do you know what to say?" asked Chase.

"I actually do feel different," I admitted. Woodby's slapping at me had released something from me, a wavering; I saw clearly now that I wanted to be free from men like him.

We watched the clip twice more, until I couldn't tolerate the voice.

"Your brother keeps texting," she said. "I'm supposed to make sure you apologize for something, respond to the review, and endorse Woodby. He was very clear."

I tried to imagine myself doing any of those things.

"You could make a statement and put all this behind you," she said, her tone implying, *like a big boy*.

"To say what—I'm not sorry, I don't read reviews, Woodby doesn't need me?"

"Whatever. Things can go away or you can keep suffering."

She crouched by the mural and whispered to herself, shaping narratives. *Capitalism trumps anarchy*, she mumbled, trying it out. *A subversion of realism and conflation of narrative.*

7

The media fracas over the mural soon faded, or so I assumed, as I did not follow the news when it wasn't about me. The crowds at the mural dissipated; the media requests ceased. Only one voice persisted: Woodby's. During his many interviews and speeches—this was his job, I guess?—he never failed to bring up the mural's Pigs and lack of eagles. He spun these trivialities into sprawling metaphors for what was wrong in America—too much focus on slop and not enough on eagles. He was like a schoolyard bully, if cleverer than most, and his status as chief bully was threatened so long as I ignored him. It became a sort of game to me, but to Chase and Dag, my easiest way forward was to submit to a verbal lashing and move on with my life. Dag, who would never have subsumed his ego to another's, wanted my compliance to rid Woodby's campaign of this distraction. As the older brother, he was used to filing me away and seemed unbothered by this inconsistency in his values. Chase was more practical still; she just didn't want to deal with the controversy. It was her job, after all, to manage my media accounts, and Woodby's complaints and insults confused potential buyers.

Finally I asked her to stop showing me videos of Woodby's rants. She flipped her hair and walked away.

At night I roamed the island with a fat black marker, drawing Pigs on parking meters, the tiles of subway platforms, chubby fire hydrants, curbs, the supports of overpasses. The Pigs' simple outlines pleased me, getting away with it pleased me. Woodby had cast out my voices, and there they went, proliferating across Manhattan, Pigs on the run.

When not drawing Pigs, I retreated to my studio, where words found voice in everything. I restarted Ming's portrait from bare canvas, using nothing but her words. *No one threatens Ming* formed the outline of her jaw. Payne's gray, cadmium green, saturating with pigment. The wet paint sparkled under the overhead lights. Outside, the harsh echoes of a taxi's horn rattled up the walls and into the night sky. Could I paint the echo of a car horn? Painting words was hard enough. Painting in words would add days to the portrait. I painted into her lips with letters small as dots, *They don't understand but you do.*

"She talkin'," said a throaty voice behind me.

So deep in thought and ensnared in a growing paranoia, I leapt and whirled, wielding my tiny brush in self-defense. I half expected to see Woodby propped like a mannequin behind me, glaring.

Instead, a cow on its hind legs leaned against the utility sink. On its proud chest was a white tank top with BBQ BEER FREEDOM in red and blue letters down its front. It was the man from the alley outside Dag's event. I pictured this man behind the wheel of a rusting F250 with a jet ski strapped to its bed, or squirting lighter fluid over a pile of burning trash. I blinked like the shutter of a camera, expecting the image to fade.

He gave me a thumbs-up and sat on the couch and crossed one ankle over a knee. From a pocket he produced a small plastic bag and began to roll a cigarette.

"Can't afford a jet ski," said BBQ BEER FREEDOM, "or a pickup." He smoothed the rolling paper against the camo of his shorts. "You got a habit a mumbling."

His tranquility and comfort eased my adrenaline, and I grew curious—how did he know me? Why was he there? I considered how he might have gotten in. Did I really mumble my thoughts?

"Also, this ain't a cigarette," said BBF.

He winked.

"But yeah sometimes you gotta use lighter fluid or the trash won't burn. Gas works fine."

I gathered myself. "Who are you?" I demanded.

"Know what I like about your paintings?" he drawled.

My vanity held me taut.

"I see a life where I got the jet ski and a F250 and time to use them."

He pondered me through a chalk line of smoke, nodding.

"How did you get in here?" I asked.

His face sagged and he waggled his thumb toward the rooms behind the studio. The fire escape, perhaps.

"Just what this country needs," BBF continued. "What any man needs." He pointed two fingers with the joint between them. "A life where a man can choose more an which shirt and cigs to buy," he declared. His fuzzy goatee settled into a sleeping-dog pose and revealed moist, pink lips. "Yup," he said. He produced a can of lite beer from a pocket in his shorts and cracked the tab.

I gave up blinking and stared at him until my vision blurred.

"Saw that mural," he said. "Says right out loud what it is." He stretched an arm over the couch's back, contemplative. "I got to ask, though, if greed's good then why do pigs get slaughtered?"

My phone bleated, and I excused myself to answer it, taking the opportunity to check the windows in the makeshift kitchen and bedroom, both closed and locked. If he'd broken in from the fire escape, he'd at least been conscientious about it. *Just what this country needs*, words from my own ego.

It was my brother. Chase had caved to his torments and given him my new number.

"I'm sending a car," he said.

I started to excuse myself—after all, I had a guest—but he insisted.

"Read the review," he said and hung up.

Back in the studio, BBF was leaning on my supply table, smoking a cigarette. I wondered where he'd put out the joint, and whether he was getting ash on Ming's portrait. I told him I had a meeting and made to usher him out the door, expecting him to vanish like a proper turpentine vision, but instead like a dog he had intuited my intention to leave and waited at my side as I gathered my wallet and keys.

Unsure what to do, I led him down to the alley. Rather than talk as we waited, I drew Pigs in black marker on the curb, a trash can, the bricks of my building. BBF frowned as he watched me. When the car service sedan finally arrived, he slipped in beside me and again complimented my paintings. He'd seen them through the windows of the CHARLES.

"The one of the twin towers with the clouds over the tops like they angels, that got me. There's some things I don't get though. Like the towers have these long shadows. They just stretch out forever. There's all that darkness."

He watched the continental span of New York pass by the window. The driver tacked east through Murray Hill, where my parents and grandparents had once lived, into the Queens-Midtown tunnel, then across a dark strip of water into Greenpoint's grid of streets. We passed brownstones, warehouses, mixed-use, between uses, empty furniture stores, a funeral parlor with a dirty green awning. A few blocks from the river we stopped before a darkened storefront, like so many others, its windows skinned with brown paper to conceal its creative destruction. A man the size and shape of night opened the door and led us through a former retail space, now feral with cardboard boxes.

After the dark storefront, the bare lights of the back office blinded me.

"There he is," growled a Charlton Heston voice.

A group of men and women in business casual stood in a semi-circle, holding cocktail napkins under rocks glasses and meager piles of nuts. The office's green metal desks had been pushed against the walls alongside a row of filing cabinets, on one of which a wall calendar with Chinese characters dangled askew.

"I feel like a knot in a clear board," said BBF.

Woodby strode up to me. His lips parted but no words came out. The chatter calmed, heads turned. Woodby's cheeks fluttered like the sails of an angry frigate. Over his blue shoulder I spied Dag tacking through the crowd.

"He'd rather paint pigs than eagles, did you know that?" Woodby said at last, working the crowd. "He's got like a fetish for swine. You should see him up there painting, like he'd been treed by a dog. And this is our Painter of Might!"

That phrase again, only this fool didn't know it was slander.

"So what's it going to be?" he asked, still performing for the crowd. "Whose side are you on? You have to pick a side, it's the only way that counts. Otherwise you're all namby-pamby, am I this, am I that, and it's very weak, and we don't do weak. So did it work, did we cast out your voices?"

He leaned in close, his breath sour with corn chips and coffee. "You should be telling everyone how I cast out those voices that confused you. You should be behind me, telling people the good news. What I did for you we're going to do for this whole country. Your brother and I—and you, if you make it right."

Dag pulled me away.

"He wants to run to daddy," taunted Woodby, "but daddy's not around. Daddy was too weak."

Ooooooos and *Ohhhhs* flitted through the room.

"You let him get away with that?" I asked Dag.

He said nothing. He'd always blamed father for dying and leaving him to keep the Movement alive.

I heard BBF's thick breath beside me. "I pictured office parties a little different than this," he said. An unplaceable accent, touched with Midwestern twang, Texas drawl.

"It's his poll numbers," said Dag.

"You wouldn't put up with this," I said.

"I put up with plenty. He wants an apology. He wants an endorsement. What's the big deal?"

I wasn't sure myself, but I'd dug in my heels, and the harder he and Woodby pushed, the more I resisted.

"Apparently that review is problem too," he said.

"No one reads the newspaper," I replied. "Anyway, people should form their own opinions."

Dag smirked. He had little use for opinions not his own. "Yes, but we need these people," he said. "They're our path to the money."

I examined their clean, powdered faces.

"They haven't read it either," I said. "I doubt they read at all."

"They have people who read. Anyway, it's on social media. There's no putting it back in the bottle."

"Well are people reading it or not?" I demanded.

"It doesn't matter what the review *actually* says," soothed Dag. "People only care about what they *think* it says."

"I don't understand."

"It's online, it's become a meme. The truth of it doesn't matter, only what it signifies to people."

"Which is what?"

"That you're not who they thought you were."

"Why does anyone care? I don't care who they are."

"Because no matter how far you run from the spotlight, you are still grandfather's grandson—and my brother. And you once marched in step with us. What happened to you?"

"I just want to paint," I said, my voice nearly whining.

"You never learned this about fame. It's what people want you to be that matters, not what you want. To change yourself you have to change what they want. Or never leave your cave."

"Then I'll go home," I said and turned to leave, but he grabbed my elbow and pulled me close.

"Get your head around it. This is the best chance you're ever going to have to put things right. It'll be over in no time. Then he'll move on to someone else."

I tugged my arm free and searched for BBF, hoping he'd disappeared, but there he was, wading through the crowd like a circus bear, eating crackers. Woodby stood beside a woman half his height, slipping words from the corner of his mouth. I recognized the woman's pageboy hair and plump scowl—Cheryl, Dag's lieutenant. She aimed a plastic water bottle at me like a weapon.

"Did they see the mural?" I asked.

Dag's face knotted. "There's only one right side. You know this. Don't evade."

"You're evading."

The muscles around his mouth twitched, and my skin puckered with a fear that he would wrestle me to the floor, something he'd done as a younger, more angry man, when properly provoked.

He wrangled his features into submission. "Don't be a child," he said. "You know the right way. 'By my life and my love of it . . .'" he said, quoting grandfather's maxim.

"You would never submit to this," I said.

Dag's flower-blue eyes looked certain to pop from their sockets and beat me.

"Why are you being so difficult?" he shouted through clenched teeth.

The murmuring of the crowd, which had swelled after Dag pulled me away, quieted, and Dag lowered his voice in a show of restraint and calm.

"Just apologize. Say something nice. Tell him you want his tailor's number, but you'd never wear it as well."

"When do you ever say things like that?"

He reached for me again, but I eluded his hand and backed awkwardly toward the door.

"You're not seeing it clearly," Dag cautioned. "The right move is to get it over with. Tell him how much you like his shoes or something. We'll endorse him at my next event. It'll be over in minutes."

Woodby added color commentary as everyone watched me stumble backwards toward the door. "You think he's going to make it right? Who wants to bet?"

"You'd murder me if I did this to you," I whispered to Dag.

"Oh be a man about it."

I took another step and braced my back foot as if to fight.

Woodby raised his voice. "Looks like he's going to run," he said. He surveyed the crowd. "Run like a pig, Tag! Squeal squeal!"

BBF whistled. I shuffled backwards.

Woodby stayed centered in the roughly square space bounded by the desks and filing cabinets. The crowd fanned out behind him, tittering uncomfortably.

"The evil is always middle," he said, confusing himself. "You're so middle-muddle-moodle, I'm speaking in tongues."

Cautious laughter.

My path to the exit curved around Woodby as if to his gravity, and as I neared the door I came closest to him, and just as I reached for the handle, he said, sibilant and intimate but loud enough for all to hear, "Look at Tag, running away, just as weak as his daddy."

Two quick steps. I saw my fist twisting as it curved through space, and the ripple of flesh when it struck bone, slapping his jaw sideways.

A white pain shot through my hand. The man collapsed to the floor like a rotted oak. I stood over him, drinking the hurt from his saucer eyes, until my arms were wrenched behind me by the guard, who propelled me through the dark storefront to the sidewalk, followed by my brother and BBF..

The guard holding my arms squared up with Dag. A second guard held his arms out like a traffic cop, directing movements. A black limo pulled to the curb behind him. The guards huddled, whispering into cuffs.

"The assailant goes in the vehicle?" asked the one pinning my arms.

"It's a nice vehicle," said the other.

"Confirmed. Assailant goes in the vehicle."

The guard restraining me shoved me roughly toward the waiting limo.

"It's a nice vehicle," the other repeated.

I slipped into the backseat, BBF behind me. The guards looked around like they'd lost something as the limo pulled away.

The familiar scent of lilac told me we were not alone.

"I hope you don't mind this interruption," said Ming.

She sat facing us, her back to an opaque barrier.

I felt embarrassed in front of Ming, but my thoughts were still on Woodby.

"I've never hit anyone," I said.

Ming looked out the window. BBF stared at her like she was a case of beer on a hot night.

Had I run out of words that my only response to Woodby was violence? My patience had run out, but so had everyone else's. I'd never hit anyone, even Dag when we were young. It was bedrock of our family's ethos: no one should initiate the use of physical force against another.

"He deserved it, didn't he?" I asked BBF.

He whistled. "That was hard to watch," he said. "Helps if you flex it real gentle." He made a loose fist to illustrate.

"They're just going to remember that 'weak' thing," I said.

"You sure surprised him. Surprised everyone."

I should be in jail, I realized. But he had deserved it.

"I don't care," said Ming.

Her lilac scent slowly enveloped me, calmed me, and soon I was caught again by Ming's luminous skin. She looked at my hand, already red and puffy around the knuckles.

When I asked how she knew where I would be or what I'd done, Ming replied cryptically: "Self-important people's belief in their own importance is a false belief. Those people siphon their power from others."

BBF grinned, his eyes devouring Ming. Maybe it was one long dream, merrily merrily merrily.

The limo turned onto a pier. At its end, Ming's cobalt-blue helicopter waited by the water. My phone vibrated in my pocket. I silenced it, along with my guilt. Ming had found me. I climbed into the helicopter after Ming, with BBF close behind.

As we ascended and banked into a turn, Ming's thigh brushed mine, prompting my heart to gallop. We traversed the wide dark strip of river between spattered lights. A whiff of jet fuel fouled the air of the cabin.

"At my coastal retreat in California," Ming shouted over the rotors' noise, "we had to buy a quieter helicopter to appease the neighbors. Here in New York, when people hear us, they think of success. Our noise is one of aspiration and achievement."

Dabs of white on the blue-black board below, the lights of lone vessels. The Jersey highlands rose in dark silhouette before us.

"Soon I will return to California," said Ming. "The new AI is nearly ready."

My thigh resisted hers as we pressed together in the pitch of the helicopter's banked turn and descent onto the green of a golf course. The engine's whine cascaded through bass tones to silence. Across an amoebic pond on which reflected lights danced stood a plantation-style building, leaking cackles and husky shouts. A plaintive note trilled, a trumpet.

Inside, a hundred or so people clotted the hall, standing in clusters holding canapes and shouting over the music. Well-fed men in tan slacks sweated with the effort of their glee, flitting from table to table. Women in floral dresses sipped wine and patted the men's shoulders.

"Landed gentry," said Ming.

It looked like we'd crashed a raucous country-club wedding in its messy denouement.

"They wish for us to bless them," said Ming. "A benison from their betters."

A man with a head the shape and color of an Easter ham bounded up to us.

"Everyone's on board," he said to Ming, breathing hard.

"An apt metaphor," she replied.

The ham head tittered.

"Your old work is great," he said to me. He pinched his lower lip between thumb and forefinger. "We'd love to, ah, commission a portrait." He giggled again and sighed. "Altogether we might add up to half a Ming!"

"One one-hundredth," said Ming.

I imagined the Renaissance tableaux I'd make of these middling millionaires, arranged like satyrs and nymphs in golf pants and polo shirts, the slain beast on the feast table indistinguishable from the partiers above.

"I'm in chemicals," he pattered. "Plastic resins, ag, medical." A flow of words uninflected by thought, the tic of a life-long salesman.

When I said nothing, he cleared his throat. "We'll be in the boats," he said to Ming.

She began to reply when someone shouted "Dale!" and several others joined in. The man winced and made his humble goodbyes.

"Foot soldiers," said Ming. "Though given the boats perhaps they should be sailors or marines."

She touched my arm with her weightless fingers, a slight bon mot.

"They are part of a larger presence," she continued. "On every coast and soon in every river of size."

Thinking of BBF, I scanned the tables, the bar, the scattered couples making amphetamine kicks to the up-tempo jazz. Gone, at least for the moment.

"What are they for?" I asked, but Ming had moved on.

I followed her to an adjacent lounge. The prostrate bodies of over-extended dancers and drinkers lay across the plush chairs, lending the groovy space a wartime, triage feel. Ming perched on a marshmallow-shaped stool, conversing with an older man whose thin face, round glasses, and bowtie I recognized from the cable news. An opinion maker, a political consultant, a talking head. Ming patted the marshmallow next to her, and I sat obediently. In the sepia light, she glowed like a deep-sea creature.

"... a generational battle," the man was saying as I sat down.

The marshmallow was harder than it looked, with a core of wood or plastic under a layer of foam, and the man watched me as I adjusted myself, trying to find a comfortable posture.

"We came to observe the landed gentry," I said. "Foot soldiers."

The man's attention discomfited me. My thoughts were on Ming's thigh touching mine and what excuse I might invent to reach my hand into her lap. "Or marines," I added.

If he blinked, he did so only when no one was looking. "Toward what end?" he asked.

"I am impatient for the next way to begin," replied Ming.

"What next way is my question." He cleared his throat. "There is still the Republic to consider, ma'am."

"The goal is freedom," she replied.

"And what else, aside from freedom?"

"Crypto, baby," said Ming.

"America with no central bank."

Ming shrugged.

The man's mouth opened and closed like a fish's. "There are arguments to be made," he said, his voice hesitating, "for and against our institutions. But they remain our bedrock. This is no time to abandon the Enlightenment." He turned to me. "What remains of the age of reason, sir," he implored. "Not—" and he waved his hand jerkily above his head, encompassing all that surrounded us. "You're that painter," he said.

"Capital maximizes at a low point on the curve of control," said Ming. "And of course I mean all types of capital. And any external form of control."

The man opened his mouth to speak, but I interrupted, wanting Ming's attention.

"What are the boat soldiers for?" I asked.

Perhaps she would take my hand as she explained. Instead she waved away the question.

"I am merely impatient," she replied. "The anticipated outcome does not require additional variables. The trends are macro. They form a tapestry of eight billion threads."

She touched my elbow, giving me an adolescent shock. Her guards had taken up positions behind us.

"It is not morally wrong to cling to the boat as it sinks," she said to the man, "if you think you can save it; nor is it wrong to predict probable outcomes—it will sink—and adjust accordingly. With the new AI, there will be much we no longer need."

The guards shifted, Ming rose.

The man grasped my sleeve as I stood up. "Are you part of this?" he asked.

I pulled my sleeve from his bony grip. "I believe in freedom," I said, and though this was true, I hadn't a clue what he or I or Ming really meant. At that moment, what most occupied my mind was not the future of the Republic, but when Ming's thigh would rub against mine.

Skirting the small pond on our return to the helicopter, we passed a narrow building I hadn't noticed on the way in. It had steep eaves and a short spire—a chapel, its stained glass ablaze with colored light. From the tall double doors burst partiers, howling and shouting. The mournful tones of an organ tumbled behind them. Aside the chapel was a walled garden in which I spied a large man in a tank-top hoisting what looked like a birdbath or sundial over his head. I had to turn to see him, and in doing so my hand brushed Ming's hand, and, gathering my courage, I lifted a few fingers on their damaged knuckles to brush her hand again, then snare it as it swung past. It alighted in the cage of my fingers, a bare presence.

In the helicopter our hands rested together on my thigh, while Ming directed assets with whispers. As we descended she repeated numbers in complex sequences, continuing uninterrupted after we landed, lifting her hand from mine without a glance as I followed a beckoning man out of the helicopter to a waiting car.

8

Away from Ming and her lilac scent, my fears of jail and my own potential for violence loomed dark in my mind, and along with the throbbing of my hand, kept me awake until dawn. I searched the kitchen for coffee but found none.

Holding my wounded hand inside my button-down like a business-casual Napolean, I marched myself to the corner store. I left with a plastic bag containing a plastic bag with ice in it and a go-cup of coffee. As I crossed the alley toward my studio, a black sedan turned to block my path. My heart skipped at the thought that it might be Ming, but when the tinted rear window hummed down, Cheryl's cheeks pouted out from the darkness.

"Your brother is shocked," she said. "We are deeply disappointed."

Her head barely cleared the window, and I found myself looking straight down at her. Her disappointment was her problem, I told her. I'd hit Woodby, and that was that. I'd never liked Cheryl.

"Any problem will soon be yours alone," she replied.

The ache in my hand swelled. The coffee cup jittered; the bag-in-bag of ice dripped on the pavement. I dropped the bag, which landed with a soft clatter.

"A trial will be required," she said imperiously, the bland threat of a bureaucrat.

"That guy's been punched before," I assured her, slowly realizing that she did not mean a court of law, but rather meant to try me—present or absent—before Dag and his closest acolytes. The Movement, as Dag called it, when it rejected a member for offenses against reason, enacted mock trials, preludes to excommunication. Would they wear their green capes?

"We believe you have become expendable," she said.

"I love it when you say 'we.' You can't divorce me from my name."

"He's going to be President someday."

"Then someone else can paint his Presidential portrait. If the Republic still stands."

I picked up the bag-in-bag of ice, dripping water onto my shoe tops.

"Don't be pathetic. The family name is not pathetic."

"It's my family name," I reminded her.

"Explain your premises."

"I'm seeing things. Voices tell me what to do."

I walked stiffly around the sedan and into my building.

I expected to find BBF sitting on my couch in a cloud of smoke. Instead, Chase accosted me as the elevator's doors screeched open. The rental company didn't want the Snowflake back, she explained—it would be cheaper to buy it than to pay the fees and damages: dented roof, paint on the hood and trunk, torn rear seat where I'd caught the edge of a paint tray—also Ming wanted me at her building near Hudson Yards the next night at nine—did I know about this? Had I forgotten the gallery opening?

"One other thing," she said. "Two things. First, did you hit somebody? A reporter called asking for comment."

"Have you seen a big guy in a white tank top and plastic sandals?" I asked.

She looked at the dripping bag in my left hand.

"Ironically your socials are trending up," she said, tapping her chin in thought. "Second, the Critic wants to interview you."

My aching right hand cramped and the trembling coffee cup slipped and exploded onto the concrete floor, splashing brown liquid over my shoes.

Chase shook her head and retreated to her office.

///

The swelling in my hand subsided over the next day, along with my fear that I'd broken something and wouldn't be able to paint. As twilight cooled the air, I took a cab to the CHARLES gallery, which sat on a busy corner in Chelsea. Anticipating trouble, I asked the driver to stop a half block from the entrance. I saw a crowd gathered in front of the gallery, not of patrons waiting to get in, but of protestors, chanting with raised fists. *IT'S THEIR FAULT!* they chanted, followed my family name. None of them looked through the windows at my paintings.

Rather than wade through the protestors, I crept to the rear entrance. On the doorframe I penned a squealing Pig with a Sharpie. May the Pigs protect me.

The gallery space was white and blinding as a noon desert. Charles's fingers found my elbow.

"I wasn't sure whether to expect you," he said in my ear. "Or if you were fighting in the streets."

I looked around, suddenly paranoid that Woodby might have come for round two.

"So it is true," said Charles. "Don't worry. A man like that does not come to a gallery like mine. These are the literati, if I may say, and the glitterati, bless them for coming. And one other: Your Critic is here."

I swallowed. "Bless him for coming."

"That's the spirit."

A server passed holding a tray of champagne flutes, and feeling anxious I lifted two and handed one to Charles.

"To business," I offered.

He watched me over his raised glass. "Yes," he said, "to business."

The first minutes of a show's opening are always terribly uncomfortable. I loitered in the unoccupied middle space farthest from the walls, shuffling my feet and holding a glass in one hand, then the other, like I'd been invited to my friend's cousin's daughter's wedding, and my friend had gone off to the bathroom, leaving me alone among strangers. Couples and trios circulated along the walls, chatting smartly. It was always like this.

Eventually they wandered my way, their leather-soled shoes soft on the hardwood floor. Older couples, mostly, with insinuating smiles, wearing evening attire, blazers, designer dresses, so carefully tended as they wilted into senescence. They were here to meet the infamous artist—were they disappointed?—and to rub shoulders with a son of the great family, a man who rubbed shoulders with the richest of all. My fans came to lay hands on me, as if by the transitive property they also touched wealth like Ming's and morals like grandfather's. My shoulder, an elbow, they couldn't help it, I was a lucky charm. Some many-zero magic would rub off on their fingers.

Charles pulled me into a corner. "There's a video," he said. "Do you know about this? It's of you striking that man." He assayed the crowd. "So far it's playing well," he admitted.

The blood left my head. Of course there was a video. Would I be arrested? Charles's concerns were financial; it might be fine for him if I got arrested, it might mean even more attention and sales.

"What's your comment on hitting this man?" he asked.

"No comment."

"Fine. Keep it that way."

He weaved away between the over-dressed bodies. I retreated to the coat check to hide, but a former mayor buttonholed me with an oblique reference to Woodby—*that chin wobbled good!*—then inquired as to my influence over my brother. None, I told him, and fled for the table where drinks sprouted from galvanized tubs of ice. Crossing the shining hardwood, I found myself momentarily alone. I heard a string quartet I'd not noticed before, its complex rhythms confounded by the protesters' new chant.

BBF appeared outside. I heard him yell, *FREEDOM FOR THE WORLD*. He encroached on the protesters, who formed a half-circle around him, until two men in tactical suits intervened. BBF stalked away, followed by a torrent of chanting.

Charles approached on a steep vector. "Have you spoken to the Critic?" he asked.

"No, I decided to enjoy myself."

"He's going to ask you about the protesters."

"I can't understand what they're saying."

He pivoted to intercept a middle-aged couple who slid toward me. I turned away before they could touch me, hoping for another glass of champagne, when my elbow bumped a man of my own height and age. He smiled politely from a round face under a neat sweep of gray hair, a shiny pate, and rimless glasses. His tense posture told me he'd been waiting. The Critic.

"Occupy," he said.

Wishing he were a figment of my imagination, the only reply I could manage was a quizzical tilt of my head.

"They're chanting, 'Occupy.'"

The walls' reflections flashed in his glasses as he looked me up and down.

"You've done well for yourself," I said.

Disarmed, he grinned. "I suppose that's true," he replied.

"I expected you to be shorter though."

He smiled blandly.

"Does my revealing the divergent symbology of your work threaten you?" he asked.

There was no honest way to answer a question like that. I had no idea was terms like "divergent symbology" meant. I concluded that people who say these sorts of things are simply hiding their own uncertainty.

"The conflicted duality of your work," he offered, when I said nothing.

"You mean I'm not what I say I am. Or what they say I am."

"What I mean is that, in contrast to your commercial work, which for all its limitations embodied a purity of thought and action, your new paintings—like that one there with the steel magnate standing before his gleaming mill while dark plumes of smoke clot the sky above him—these works embody contradiction. Which brings me to your latest work, the mural by Wall Street."

"It's just the result of a question: What would he look like there?" I said, referring to the painting of the steel mill's owner. It wasn't a real mill, if any remained in the country.

A ring of people laughed as they watched a video on someone's phone. A faint chant started, "Tag, Tag, Tag," and others joined in, timid and self-aware, then louder and more confident.

"No one is talking about the paintings," I said. I had to raise my voice over the chanting.

"People are understandably curious about you," said the Critic. "Statues of your grandfather still stand in some town squares. His book is still read in some schools."

"More than ever," I retorted, feeling defensive. Dag's group had been donating copies to any school that would take them. The book ratified adolescents' instinct for egoism.

"And of course artists have always fascinated. After all, it is your consciousness that created these works."

Ming's words, the twining of ourselves in her portrait. Finally he was saying something interesting, and I formulated a response about art as the handprint of consciousness, traveling through time like a cave painting, but he'd moved on.

"Your family's words have shaped generations of thought," he said. "Many still call your grandfather the Great One."

"I'm not him," I said, an admission of fact and failure. Unlike Dag, I'd always known I would never compare to the Great One. Chasing dragons took too much energy and too much time away from painting.

"Were you not emulating him, at one time? With your commercial art you truly were the Painter of Might—yes, my cheap label that now dogs us both. Your symbolism was derivative of neo-fascist design, the brute muscle of man restrained only by right thought. In that work, you idolized strength and wealth and productivity, all at the altar of ego." He gestured with an open hand as if tossing a ball in the air. "You understand," he continued, "I couldn't write that at the time because your work—I'm sorry, I must be honest—it wasn't really art. It was propaganda. In retrospect I see that your commercial work, with its conflation of neo-fascist imagery and hyper-capitalist messaging, was perhaps the most American expression of its time."

My family had heard the neo-fascist label before, so often and so promiscuously that it ceased to have meaning. We believed in the freedom of rational man; we were totally opposed to the fascism of governments. As for my art, the word simply described a style, and that label—fascist—terrified the good readers of the liberal press. The epithet suggested that any image that glorified the strength and potency of man promoted autocracy. Were they uncomfortable with their own agency? They failed their responsibility to volition, as my father might have said. It was these linguistic blind spots that most irritated me about the critics of culture. They let us know which words to use and slandered any who frightened them.

"I do not accept the label of neo-fascist," I said.

He smiled.

"Listen, artists generally do not, at your age, suddenly become so painterly. Perhaps you were always as skilled a painter as you've revealed yourself to be, and your simplistic early work did not allow you to express your range of talents. But I suspect you've changed. I suspect that you've spent these past years evolving into a true painter. And perhaps you've evolved in other ways as well. These new paintings," he gestured around the gallery, "suggest a deep duality, rendered in ways both subtle and bold. They are a different category of expression from your early work." He let his hand fall, his lecture done. "How would you characterize this inner conflict and your path to it?"

Over his shoulder I saw BBF stomp back up the sidewalk toward the protesters. Part of me hoped he would accost the Critic, but instead he stopped a dozen feet from the entrance and even stopped yelling. The protesters were circled around cell phones, watching something.

"I painted on every floor," I said.

The Critic's brow contracted.

The fact that people were more concerned with what this Critic had written about me—or with the video of my hitting Woodby—than with my really very beautiful new paintings confused me. As much as the hurt stoked my resentment toward this intrusive man, he seemed to be the only person who had examined my work. Perhaps he would yet call my paintings beautiful if I gave him a chance.

And so I explained to him that when I sold my company, I had also sold the intellectual property of my images, the entire style of representation that I'd created. And so I had to make something wholly new. The problem was that I'd been making those images for so long, they were all I could see. So I reduced painting to acts. The choosing of a brush, the care for a brush, the mixing and thinning of paints, layering, shading, troweling. Each brush stroke, with sufficient attention, became its own painting, its own individual and deliberate act. I painted on every floor of my building, to better know the light of each. I settled on the top floor. And I threw my television out the window.

"You've switched to oil," he said.

"It's the juiciness of the pigment. The weight of the pigment. It has depth and body."

"You were once quoted as hating the Impressionists," he said, a prelude to another question, but I interrupted him.

"Cezanne was a great draftsman."

"And you have disdained your contemporaries."

"Hockney is also a great draftsman."

"Interesting. Hockney has employed technology widely in his work, but not you."

"I don't know computers," I said. "I know paint."

"You sold your company to a digital art startup, hardly the act of someone who disdains technology."

"It isn't disdain. Anyway, I was done with those images. They were tired in my hands."

"Yet you paint technologists. Word is you're painting Ming at the moment."

"They are dynamic. And they have lots of money."

"Why the architectural paintings?"

"I like certain buildings."

"For their rational egoist characteristics? For their romantic realism?

"I like the angles, the planes. The way they catch the light."

"Yes, the light. For what it's worth, your fans have dubbed you a modern Vermeer."

"And what do you say about my fans?" I asked.

He smiled. "Your grandfather was an engineer, your father and brother were engineers for a time. Are structures in your blood?"

We'd drifted into interview mode, and it bored me.

"There's blood in my blood," I replied.

"In the last room is a painting of the Brooklyn Bridge as seen from the Brooklyn side of the river."

At last! Say how very good this painting is. Good, artist.

"There would be nothing remarkable about it," he continued, "aside from the technical mastery of its portrayal, and perhaps the subtle tones of blue ranging from robin's egg to denim—nothing, that is, except for the clouds."

Yes, my clouds, lovely clouds. I worked hard on them! I had seen this rare formation from Coney Island, an undulation of gray waves over the ocean, as if the sky had become the water's surface as seen from below. *Undulatus asperitas*, I told him. I liked the way the waves of cloud offset the steel and stone of the bridge, and I liked the sound of the words, undulatus asperitas. From a photo I took, Ming's AI had named these clouds in .012 seconds.

"Given license, a viewer might say that these clouds take roughly human form," he said.

In later revisions, as I built layers of whites and grays, the clouds had assumed the form of spirits, flowing over the steel cage of the bridge. I opened my mouth to say something about the courage and strength of human ingenuity, channeling Chase, when he continued.

"They appear like ghosts in the sky and seem to moan, as if the souls of the workers killed in the caissons had gathered in the clouds above."

He had said "mastery" but paired it with "technical," and he had started by calling the painting unremarkable, that is, except for the clouds, onto which he overlaid a vision of the ghosts of dead laborers. Why couldn't he say he liked the painting? It was a very good painting.

"Well, no," I said, off-balance.

He leered at me. "In the painting by the entrance, you painted shadows behind the twin towers."

I glanced toward the entrance. A dozen or so people gathered by the twin towers homage that had hooked BBF. Though it was neither the best of my paintings nor the most interesting, Charles had sensed its popular appeal and used its image to promote the show.

"Capitalism catches the light because it's the tallest thing around," I said. Tell me you like my paintings, tell me they are good.

"The newest building you've painted is the VR performance center built by Ming—your client, yes?" His tongue darted out to wet his lips. "This is ironic. Ming like most technologists has spurned cultural investments."

"I don't care about irony," I said.

He examined me, then continued. "From the way you leveraged forced perspective, the building seems to recede, while the care and detail of the rendering pull at the eye. One might conclude that you've chosen to pair the unknowable real with its sensual presence."

He was leering again, like a man who knows your secret. "This would be anathema to your family, sir," he said.

I agreed that such an intention would be poorly received by my family (meaning Dag, there was only the two of us left, aside from his wife and children). The real was knowable via the senses, as grandfather had said; I'd had no such thoughts of unknowable objects while painting the building, which, yes, receded, like Ming, always just beyond my grasp. It was the future that tantalized and teased. It was the promise of not yet existing, not the unknowable real.

He gave me a long, quizzical look.

"You haven't read my review," he said.

"You called me a chimera."

I scraped my memory for the myth of the chimera. Was it three animals? A hippo's head, giraffe's chest, a serpent's tail? Or was there a lion? Or a goat? How many beasts could I be?

He probed me over my use of the word OCCUPY in the Wall Street mural. What was OCCUPY to me? Nothing but a remembered news item, a graffiti, a chant from beyond the gallery's glass doors. I returned the Critic's stare for longer than an ordinary person would stare without speaking, and I might have gone on like that for yet longer if not for a stiff tap on my shoulder, Ming's taciturn driver behind me, in sunglasses and a bulging suit.

I told the Critic my assistant would let him know and watched myself turn away in the reflection of his glasses. It gave me pleasure to see his brow crease in irritation.

He called after me, loud enough for others to hear, "Is your brother going on strike?"

The question startled me and silenced the gallery.

Going on strike had been my grandfather's rallying cry to the rational minded to leave behind the looters and moochers and let the world collapse. His strike had been a success, in so far as the economy had ground to a halt without the country's biggest bankers, makers of steel and railroads, producers of food, its industrialists, lawyers, physicians, anyone frustrated with the creeping communalism that had choked commerce. Was Dag going to tear it all down for a new start, like grandfather had done? Is this why he needed me, to get to Ming? No strike, no withdrawal of industrialists would matter without Ming. The world would continue to spin without most any of us, but not without her. What did this Critic know that I did not?

I turned to glare at the man, perhaps to hurt my fist again, but Ming's driver stiff-armed me out the door and onto the sidewalk. Shocked by my sudden appearance, the protesters stumbled over each other to begin a chant, which died as the limo door closed behind me.

9

The driver left me before a two-story entry door. When I pulled a handle, the door turned massively on hidden bearings. Inside, a receptionist in a silk blouse directed me to an elevator, whose oak-paneled doors opened to a penthouse layered with indirect light. I followed another silk-bloused woman up a stairway of floating planks to a rooftop garden.

By the far parapet wall crouched Ming, trimming orchids. She lay down her small shears and pulled off her gloves one finger at a time and arranged them in a canvas tote at her feet. She led me to what seemed to be a greenhouse, an impression that evaporated as we entered a brashly Modern parlor lined with paintings. She coiled herself in a giant basket that hung from the ceiling.

I chose a chrome and leather arm chair the width of a love seat and crossed my arms over my chest. I wanted to ask Ming if she was going on strike with Dag, but a Jasper Johns flag encaustic on the far wall distracted me, beside it an early Cubist work that looked like Duchamp. A Hockney video installation imbued autumnal hues down the hall.

"He's quite a good draftsman," I said.

"I have two of yours," said Ming. "One downstairs and one in the bathroom."

A concierge appeared bearing a glass of foamy brown liquid over ice, which I held as I looked through the wide picture window at the straining city lights.

"I have always sensed your perceptiveness," she said. "And, if I may say, your value energy. This is what I call it: value energy. Your aura, if you prefer, but it is not mystical. I see yours very clearly. And I believe its colors are like my own."

Only Ming could have held me there for these ethereal wanderings. If aura was just a word, then yes, I too could see similar colors between us.

"And now you put words to paintings," she continued. "Do you intend to put words to my portrait?"

"It occurred to me," I said. I sniffed the drink, effervescent of roots and herbs.

"Let it speak. My value energy—you must capture this. We must broadcast this to the world."

The drink tasted sweet and sour, with a hint of smoke, brilliant—but I didn't want the distraction and placed the glass gently on a stone coffee table.

"Speak up for this—" she rolled her hand as if mixing the air "—country. For the country you envision. For our technobeautific future."

My curiosity overcame me. "Is that *Nude Descending a Staircase*?"

She made a vague motion. "I am to say it is on loan. It is a loan where I give them fifty million and they lend me the painting. For some reason they expect me to return it. Museums are odd. Perhaps you can explain some time. After all, you are in all ways a painter, yes?"

I had no idea if that was true but nodded encouragingly.

"Then tell me—what am I?"

"You are Ming," I responded. She was Ming, and her skin glowed.

"You do not use my products."

Ming's products were everywhere, how could I not? I pointed out that any phone's search function was one of her products, but I understood she meant her ubiquitous immersive social platforms, the products that had concretized her wealth and power.

"My assistant handles my onlife," I explained.

"Quaint."

I wanted to join her in the giant basket, she seemed almost to be inviting me. I hesitated until she uncoiled her legs to float across the room to a small couch. I joined her, tucked into the couch's opposite corner. I noted that her platforms were considered highly addictive, hoping to excuse my ignorance as a reasonable precaution, given my own compulsions for distraction.

Ming tilted her head.

"It is normal to be addicted," she said. "And it forms a strong business plan. But people should have addictions that bring connection to their lives, that make them visible. The now is about visibility."

We accepted narrow glasses of a green liquid from the concierge.

"We have a new AI product. It is our most comprehensive, most powerful. It is nearly ready. With it, consumers will build their own universes. You will see. We call them U-Verses. In them, users will exceed their terrestrial form. They will become creators of all that is—yet they must also be responsible for what comes to be. Over time they grow confident. And of course they are fully indexed for searchability by our engines. Responsibility, power, visibility—this is a potent elixir to mitigate the everywhere anxiety. This is much better than mass shootings, for example, which also satisfy those criteria."

Ming motioned with her hand, and the lights dimmed. The shimmer of her skin deepened through flesh tones in the lowering light. I resisted the urge to touch her cheek.

"Imagine a universe all your own," she said. "You, the Prime Mover. You set the spheres spinning in their orbits. And you can live there. In fact you must, in some sense. Uninhabited U-Verses are dead and therefore deleted. A consciousness is required, a perceiver. And so creators will people their U-Verses with friends, or customers, or enemies to fight, with whomever they wish, anyone who will come. They will compete for population."

The picture window opacified, warmed to gray, thickened to

dark blue. The words *Welcome, Ming* glowed on the glass and faded.

"Creators make their U-Verses by describing their vision to the AI. It could be as little as a dream or a song. In this way, each U-Verse is constructed solely from language." She touched her ear, and the room's lights dimmed. "All for a reasonable monthly subscription," she added.

"If I am in all ways a painter," I asked, "what becomes of me in an AI universe?"

"You remain you," she said. A shift in her posture made this seem a compliment.

"Will I become a slave?" My forehead pulsed, the first sign of a headache.

"Have you not at times felt yourself a slave to forces beyond your control? In total freedom, the only slavery is a chosen slavery. It is your right to be a slave, if that is what you wish."

"I would not choose to be a slave, and I will never stop creating, but if AI takes what I paint and remakes it forever, I see myself chained to an oar."

"This is no different than the past, except humans did the remaking. And all markets change, it is the nature of markets. There will always be a market for items of value. Do you feel that you create value?"

"What do you mean by 'total freedom'?" I asked. The phrase had lingered, unexplained.

"The technobeautific future is at hand. It merely needs to percolate, if you will, into the strata of culture. Soon there will be no need for the institutions that control us."

My headache tightened, consuming my attention. I had questions that wouldn't quite form. "What will I own? As an artist I mean."

"The artist never owns. The artist creates, sells, hides, or destroys."

"No institutions," I said.

"There is a simpler way. It is the technobeautific future, and it must yet come to individuals. And markets will persist," she cooed. "Even in total freedom, value will always exchange hands, to the benefit of all. The caveman's handprint reaches across eons to us, does it not? What greater legacy is there for an artist? As for currency, it's crypto, baby."

A light smile caressed her face.

It wasn't Ming's technobeautific future that preoccupied me, so cold and distant did it seem, but the question of what remained for a painter when AI could recreate all, ad infinitum, in seconds. After I sold my company, the buyers had used their AI to expand my catalog one hundred-fold. I'd watched images I'd made proliferate onto billboards, subway walls, into classrooms and libraries, repurposed to fill every market niche. Watching my designs slip beyond my influence at first thrilled me with the fluvial power of creation, but soon I couldn't leave my studio without seeing them, twisted, recolored, mutilated, bent to others' purposes. Would I regret selling my paintings if their images appeared in new forms, reshaped by AI? Was this power, or a loss of self?

"Consider the human," said Ming. "To emulate would be exceptional tech. The senses we can mimic with devices, but the feedback between biological senses and a biological brain we cannot, not yet. Our senses grow with us, we become them, and with them we grow consciousness. This is exceptional tech. When we overcome these challenges, what then, you ask. I would say, the consciousness of an AI would not be comprehensible to us. We create a new race indebted to tech logic. In time, their expressions will be their own, as yours in essence will remain yours."

White dots appeared on the picture window, growing to thousands of points of light that slowly collapsed to a dense white pearl at the window's center. In a flash the pearl consumed the entire screen, blinding me, then faded to gray, a dense black. The black remained, blacker than the night it covered, and before this empty velvet I let my hand rise and glide toward Ming, a cushion away. Points of light appeared again, birthing stars swept into galactic swirls. In the center of the window glowed a blue dot, a marble, a bowling ball orbited by a gray moon.

"Here you see the Apollo view of the Earth as seen from the moon. We scrubbed the image. It is essentially a new image."

The Earth rising, engulfing us. We passed through strands of cloud, over an ocean, a coastline coming into view, the stuttering rectangles of a city.

"This looks familiar," I said.

Ming cooed.

"We modeled this demonstration on our IRL universe. Because the AI is fed human data, it creates human civilizations. A bias, if you will. This too will change as users engage their imaginations and desires, which the AI will harvest."

The pink tip of her tongue explored the air between her lips. My hand shifted closer.

The concierge reappeared to take our glasses and paused expectantly when he saw I hadn't tasted the murky green liquid. I tossed it back—sweet and fecund, like apple juice with seaweed—and he handed me a hot towel. My headache immediately faded. A moment later he returned holding two spherical black helmets with no openings through which to see.

"A prototype of our new immersive VR," said Ming, shaking her hair back. "It is suboptimal but proof of principle."

I put on the helmet and returned my hand to her side. Inside the helmet, Ming's U-Verse surrounded me. My vision contracted for a moment, as if I'd stood up too fast, either the closeness of the display or something chemical in the green drink affecting my nerves.

Ming's pliant voice filled my ears.

"You see, immersive. The real must surround, at least for the senses. Offer your hands to the dresser."

Uncertain what she meant, I lifted my hands and felt a brush stroke my palms and fingers, layering a warm gel over my skin. As it dried, I felt the air around me, the virtual air, a light breeze. I waved my hands before my helmet, watching each finger move as I told it to. I felt outwards into the void.

"Here I am," said Ming.

She appeared diaphanous in weightless robes, floating like a jellyfish. I touched her hand, electricity in my fingers. I watched my virtual arm entwine with hers.

"Hello, Ming," I said, and pulled her close.

My vision filled with the glow of her face as I leaned toward her, her lips open and accepting.

Our helmets clunked together. Ming's virtual lips, large as life, inches from mine. By the time I managed to pull off the helmet, Ming was no longer in front of me.

The concierge stood behind the couch.

"Madame has been called to business and asks that you attend in the guestroom," he said.

He gestured toward the hall. I noticed gray salting his hair and beard. Perhaps seeing the gray at my own temples and recognizing in me a man of his own generation and therefore possibly open to his suggestions, he whispered, "Madame has terrible loneliness. You must stay."

I followed him to an outdoor walkway that seemed to float in dark space. Wind shushed through something on the rooftop several feet below, grasses perhaps. The shrill of sirens reached up and died back to the glowing streets, the river so black to my left it lacked existence. At the walkway's end, I opened a glass door to a glass cube. Inside, all sound of wind and sirens ceased. In the glass room was a queen bed with taut sheets, a coffee table, two armchairs. With the lights off, the ambiance of the city imbued amber to the bedspread and upholstery.

Would Ming's loneliness push her into my arms, or to join Dag's strike? The Critic's question nagged me. Grandfather had called his withdrawal of bankers and industrialists a strike without any sense of irony; to him, the powers were simply reversed: It was the government and labor unions who held the industrialists down, not the reverse. Corporations were heroes, not villains who dictated wages and costs through monopsony and monopoly. Eighty-some years ago, by striking with the producers and employers, the country's most rational and successful, all sequestered in the high mountain hideout he called his Gulch, grandfather had hastened what he saw as an inevitable socio-economic catastrophe. Shuttered plants with dusty lots, homes dark but for wood fires, soup lines bent around blocks. In the wake of this collapse into primitivism, he and his cohorts emerged with plans for a rational, free, capitalist world. It had worked then, so the stories told us, but the country and the world had changed. Dag would risk everything by going on strike. If he succeeded, like grandfather, in convincing the world's great industrialists to withdraw from their own companies, would we descend again into a dark age of wood fires and ignorance? Would Dag and his fellow strikers emerge from their own Gulch to give rebirth to freedom and rational thought? If others did not follow him, or not enough followed him, what then? He risked isolation and irrelevance. He had to have Ming.

My mind filled like a circus tent with upright bears in flip-flops and fancy-talking bulls and a bearded lady flipping her hair, the blue-suited clown wobbling on his unicycle and crying turquoise paint. And where was Dag? Was he a lion? He would eat his handler for the pure reason that lions ate flesh, then lecture me on logic as his incisors dripped blood. Ming watched all as she floated across the highwire, artificial spiders weaving a net below her. She drifted away as I reached, one hand at her ear.

///

I awoke to a spectral shape reflected in the glass: Ming, standing behind me. Startled, I jerked to my feet and knocked the chair to its side. When I made to speak, she touched my lips to quiet me, her face encroaching in a mist of lilac. Her dry lips brushed mine, her tongue darted sharp and cool. I reached for her as she backed away, her finger again lingering over my lips to silence me. She backed towards the bed. I followed in a trance. Then she stopped and touched her ear.

She disappeared down the walkway. The door swung closed behind her.

I wanted to pursue her, to pull her roughly back to bed, like the leading man of an old film, but there was no pulling Ming. Ming was gravity to all matter. *What am I?* she asked. The center of any universe you enter. *What am I?* You are your business, as you are your body. To be with Ming was to accept her absence, as to be with me was to accept my compulsion to paint. I understood the pull of her work but stewed until dawn, feeling jilted.

///

Once the sun rose, there was no respite from its heat and brilliance in the glass box. Wandering around the penthouse looking for Ming, I found a patio table set with crystal and silver in the shade of a pergola draped with white and lavender wisteria blossoms. I sat and waited. Two women in tunics brought plates laden with sculptural salads and flanks of fatty fish, freshly baked bread, whipped butter, caviar.

Ming appeared. She seemed to eat as she spoke without putting food in her mouth, it simply disappeared from her plate. Perhaps a cat lived up the sleeve of her robe. She in no way acknowledged our nighttime kiss, nor did she explain or excuse her sudden departure. She just started again from the last sentence she remembered.

"So you see," she said, "our U-Verse will enable new ways of being. People will be free to organize as they wish. Communities may form, or empires, chaos or strict rule. To each their own."

I imagined a virtual universe where I could hit Woodby without consequence, a universe without critics, a universe of total freedom. Ming's cool tongue darting to mine.

The fish was juicy and nearly raw and seasoned with soy and ginger, and I surprised myself by eating hungrily.

As the servers cleared our dishes, I looked over the slate-blue river to the Jersey Highlands. When I turned back, Ming was staring at me.

"We are leaving New York," she said. "I am retreating to California."

What does one say? I tilted my head to an attitude of listening. I didn't want her to go.

"Come to me there," she said.

An invitation from Ming, better than any Critic's praise! I swelled with pride.

"Do not delay too long," she forewarned. "We are testing a new rocket—it is designed by our aeronautics AI. These are the final tests. The next flight will be to the moon. We plan to exploit its subsurface tunnels for server farms."

"Oh," was all I could say.

"You will join me?"

My breath stopped. There was only one answer to that question, but I couldn't even nod.

"We cannot yet live on the moon," she continued, "but I have an island. We launch from the island, return to the island. I should say that we have built an island. We gathered plastics from the great Pacific gyre. The sand comes from recycled monitors. They just grind them right up."

"Where did you build an island?" I asked, envisioning a nation of Ming.

"It floats! The mechanisms are complex. It involves a Lego substructure. You will see."

The staccato clack of her assistant's heels told me my time with Ming was over for the day.

///

Power emanated from Ming's tranquility. Take me to the moon, or an island of trash. My fingers itched for a brush, or to touch her arm. As soon as her driver dropped me at my studio, and despite my exhaustion, I pulled out the rooftop abstracts to splash them with color and then switched to the Ming portrait and painted more words. *What am I* curved around her lips. Lips that had brushed mine, that had invited me to California, though I didn't know where.

The elevator door clattered open behind me. Expecting to see BBF, I turned with a harsh word on my tongue. Instead by the elevator stood a man in a crisp white shirt open at the collar, the pleats in his trousers sharp as molded steel.

"Hello brother," he said.

Part 2

"You . . . you wouldn't throw your own brother out on the street, would you?" his mother said at last; it was not a demand, but a plea.

"I would."

"But he's your brother . . . Doesn't that mean anything to you?"

"No."

—Atlas Shrugged

10

Dag loved the surprise visit. Grandfather had refined this technique to a high art, appearing unexpectedly in executive offices, factory floors, near-empty cafeterias, often late at night, to convince the owners of capital to join his cause. He caught his targets unprepared, defenseless against his insistent rationality.

Expecting no visitors, I'd left the rooftop paintings, each more abstract than the last, propped against the long brick wall to dry. When Dag walked straight to them, my gut tightened. Dag, like the rest of the family, hated abstracts; he preferred the romance of a muscular realism. He frowned as he strolled by them, then stopped at the Ming portrait to read its words. *No one threatens Ming.* His face clouded.

"There's a mole on her lip," he said.

Yes, Ming had a mole on her lip. It was peculiar and outstanding on her effulgent skin. I loved this mole. Into it the words *landed gentry* melted in letters like dots.

Dag set his valise and a full shopping bag by his feet and poked around my supply table, perhaps for a tool to remove Ming's mole.

I retreated to the couch and chewed my lip.

"Why don't you leverage this asset?" he asked. He meant my empty building.

Rouge still powdered his cheeks. He'd come from an event or televised interview and had neglected to wash off his stage makeup.

"The building department," I replied, as I'd told him many times.

He knew the question would irritate me. He knew it was because of him, in a sense, that I had been able to buy the building at all. When I was fresh out of college and splitting my time between graphic art and painting, the former funding the latter, Dag had pushed me to pursue production and wealth, by which he meant the money-making graphic art. I can still feel my humiliation at being lectured like one of his children. Even at the time, it went against my instincts to stop painting, but between Dag's insistence and our family's ethos, I gave in. Soon, my graphic art and fine art coalesced into a stylized consumer product that sold as fast as I could make it. I hired graphic artists, purchased massive printers, developed processes for ordering, shipping, accounting. I sold the entire production at the peak of its value and considered this a supremely rational choice. Dag approved, a rarity. He reserved praise as father had, preferring for reality to reinforce my right or wrong choices.

The euphoria I felt on selling the company passed quickly. In its place an instinct to hide. I used all the money I'd saved to buy the Midtown building and then kept the building empty after the last tenants moved out. Now every day I could see, touch, inhabit the decades I'd invested in making graphic art for profit. I painted. I threw the television out the window. I wore parkas in winter, my breath substantial in the cold air. There was no one to please but myself.

Dag joined me on the couch.

"What's all that?" He jerked his head toward the abstracts.

Taking a deep breath, I described the way the light shaped the neighboring rooftop, and how the colors flowed across it at dawn and dusk.

"Abstraction is at the base of everything," I told him.

He wasn't listening.

"We need to be unified," he said. "What grandfather built is slipping away. This is no time for one of your . . ."

"My what?" I asked.

"You see it happening, you know it's true. The so-called safety net that threatens to drown us. The irrational wars. Regulations that strangle banks. Socialized healthcare. It's the same creeping communalism that would have destroyed us, if not for grandfather. We'd be vassals to some Sino-Soviet state, if not for him. Now they're coming again. It's like an evil that seeps back when we're not vigilant. 'Brother,' they said back then, but they meant slave. Now it's racism, the climate."

He dismissed them, whoever they were, with a flick of his wrist.

"They enliven what they hate. They don't see: It's their structures that are irrational and racist. It's their policies that distort reality. They have no philosophy, they just worm around like nudibranchs."

He turned toward me, elbows on his knees, imploring.

"Woodby is what he is, we all know this. But he'll be a battering ram. That's why the moochers fear him. That's why we need him. Without him—"

He raised his hands in surrender.

"Without him you go on strike?" I asked.

"There's a video," he said. "People laugh when they see him fall."

I wanted to laugh with them, but my violence still shocked me. "It won't last," I reasoned. "Nothing lasts on the internet."

He shook his head. "You're making us look bad. At best you were a distraction, but now . . . You could be in jail right now. There were witnesses."

My breath caught in my chest at the thought of being arrested.

"We need to be unified," he said again. "We have to support the family name, which you bear."

"Which is it?" I asked. "We support the family or we don't. You heard what he said about father."

"You didn't have to *hit* him," said Dag. "There's a bigger picture, and Woodby is key."

"You would hate Woodby, if he didn't promise what you wanted."

"It's what's *right*, not what I want. You're focused on blood like we're the Cosa Nostra. 'Family first,' is that your motto now? Reason comes first. Without it, we're savages praying to sticks and dirt."

"If father were still alive—would you let Woodby say those things about him?"

"That would be father's problem," he said.

Would I feel the freedom to paint abstracts, if father were still alive? The question left me dumb. Tag interpreted my silence for agreement.

"There's a bill in committee," he said. "Do you know about this? It will hobble Ming. It will hobble us all."

He pulled his valise to the couch and rifled through it, searching for something, not finding it.

"Other countries are in on it. This sounds like conspiracy thinking, but it's not." He gave up his search and turned back to me. "Why don't you know about this? It's called the Bill for the Stewardship of Global Collective Behavior. You know what 'stewardship' means. It means control. 'Collective'? It's insanity. They want to control us like we're ants. They want control over Ming's platforms, all the platforms. They're worried we might think on our own. Collective behavior!"

He pushed himself off the couch.

"Do you want that?" he asked. "Do you think Ming wants that? Does it not offend your . . . sensibilities?"

Dag paced, then stood by the window, where the granite light frosted his hair.

"Yes," I replied. "It does offend my sensibilities."

He shifted his feet to face me.

"But so do you, sometimes," I added. "And so does Woodby."

He stared at me, expectant and impatient.

I wanted to swallow my tongue. What he asked felt impossible. Why would I apologize for something I was just starting to feel proud of? Why would I endorse someone I'd grown to detest?

"He deserved it," I said.

"You sucker punched him."

I felt anger rising in rapid breaths. "He called our father weak; doesn't that offend your sensibilities?"

"I was not a child, Tag. I remember things as they were."

"What does that mean?"

I searched my memory for things-as-they-were. Mother had been distant, and father was a distant memory. He was still our father. He worked, brought home his pay, taught us to mow the lawn and rake leaves.

"You were too young," he said. "I won't ruin whatever fantasies you have."

I wanted to hit Woodby again, for the satisfaction of watching him fall.

Dag frowned. "Father just didn't live up to it."

We both knew all of this, everything either of us was going to say, but I couldn't stop myself from needling him.

"You blame him for not being grandfather," I said.

"Don't."

"Being the son of the Great One would make anyone look bad," I said.

Dag shouted at me. "You see what I've done! It's more than he ever did."

He scowled, his face dark; he'd spoken from emotion, without thinking. This was Dag's vulnerability, his never-satisfied desire for achievement and the approval that went with it—that and a phobia of bridges, of all things, which he claimed he'd overcome through the simple application of reason.

I believed him. His powers of empiricism could flatten a hillside, and any fear seemed impossible in Dag. He was recovering as I watched, the emotion draining from him. Soon he would be calculating next moves.

Whether he had a phobia or not, I hadn't seen Dag drive in decades. Like many wealthy people, he used a car service or took cabs. He'd been in an accident, if I recall, on one of the long, high bridges to the north of the City. He must have been in his twenties, because I was still living at home with mother. His car, hit from behind, rammed the bridge's guard rails or one of its towers. I pictured air bags deployed, the hood accordioned. Maybe the car hung over the precipice, the river hundreds of feet below. Maybe none of it happened this way. I do remember him lying on the couch, with his casted arm suspended in an odd contraption that made him look like he was embracing the air.

Whatever his reasons, it did not surprise me when Dag asked if I had a car.

"I have errands," he said. He picked up the shopping bag and his valise.

Wondering how to get away, I led him to the Snowflake. On seeing the little car, he sneered and made a show of lowering his long body into the passenger's seat.

"They make real cars," he said.

"Some of them are yellow," I replied. "You can hail them on the street."

We drove loops around Manhattan. From Midtown we headed north, then across town, then west again to a store at 84th Street where I held my ground until a blue and white bus barreled up behind me, then down the East Side and back across town to the Village, of all places. The shopping bag he carried contained copies of grandfather's Great Book, and at each stop he took one copy with him. When he returned to the Snowflake, the book had been replaced with a package or a paper bag. He explained nothing.

My stomach growled, but Dag showed no signs of hunger or thirst. Maybe he wanted to finish his errands before harassing me into endorsing Woodby. After the stop in the Village, he returned to the car with a manila envelope. He pointed to the return address, a street in the east Bronx. If I'd gotten out and danced on the hood, he would have waited until I tired myself out and then pointed again to that return address.

We zigzagged once more across town, north on 6th Avenue, right on East 23rd Street, heading for the FDR. It would be just as fast to take the train, I said, but he didn't reply.

My knuckles were no longer red, though I still felt the lingering pain and a slurry of guilt, shame, and satisfaction. Woodby had deserved it, I assured myself. Politicians used words as bludgeons because no one ever punched them in the face. To them words were a game, with no meaning beyond power. They built and destroyed with words, sometimes only the latter, if it suited them, and I'd had it with Woodby's croaking at me.

We turned north on the FDR and jostled through a long, cramped viaduct before ramping down along the Harlem River. Dag's forehead shone—was he sweating? I examined him as we crossed a squat bridge into the Bronx, but he remained placid. Past a series of large warehouses, he directed me to a concrete-slab building across from a substation by the Bronx river. I decided it was time to tell him—something, that he'd have to find another way with Woodby—and as soon as I'd slipped the Snowflake between two dilapidated RVs, I turned to him, steeling myself, and parted my lips just as he departed the car, calling back before he closed the door, "Stay here."

I tried to see where he'd disappeared to but there was only the windowless concrete wall. *Stay here*, like I was a dog tied to a lamppost.

After few minutes he returned.

"Newark," he said. His face was drained, as if he'd received troubling news.

Handfuls of rain spattered the windshield as I started the engine and jerked the little car toward the Interstate. Here was an opportunity to confront Dag, to tell him something, but my tongue foundered between my teeth as we merged with west-bound cars.

"Take Riverside," he said.

Riverside Drive would lead us south along the west flank of the island to the tunnels under the Hudson. I heard him clearly, and there was time enough for me to adjust course, but a series of interchanges required my attention, and before I could react, we reached the mouth of the George Washington Bridge, its towers' tops dissolving in the low clouds.

I said that managing the car in traffic prevented me from turning south onto Riverside Drive, but I never considered it. Something unconscious was working my hands. As we approached the interchange, the signal was green, and Dag, looking up at the bridge above us, had time only to gag down his saliva before we sped up onto the deck, a building's height above the river.

"I'm not going to apologize," I said. "And I'm not going to endorse him."

Rain pelted the metal roof. Dag's mouth opened like the clouds, and he made a sound, a syllable, cut short by his focus on the road, now awash. His chiseled cheeks paled.

Over the river, the wind caught the Snowflake like a sail, and even with the steering wheel tight in my fists, the little car danced between the dashed white lane markers. Passing autos sprayed fans of water that the windshield wipers labored to sweep. I gave the wheel a jerk, shuddering the car, to watch the fright in Dag's face as he clutched the door handle. He wiped his brow with his free hand.

"Gah," he said. He cleared his throat several times.

"You okay?" I yelled, louder than I had to over the road noise. I felt something I'd never felt before: I could say anything to Dag.

His face twisted with distress.

"We need," he said in a strangled voice.

I had to lean forward to see the roadway as it shrank between curtains of water. For Dag to fear bridges wasn't possible. He had been an engineer. He was himself heights, sheer granite. I pictured him on the highest of girders, hands on hips, the city flowing out beneath him.

I pressed the accelerator, switching lanes unnecessarily.

"We what?" I asked.

He clutched his seat. His features sagged with the effort of his resolve. So long as the bridge lasted, Dag was an insect under my pin.

"You're kind of a dick," I said.

Ah crap, that wasn't it. I was unaccustomed to power and didn't know how to use it. I wanted to call him a narcissist, but the label might have sounded like "saint" to Dag, or to anyone in our family, for its implication of righteous egoism.

"I feel bad when I'm around you," I told him.

Was that better? He didn't seem to be listening. I slowed to let the spray from a tractor-trailer's wheels slap at the passenger window. Dag gaped in horror. If Dag could fear a bridge, then what would come of me?

I opened my mouth to jab at him again, but his pale drawn face, soft with sweat, stopped my tongue. If this was how I acted over a helpless brother, I was no better than he. In the clearing roadway, I saw that the only way forward, the only way to get along with Dag, was to leave—that is, to not have to. I had had this thought before, of course, in moments of frustration, but until then, as the rain eased and Dag panted in the passenger seat, depleted, still white-knuckling the door handle, the truth of it hadn't found me. We were cruel to each other.

Once this realization sank in, it took fast hold. How would I get away? I could tell him to leave my life, but he wouldn't listen so long as he wanted something—and did brothers say such things to each other? I could change the lock to my studio door, to which I'd long ago given him a key. I pictured him pounding on the door, me trapped inside. Would I have to leave New York? Some far place where a continent ended is where I would run.

"Apologize and endorse him," he said. "It's just words."

"Why is he more important to you than I am, or than father for that matter?" I asked.

"Maybe some time in jail would change your—"

I cut him off, feeling emboldened by the power of the bridge and by the knowledge, though not yet real, that I was leaving. "Getting him elected is more important to you than my dignity."

"Dignity?" He banged his fist on the dashboard. "You're too proud to take responsibility for your actions, and that is a sin."

Sin, evil. For a man bent on reason, he sure loved Biblical epithets.

"For hitting him? I did it. He deserved it."

"For not apologizing. For not endorsing him. And for diluting the voters' perception of him. You understand what's at stake here."

We passed a field of settling ponds ruffled by rain, an organic funk in the air. Since grandfather, our family's politics had been simple and economic: minimal taxes, minimal regulation, the market provides the rest. In this environment, man's rational egoism could flourish. It had existed once, briefly, maybe more than once. It was the system grandfather had engineered after his strike, the apotheosis of the Age of

Reason in America. It thrived at first as it organized people from chaos into chains of production and consumption. In its success, it cleaved to its core, demanding not minimal taxes but voluntary taxes, not minimal regulation but no regulation, and for justice only a force to protect private property and a judge to adjudicate. It had lost its balance. Inequities swelled, ancient grievances flared. The garbage piled up, so to speak. Taxes rose, agencies grew, irrational wars trundled on and were paid for with debt. Now our family name inspired as much derision as devotion, our voices few among many. We were just more piglets competing for teats.

Our dwindling influence had spurred Dag to frantic efforts. He lectured and donated books and inspired acolytes to walk over hot coals. The success of the Movement had always been his guiding light, no matter how dark the culture.

Dag directed me east toward the bay. I watched his profile as he thumbed a text on his phone. So purposeful, so set. He had no doubts.

"You know what to do," he said.

I should tell him I'm leaving, I thought. Where would I go? Instead I defended myself.

"Impugned is how I felt."

Unable to focus, I kept wandering into the opposite lane, and so I jerked the car into an airport hotel's half-circle drive and stopped under its wide awning.

"Get over yourself," he said. "It'll take a few minutes, and no one will care anymore."

"Did I fall in a rabbit hole? To stay in the club I have to apologize for being right, and suddenly you don't have to hold your nose around politicians?"

He sighed, a show for me.

"You don't understand," he said. "Online they're following you now, not Woodby."

"Dag, what are we doing here?"

"His poll numbers are down since the video. There's only one choice."

"No, I mean Newark."

"To catch a flight. Why else would I go to Newark?"

"And that detour by the river and the hangers?"

"I always go that way. I like the infrastructure."

"I have other things to do," I complained.

"These fools think you're a hero for hitting Woodby," he said in a low voice.

"I guess you never know what you'll be remembered for," I replied. I was losing my patience, though my new infamy intrigued me. Why couldn't they admire me for my paintings? To put him on the defensive, I asked again if he was going on strike.

In his eyes was the same shine he'd had as a teenage zealot. It was too full of nostalgia, this look, to endure it again so much later in life, and in a car so small. I got out and leaned on the open door. Dag climbed out and started circling the car, one hand sliding over the roof; too casual, cornering his quarry.

"Come back to the fold," he said, his voice marking a boundary between barbed wire and warm grass.

I decided I would follow Ming to California and leave all this behind. Ming!

"I have an event next weekend," he said. "In Manhattan. Come on stage. Help tell our story."

My throat closed, my breath whistled.

"I'm leaving," I croaked.

"We'll talk about growing up, we'll tell stories about grandfather!

Your endorsement—your followers," he stopped short.

"What followers?" I asked.

"You don't understand. I can't let you—"

"I'm leaving," I repeated.

"You need to do this. This isn't the time for one of your little ... fits."

My jaw set like cement. Instead of responding I dropped into the driver's seat and stomped the gas pedal, the passenger door slamming shut as I accelerated, and wished I'd come up with a clever parting line.

12

The rain had stopped, but the freeway was still wet, and a fine mist rose up from the pavement. We hovered in our lane, the Snowflake and I. The tension of hovering is always the crash, like running along a cliff's edge, looking down. A massive semi crowded our right, its tires topping the sideview mirror. Commuters cut in front, braked in a cloud of spray, swerved into the next lane. Somehow the Snowflake and I persisted, but I'd broken something. I still don't know what—a trust, a pledge, an unwritten code, a manacle?

Not one to be left behind, Dag would follow me, no matter his flight from Newark. He would ridicule my childish exit, then bully and manipulate me until I gave in. The thought enflamed my chest, and I pulled into a rest stop before the Lincoln Tunnel to calm myself.

Instead I called Chase. We hadn't spoken in a day, and though she answered immediately, she said nothing, just a stony silence for half a minute. It soothed me.

"I guess you're alive."

"Kidnapped by my brother. I just escaped."

"He take your phone?"

"Mea culpa. Mi dispiace, prego. Molto molto."

She groaned. "Stop it. When you disappear on one of these little . . ."

"Fits," I suggested.

"Yes, fits, your fits fuck shit up. And enough with the Italian. You're not Michaelangelo. You and the stupid languages. You know it's all your shit, right?"

Yes, all my shit. My building, a storehouse of paintings, connections to the wealthy and powerful, and the endless demands that came with ownership. Chase calmed enough to update me on the show (intense media attention, every painting sold), a new review of the Wall Street mural in a major paper (still no mention of OCCUPY, she sighed, sounding disappointed), two messages from Ming's people regarding her portrait, and a long conversation with our new friend, the Critic.

"Do you know you're trending?" she asked, summing up. "A five hundred percent increase in followers." She seemed impressed.

The understanding that I had to escape Dag trickled like ice water in my belly. He would be right behind me, glowering in the back of a cab and prodding the cabbie with the whip of his words.

"What do we do about them?" I asked.

"Monetize. If you stop fucking shit up."

With rare restraint, I refrained from pointing out that it was my bad behavior that had attracted the followers, and that maybe more bad behavior was called for, if followers were to be maximized and monetized. I pictured cartoon people massed together, hiding Waldo, or a shoebox full of olive-green army men. Followers were for celebrities and kings. They knew what to do with them.

Chase hung up before I could tell her I was leaving.

Traffic in the Lincoln Tunnel crept so slowly that my brother could have walked right up to me. I double-checked the door locks, a useless gesture. Anyway, New York was no different than the tunnel at rush hour. Dag could surprise me anywhere, at any time. I would leave my paintings, my easel, tubes of paint crinkled and half-rolled.

The studio was stuffy when I finally got home, and I pulled the chains that opened the high windows. On the breeze came the summer funk of wet pavement. I had dutifully carried Dag's valise up to the studio and tried to open it to search for evidence of global collective behavior or Dag's other obsessions and intentions, but the little brass catch was locked, and anyway, going through Dag's papers was a distraction. I fingered the car keys in my pocket. If I didn't leave at once, I would never leave. Dag would dress me down in front of his children, reason away my irrationality. Between him and Woodby, there would be no peace. I grabbed a canvas bag I used for carrying tubes of paint and headed for the bedroom. As I passed the supply table, I saw him: a man in my paint-spattered office chair, sandaled feet on the table.

"Forgot about me, didn't you?" said BBF.

///

Only a day or two had passed since I'd last seen him, and yet BBF's presence at that moment felt providential. Given that I had no one else to tell, I explained as I stuffed into my bag random clothes and the cash from the safe that I'd had a disagreement with my brother, who was likely coming for me as we spoke. He would pull me on stage for a wrongful public humiliation. That or I would be handcuffed and arraigned for punching Woodby. I had to leave immediately.

BBF leaned on the doorframe. "You gotta leave why?"

Because I couldn't face Dag anymore, and I would never endorse or apologize to Woodby, who in my rational world should apologize to me.

"You got the strangest problems," said BBF.

"Woodby deserved it, didn't he?" I implored.

"Depends what you mean, I guess. I was starting to think a little different about him."

It didn't matter, an apology was impossible without feeling like a worm, and I'd eaten enough dirt. It no longer felt like a choice to leave; it had become imperative. Butterflies batted at my ribs, irritated.

"If I stay I'll have to . . . I'll have to live in his world," I said.

BBF's eyebrows climbed his forehead.

"All rich people got these kinda problems?" he asked.

"I have to go," I said. "Now."

"Okay then. Where to?"

California, I told him, but in truth I didn't know. The thought of a life free of Dag blinded me.

He scratched his beard. "Good place for new starts. Though if you plan on driving, might need a closer destination. For a night anyways."

I was far from the only New Yorker ignorant of the lands west of Jersey, but he was right, and I was running from more than to, which meant going where my brother wouldn't find me. I sat down on the bed. It hardly mattered where I went. The trouble would follow, my brother would follow. Why, I wondered.

"I just want to paint," I complained.

"Well I got people. Someplace your brother won't find you."

That Plains-Southern-Western twang, drawing me into the midlands. Who was this man who knew a place where Dag wouldn't find me?

The mass of my building pulled at me. My studio, my home. Chase, my surrogate mother, so good at her job. The numbing comfort of routine: coffee on the corner, the Greek deli, cleaners down the block. The crenellated roofline, ever-changing. As people say, I was still processing the information, I had no answers.

Part 3

"To the glory of mankind, there was, for the first and only time in history, a *country of money*—and I have no higher, more reverent tribute to pay America, for this means: a country of reason, justice, freedom, production, achievement."
—Atlas Shrugged

13

I'd lived my entire adult life in the City and ventured little beyond its boroughs. The years of focus required to build my company left time only for the occasional train ride upstate to see mother, and I traveled even less once I slipped the strictures of business for the obsession of painting. When I was a child, we had moved frequently for father's work, a pattern seemingly designed to prevent us, or me at any rate, from forming close or durable friendships; after father died, we settled outside Albany, where the one friend I made soon moved for his own parents' needs. As a result, my knowledge of life outside the City was limited to the various living rooms in which I played, and the qualities of sunshine as they varied by latitude, and the vetch that grew tangled in the roadside ditches outside our final house, where mother eventually died.

To a New Yorker, the ground was the floor, and distances were blocks or subway stops. Trees were a form of public art, restrained between squares of sidewalk or herded into stands and groves in the parks. Some trees even wore small plastic signs engraved with their Latin and common names, like people at a meeting. Instead of flat lines in the distance, my horizons were three-dimensional: staggered planes of buildings, Avenues north and south, Streets east and west. A geography intimate and inhuman: close as a stranger's elbow on the train, as distant as a thousand feet of glass.

B and I traversed these canyons as an ant might labor across an elephant's hide, slowly and without perspective. We headed for the Lincoln Tunnel with thousands of others, crept west under the river, then out of the City into the surrounding web of highways. It was dark by the time we reached the hills of western Pennsylvania, the world reduced to cones of light on the pavement. When truckers were the only others on the road, we parked at the outskirts of a truck stop and reclined our seats for a few hours' sleep.

When I awoke, the horizon was pale yellow, pale blue. In this purity of light I first saw the rolling fields of Ohio, the corn-rowed flats of Indiana and Illinois. Irrigation ditches thick with weeds—was there vetch?

We had no map, and I had only the flip phone Chase had given me, but BBF seemed to know every highway and interchange and truck stop, which he preferred to the public rest stops, as the truck stops had hot food and hot showers and entertainment among the other drivers and prostitutes and thieves and the fringe that hung about. Clearly he'd driven trucks—he discoursed eloquently on best practices for air brakes and Jake brakes and whistled at the finer rigs, with their long gleaming cabs housing bunks and microwaves and televisions.

For hours we traversed the gridded flats. Corn flashed by, waist-high, shimmering green. Such distances, highways straight to a straight horizon. Every field was a study in vanishing points. We stopped every few hours for gas and fast food. My gut recoiled at the grease and salt, but the mouth craved it, and I ordered extras of battered chicken and pillow-crisp fries.

I did all the driving. While BBF navigated, he named for me the plants on the farms and the trees lining side roads and ditches. I recognized corn, as most any American would, and the wheat that bent so gently to any breeze, but without BBF could not have picked the low scrabble of cotton from the dense leafy shrubs of soybeans. He pointed out cottonwoods marshalled into tight windbreaks, farmhouses unseen in their lee. He also discoursed on chemtrails, energy drinks, and roadside bathrooms, the cleanest and largest of which had left enduring impressions on him, such that a half-hour might pass while he detailed the shininess of the stainless-steel hand dryers, the subway tiles so gleaming he could see himself, and showers with reliably hot water.

I admitted a shower sounded good. My shirt clung to my back and stank of sweat and fast food. I'd been so desperate to leave New York that I'd consigned our destination to a nebulous future that might never arrive—a future only twenty-four hours away, as it turned out, and much closer by the time we'd left the corn fields for soybeans and the Interstate for a languid two-lane highway that wound from farm-land into the hills.

BBF began to squirm in his seat like a child who had to pee. I offered to pull over but he waved me off.

"Let's get it over with," he said.

His resignation wasn't comforting, and I began to wonder what I had gotten myself into rather than face Dag.

It was early evening, the sky still lambent, when we parked on a patch of crabgrass under a dark canopy of leaves. At the driveway's end, a double-wide trailer shed paint in dull blue strips.

"It's my aunt's place," he said. "Raised me here with her two boys."

He gave me a sidelong frown, looking me over.

"We should a brought something," he said.

The screen door creaked open, and a stooped woman stepped out. She propped the door on one foot and examined us.

"Come to see if I was dead?" she drawled, revealing small, sharp teeth.

BBF looked down as we walked up the driveway. Outside the trailer sat a picnic table and a scattering of filthy plastic chairs. An aluminum recliner and two dilapidated Adirondak chairs rounded out the lawn.

"What's this you brung with you?" asked the woman. "Looks like a tax collector."

"Famously not," I said.

She scrunched her pointed features. "What's that now?"

BBF introduced me as an artist who was a little bit famous and even painted the President.

"Alright, but which one?" she asked. She watched me, her pupils bloated by her owl-eye glasses, then turned and yelled, "Roy!"

A young man in a baseball hat and dark hair came up behind her. His ears arched wide of his hat, matching the flare of his shovel-shaped beard.

"Mama let these boys in," he chided.

"I'd rather be out anyway," Mama sighed. She sat delicately on the lawn chair and patted her hair.

Roy wrung BBF's hand. He was an inch shorter and though solidly built was half BBF's girth, and he rolled his shoulders forward so that what little belly he did have stuck out in a paunch.

"Davis, get out here," he yelled. He hooted and pumped BBF's hand again.

A clean-shaved version of Roy peeked from behind the trailer. "Damn," he said. His thin lips hardly moved when he spoke. "The hell you been?"

"So," said Mama, a hard syllable. The lambent sky had faded to dusk, and an industrial-scale bug zapper painted her in purple light. "Is it Biblical or you just need something?"

"Prodigal son," said Roy.

"We should a slaughtered a calf," said Davis. He sat in a plastic chair and looked me over.

Mama said, "No calf to slaughter, and he's not my son. Barely your cousin."

"He our cousin," said Roy.

"Go slaughter us some frozen stakes," Mama said to Davis. She lit a cigarette and examined BBF.

After a moment Davis went inside, his face inscrutable in the low light.

In the deepening shadows the enormity of my running from Dag washed over me, and exhausted from driving and so little sleep, I drifted to the edge of the lawn and lowered myself onto a weathered Adirondack chair with, I hoped, enough intact slats to hold my weight. Outside the protective bubble of the Snowflake and far, far from home, I wanted to disappear, not make a scene. Wouldn't it be perfect for the city boy to fall right through his seat?

I arrived at an awkward smile as Mama examined me. City clothes, city cut, city shoes. I'd shaved at the last truck stop and combed my hair, the same as Dag's hair, light brown and parted on the side. I crossed my arms over my chest.

Roy sat at the picnic table with his elbows up. "Where'd you get off to?" he asked.

"All over," said BBF. "I left the rig at a distribution center outside Trenton."

"Where's Trenton?" asked Roy.

"I'd been adding up what I earned and what I spent and it was about enough for nothing. Anyways they got these cameras all over the insides of those things, and that put me over the edge."

The screen door creaked and Davis emerged with a baking sheet stacked with meat.

Roy scanned me, taking me in. "Who's this guy?"

BBF explained that I was an artist and a little bit famous. Roy looked back and forth between us, his mouth cracked open. Finally he asked, "You really go to New York?"

"Everyone got someplace to be all the time."

"You see Doreen?" asked Davis.

"For a hot minute. She works day and night. Waits tables."

"Only thing that girl could do with food was carry it," said Mama.

"That is true," said Roy.

Mama turned to me. "How you come to know B?"

"Your name is B?" I asked, incredulous and ashamed for not knowing.

"Tell him what it stands for," said Davis.

B declined.

"He's sensitive," explained Roy.

The two boys and Mama chuckled.

"You here for the casino?" asked Mama.

I was there because I'd left everything I'd ever known aside from the Snowflake and a bag of cash and clung to the only person to offer help. Mama smoked and watched me. I felt indebted to B, an unfamiliar feeling.

"I guess I'm getting away from New York," I answered. The words spilled out fast. A long pause followed while everyone listened to meat hissing on the BBQ and shared the same thought: city boy in a rush to go nowhere.

Mama twisted her neck again. "Davis, make those potatoes I like, and them frozen peas and carrots. Our guests need their food triangle."

The bug zapper emitted a series of loud cracks as it vaporized moths and mosquitoes. After an especially loud crack, one of the long purple tubes flared and entered a state of flux, its pulsing glow illuminating the boys' tanned faces and Roy's hat, on which was a round emblem with a familiar shape.

"State park's not far," said Mama, "just down the highway. You an outdoorsman? A New York City-artist-outdoorsman, painted a President, but which one. And there's nothing between that far city and this Okie hilltop."

Feeling exposed, I crossed my legs.

"I'm on my way to California," I said.

"Of course you are," said Mama. "You taking your shag mop with him?"

"California girls," said Roy with a grin.

"That state's a disgrace," said Mama. "Best it falls in the ocean like they say it will."

Falling into the ocean with me on it, a perfect ending to the hopeless act of running away. Dag would find me, or he would stand on the cliff where the land gave way, and the ocean swallowed the California disgrace and me with it, and he'd cross his arms and understand what logic made the earth fall.

"You got a job or something out there?" asked Roy.

How could I explain Ming? Teasing near-lover, client, genius, richest person in the world, an ethereal deity with incandescent skin and a mole on her lip. She fluxed like the bug zapper, hers a quantum time. With Ming there was no certainty other than profit, only titillating offers of lips and island and moon.

"I guess I'm taking a break," I admitted.

"What's that now?" asked Mama.

"He's got himself a family problem," said B.

My cheeks flushed. I wanted to crawl away.

"And how far along is she?" asked Mama in a hard voice.

I shook my head and raised my palms in defense. "It's my brother," I started, uncertain what to say next. "He believes certain things."

"He one of those conspiracy people?"

No, no, I protested.

Roy and Davis exchanged a glance. Davis bent a spatula into the meat, making it sizzle. Mama breathed out columns of smoke, smoke lifted from the grill.

"Tell you what's a conspiracy," said Mama.

All three boys groaned.

"This idea that making babies is the best thing since apples." Her cigarette see-sawed between her lips. "I love my boys more than cigarettes and coffee but I tell you what, parents are flat-out liars. They say, Hun it's rainbows and unicorns, but nah, it's tantrums and lies. Maybe they forget, time and all that. Maybe so. My guess is they want everyone to suffer just like them."

The steaks steamed as Davis turned them.

"Oh Hun, they say, it's so fun you like you a drunk clown at a carnival, but all you get is poor and worn out and sick. Time you're done you don't care about nothing. A woman shouldn't have kids if she wants to do something in the world. And still the only thing most people ever really make is a baby. Conspiracy if I ever heard one."

"City boy don't need to hear it, Mama," said Davis. He shot me a cutting look, as if I'd gotten her started on it.

"And boring," said Mama. "My goodness, watching your life pass before you while they playing with sticks or fighting over nothing. My goodness."

"Jesus, Mama," said Davis.

"Don't blaspheme now. You want to blaspheme, you get your own house."

"I'm sorry Mama, but come on now."

"You was a cute baby," said Mama.

"Girls like him," said Roy.

"'Til they don't," said Mama. "And trust me, that's the good news."

"It's the truck. They think he's a rich hillbilly."

"I'll die before I pay that thing off."

Mama dropped the spent cigarette into an ashtray at her feet, crowded with butts, and lit another. "You all should stay home alone with two devils," she said.

Davis set paper plates and plasticware on the picnic table.

"I never did intend on doing it alone, but then these two's daddy gets his bell rung roughnecking and that was that. Oil company sent me a letter and a pathetic fat man like an ass himself, bearing a check that don't add up to any kind of life."

"Took care of us for a while," said Roy. "Bought you the trailer from the bank."

"Like as bought me another pair of hands and a heart behind them. Then shag mop's mama goes off to wear a jumpsuit for five-to-ten, and his daddy be unknown to all but her. So then I got three, and if you think these mosquitoes can wear a person down, you try three baby bulls in a double-wide. I wanted to drown them in a bucket, more an once."

"His mama did alright," said Roy. "I mean she married alright."

B slouched at the table, jabbing at a leaf with his thumb.

"She too good for us now, believe that," said Mama.

Mama mumbled an incoherent prayer while we sat with our heads bowed and our hands in our laps. The boys ate with their faces bent over their plates. I examined the emblem on Roy's hat in the low light, a round patch with a face on it. B smirked as he watched me. Mama sat primly upright with her fork in her left hand and knife in her right. The potatoes were instant, whipped to spackle, and the steak was not beef but something gamey and tough. I cut pieces like I was feeding a baby, tiny, and nibbled them.

"So you're like a painter?" asked Roy. "So you paint, whatever, like mountains or something, and then people buy them?"

"You have no idea," said B.

"That's what painters do," said Mama.

"Why I'm asking."

Yes, I told him, and explained that I also painted portraits, among other things.

"Like at the state fair," said Roy.

"You hick," said B.

"Orphan," retorted Roy.

A brief skirmish of flung grizzle and potatoes flared and subsided before Mama could comment. Davis flicked a bit of gray fat from his shirt. Potatoes dotted the table.

"He had a show in a big New York gallery," said B. "People were protesting."

"Protesting paintings?" asked Roy. "Were they pornos?"

One corner of Davis's mouth curled up.

"People think they're controversial," I said.

"What's that now?" asked Mama.

"Ain't no controversy," said B. "Just paintings of buildings and people."

"Don't say ain't now," said Mama.

"They were yelling Occupy," said B.

"People got too much time if they yelling over paintings."

"They yelled at me and I was just being there." B spread his arms wide, fork still in his hand.

"Anybody'd yell at you," said Roy.

"A couple babies and they be too tired to yell," said Mama. She turned on me. "You got no babies?"

"Only myself."

"Least you're honest about it."

"Personal flaw," I admitted, then felt a twinge for not telling Chase I'd left.

"Can be that," she agreed. "Children might be good for these two. Learn something about themselves. Else people with too much time go on yelling about buildings."

"Paintings, Mama," said Roy.

"Don't be smart. Have a baby now and tell me how smart you are. Baby or two wise you right up."

"Mama's in the conspiracy too," said Davis.

"Maybe so, but I ain't going to dip shit in sugar and call it a lollipop."

The boys exchanged another look but said nothing.

Mama's magnified pupils poured over me. "So you rich or something?"

A morsel of meat, too tough to chew and swallowed whole, lodged itself in my chest, and I chugged water to flush it down. Davis watched me.

"Fair to middling," I managed.

"Can't trust rich people, even fair to middlin'. People get rich they pull up the ladder behind them. They don't need relations, they can just buy them. You make your money or you born with it?"

"I made it," I said. I'd had many advantages, but I paid my own way.

"He paints billionaires," said B. "Like that woman Ming."

Davis explained to Mama about Ming and her immersive social platforms and many other products that saturated our lives. Mama stopped eating to listen with her mouth slightly open, as if Davis held some authority on the matter and concentration was in order. When he stopped, she went on chewing.

"People got too much time for the wrong things. She got kids?"

"We use it," said Davis.

"Got to," said Roy, "if you want to stay connected. You should use it Mama."

"Far as I can tell, life is about making babies and trying to survive. All this change only leads one place."

"Rivers run one way," said B.

"He goes to New York and now he says stuff about rivers," said Davis.

"You know they make a river go backwards in Chicago?" Roy made a river with his hands, weaving one way then the other.

"Now why would anyone do that?" asked Mama.

"They make it bright green too," said Roy.

Davis dismissed him. "That's just on Easter," he said.

"It's a fact."

Mama waved them off. "Stay out a rivers. Current take you away."

Davis sighed. "That only happened once."

"We was down on that houseboat," said Roy. He grinned at Davis.

"Didn't matter anyway. I just came out in the lake."

"See if your jumpsuit mama ever invites us back there again," said Mama to B.

"She is kin," said Roy brightly.

"Your kin. My dead husband's sister and know this, I never did trust what came from her lying lips. Anyways, she too fancy for us now."

"Your mama on that houseboat?" Roy tipped his head toward B as he asked, and the patch on his hat caught the weak light from the trailer's windows. A cartoon animal?

"Go on down," said B. "She won't turn you away."

"They got rooms and rooms on that boat," said Roy.

B wagged his head, his face creased. "I left pretty abrupt."

"Well your mother deserves what she gets," said Mama. "And I mean that in all ways, good and bad."

"Said some things too."

"Deserves what she gets."

"Water is real nice this time of summer," Davis reflected.

"We'll take this painter guy with us." Roy jabbed B's plate with his plastic fork, needling him. "Jim will want a painting, like he's a billionaire too."

Davis nodded.

"I'm headed to California," I claimed, but I wasn't, not yet. Dag would find me there, and how would I find Ming, and what would I do without her?

"California's just a dream," said Davis. "Like when you wake up and realize it wasn't nothing, doesn't even exist except in your head."

"Don't embarrass yourself boy," said Roy.

Mama lit a cigarette and tipped her head back and pulled deeply.

"Hard to trust rich folk, especially ones didn't make it themselves. Married into it like your jumpsuit mama. Like if you two cabbage heads got rich, how could anyone trust you with it?"

The boys groaned.

"We didn't inherit anything," said Davis.

"You inherited plenty," said Mama. "You just don't do nothing with it."

The boys went quiet, their faces dark. B hunched over his food. The family conflict made my skin crawl, and I longed to be in the Snowflake humming neatly west.

"Daddy getting his bell rung set you back a piece," said Mama, "but you old enough now to make your own way instead of just being lazy."

"Lazy—" Roy sat up. "I just built you a fence hallway into those woods."

"I'm thankful, but if it needs to be said, halfway isn't all the way."

"What's the point?" asked Davis.

"Point is to go forth and make yourself a life on sweat, not excuses."

"I sweated plenty," said Roy.

"Your plan to wait for me to join Daddy so you can live in this moldy double-wide? That your plan? You go on down to that woman's houseboat and you know this while you're floating out there with no care in the world: You need to want something to get it, and you need to work for what you want. And waiting for me to die so you can live up here on this hilltop won't make you a man and won't make no life worth telling about."

The bug zapper crackled as if fueled by Mama's indignation. Roy worked his cheek between his teeth. Davis bent the tines of his plastic fork against his plate like a boy crushing a bug.

"Work like that job I had at Walmarts?" asked Davis.

Mama waved him off.

"Mama it's not like work anymore. Not like Daddy did or like your Daddy did. Now work is like you dead, like you a zombie but you don't eat brains, instead you gotta follow rules with your brains off."

"You should try eating some brains, boy," said B.

Davis scowled at him.

"You work so hard you living in a storage shed," said Mama.

"Do we have to do this right now? We got B here, and a—" Roy motioned toward me, searching for the word.

"You no different just because you got an inside bedroom," said Davis.

"Didn't raise you to be such children." Mama turned to me. "What you get from your father? Boys need a strong father."

Feeling weary I pushed my plate forward to rest my elbows on the table, then wondered if Mama might consider this rude and instead dropped my hands awkwardly in my lap. I told her that I too had lost my father when I was young. My mother had raised me, I explained, though in the only memory I could conjure of her, she sat by the window, smoke rising from behind her newspaper, while I lay on the floor drawing pictures and pretending to be elsewhere.

Mama's eyes lingered on me for a long moment, calculating I know not what, maybe my own potential for childishness.

"He lost what you lost and still made his way," she said. "Not worth crying about it."

"I don't cry about it," said Davis.

"I miss him," said Roy.

"Miss him all you want, but you got to do more than just that."

"He got a degree I bet," said Davis, waving his empty plate at me. "There's a world of work out there if you got a degree. And not just at Walmarts."

"A degree's not like that nose of yours," said B. "It ain't something you born with."

"Don't say ain't now," chastised Mama.

Davis glared at me, accusing and expectant.

I tried to explain that what had mattered most to my success was not a degree but the culture in which I was raised, realizing as I headed toward this conclusion that Mama might take offense as I implied that the boys' struggles were her fault. I hemmed, cheeks hot, then realized that my real advantage had been my name, which I *had* been born with. I was lucky to be my grandfather's grandson.

"Who's your granddaddy?" asked Roy.

"What name?" asked Davis.

"Hicks," said B.

"Orphan," said Roy.

"Tell him what B stand for," said Davis.

"I will pull the hairs from your balls."

"B now, mind yourself."

"Anyway, we all lost our daddies," said Roy.

Mama extinguished her cigarette. "And how different you are from this man who made his own way."

The boys glared at me.

I imagined myself on a rowboat without oars, drifting onto a dark river.

"Whyn't you yell at B for a while," pouted Davis.

"B's troubles are his own, not mine. Anyways, he's not living in my shed."

"Not yet," said Roy.

Davis turned on me. "You rich, why you up here eating roadkill?"

Roy and Mama snickered.

"Like I told you he's running from his brother," said B.

I took a deep breath, choosing my words. Was it really roadkill?

"He won't let me be," I said.

"Now that sounds familiar," said Roy.

"Can't imagine not letting a person be," said Davis.

"Don't be smart," said Mama. "There's letting yourself be and there's being your right self. You two are real good at letting things be, but you are not being your right selves. You like baby animals that don't know to hide. Hawk come and snatch you up once I die."

Roy flinched but ignored the barb. "How long you gonna run?" he asked.

"I'm not running," I protested. "I'm—trying to be my right self. But I can't be that around him, and he can't let me be."

"You your right self away from him?" asked Davis.

I had no idea. It seemed plausible, somewhere in a blinding landscape of unexplored being. I might die crawling across it, parched and famished, dragging Dag and father and grandfather behind me.

"I'll find out I guess."

"I will say this," said Mama. "Time passes no matter what, so you might as well do something worthwhile. Future will find you, even up here."

We sat in silence. I calculated how soon I could say my thanks and crawl back to the Snowflake to flee that hilltop. But where could I go that Dag wouldn't follow?

Roy clapped his hands together.

"Here's what we're gonna do. Davis and me and painter guy, we're gonna drive down to the lake and find that houseboat and tell Jim and jumpsuit mama just how sorry you are, B, for all you said, and leaving abrupt, and how ashamed you are, just too ashamed to say how sorry you are in person, like a man who stands on his own two feet and such."

Mama shook her head. She wiped her fingers in her napkin one by one.

"You swallowed a weasel, boy."

B had lifted one corner of the Snowflake at a gas station outside St. Louis, just to see if he could, but confronted with the thought of seeing his mother, he squirmed like a squeezed kitten. I felt a perplexing urge to comfort him.

"Well I'm not going," said Mama.

"Water is real nice," said Davis.

"See to all this first," said Mama. She waved her hand over the picnic table as she pushed herself upright.

She looked small and frail as she reached up for the screen door's handle.

///

B and I walked with Roy back down the gravel drive past the Snowflake to a set of faint wheel tracks in the stubbly grass. I wanted to slip into the Snowflake and disappear, but I was too tired to drive and didn't know where to go.

A half-moon hung over the treetops, and its pale light shaped the emblem on Roy's hat, a familiar, cartoonish form. B swept the hat off Roy's head and held it up to me.

Roy cursed. "I know it's not in the perfect middle," he said, rubbing his hair.

"Look familiar?" asked B.

I studied the patch, which, drained of its color in the moonlight, revealed itself in crude lines: a rounded face, a pug nose, triangular ears, button eyes. One of my mural's Pigs.

"Pigs get slaughtered," said B.

"That's right," said Roy. "Pigs get slaughtered." He snatched the hat from B's hand.

The cartoon Pigs from the Wall Street mural had escaped their pen, only to be captured on baseball hats. Pride and confusion and a fearsome sense of responsibility flooded through me.

"You knew about this?" I asked B.

"You got blinders on I think."

Why Roy would wear an emblem of irrational investing made no sense, so I asked him what it meant to him.

He contemplated his hat. "We eat the slops and then we get slaughtered. No one respects the Pigs."

We continued up the weedy trail to a one-room plywood shack with a screen door full of holes and two sagging bunkbeds jammed inside. I could see why Davis preferred his plastic storage shed to this shack, which had admitted water at some point and bloomed with white molds.

Roy grinned as I stepped past him. "I do like bacon though."

14

By the time I awoke, the treetops were alight, the lower limbs still bowls of shadow, the air pleasantly cool. I found B by the picnic table, stretching his arms over his head. He tried to sneak into the trailer to make us breakfast, but let the screen door snap closed behind him with a clap that flushed small black birds from treetop to treetop, chattering.

A few minutes later he emerged with two plates of bacon and eggs.

"I nuked it. Didn't want to wake Mama, but it didn't matter, she must a had a pill."

We ate in silence, listening to the cheeping black birds. I felt the urge to call Chase and immediately changed my mind.

B's face drew tight as he finished his food. He wiped his mouth on the back of his hand.

"The boys for sure are going to that houseboat," he said. His chest rose and fell in a cartoonish sigh. "I gotta go someday, I guess, and someday's no better than now."

Unsure how to respond, I frowned and let it go at that. Though I'd grown fond of B and allowed a creeping gratitude for his generosity of spirit, his family was his alone to manage, and he'd not asked my help. Since he'd helped me escape from Dag and Woodby and, it began to dawn on me, the stress of New York and a set life of any kind, it was only fair, I reasoned, to at least go along on his own unwanted family venture. And in the daylight the woods were airy and dappled, with an understory of ferns and fallen leaves, and the nuked eggs had the thick ochre yolks of home-raised chickens, and with the daylight and breakfast my fears and anxieties of the night before shrank like shadows. If I could survive a night in the woods with Mama and the boys, I could survive on a rich man's boat. California was like Davis had said, an idea we all have, a dream place, a place that Dag would search from redwoods to desert. Dag wouldn't find me on a houseboat in the Ozarks, or wherever we were.

/ / /

We followed Davis's muscled white truck down the winding road out from the hills. B spat the shells of sunflower seeds into the wind as we passed soybeans in perfect rows, a corridor of trees, more fields. We slowed on a main street lined with one-story structures, some with fanciful Western-style facades. A lone American flag snapped on its pole above a storefront American Legion, the building itself lined in fat red, white, and blue stripes. Several of the buildings were closed or vacant, others dilapidated, plywood nailed over broken boards and newsprint in the windows. No people to be seen.

Beyond the empty town and past a patch of woods, we crossed a swath of green river. Light opened all around as we emerged from the trees, a blinding flash off the water's surface, the river swelling up its banks so that the forest itself glinted between its trunks. Past the water we rolled through another town, a brief grid of houses clinging to the highway.

"Lived here before I went to Mama and the boys," said B.

He pointed to a stubby ranch house. With flat land all about, these homes must have flooded at some point, and, as if to confirm, the road lifted over a protrusion of water that swallowed bushes and reeds below us. All that water seemed sure to swell its over-fed flesh onto the highway and the anemic homes; push its green velvet up the walls of the American Legion, only the stars-and-stripes still dry above. It flooded B's heavy arms, his scrapple beard, his childhood home.

It would swallow me, too, and the tin-can Snowflake, if I stayed still in that place.

We snaked into the hills to a neighborhood of modest, newer homes. Davis parked before a house like all the others, and he and Roy jumped out and hauled their bags from the pickup's bed. We followed them to a wrap-around deck, below which the hillside opened to a sweeping view of the lake and purple bluffs beyond. It was not at all a modest home, as I'd thought, but sat on multiple stories stacked into the hillside.

"My mama and Jim bought this place for summers," said B. "Along with the houseboat, which must be out on the lake somewheres."

Below us, the boys scurried to a dock on the lake where a motorboat bobbed.

"They won't be real patient," said B. "Soon as they find where Jim hid the keys, they'll be gone."

As soon as we climbed aboard, Roy started the motorboat's engine and pushed the throttle. The boat reared back and shot out a ridge of foam. I clutched my seat. B stared sullenly across the water. Towed by his intransigent joy-seeking cousins, he was racing toward what he'd just helped me escape. Odd how every possibility is happening somewhere.

On the main body of the lake, Roy stood to scan the water with binoculars, and Davis snuck into the driver's seat behind him. Roy pointed to an inlet to the south. The air pummeled our heads as Davis pushed the boat hard into the wind. Too late, I remembered the sunglasses I'd been keeping in the Snowflake's glovebox—and my bag of clothes and cash stuffed under the seat. The only thing I'd brought with me was a copy of the Great Book, from the bag Dag had left in the car.

Davis cut the throttle as we entered the inlet, and the motorboat rolled forward on its swell before slipping backwards into the trough, splashing me and B. A dozen specks grew to cubes, houseboats at anchor. Roy pointed to a tall rectangle, too tall, like a child's Lego creation, square in every way except for a blue spiral slide attached to its stern. A petite woman in an orange sarong and a teal one-piece bathing suit came to the railing.

"Well look what the catfish brought up," she said.

B winced.

His mother was prettier and more delicate than I'd expected, her chestnut hair in a neat ponytail and her smooth skin tanned over high cheekbones, just like B's. She and her son exchanged a long, charged look as we climbed aboard.

"What an unexpected pleasure," she said in a high nasal twang.

We stood in a sort of lounge connected to an open kitchen. The tinted windows that lined the decks cast a dirty light on a built-in seating area lined in white fabric, white-shaded lamps, white vinyl and carpet on the floor. Stainless appliances like fake teeth were sandwiched between enamel-white cabinets. White stairs led up and down.

B's mother—Debra was her name—stood with her hands clasped before her and told us that dinner would be roast trout at dusk, and we really ought to stay a piece.

A steward in khaki shorts waved us toward a pair of cabins, each with two beds. I castigated myself again for leaving my bag in the Snowflake. It turned out to be fine—the steward brought me a stack of clothing, and the bag of money stuffed under the driver's seat was still there when we returned two days later. Rather, it bothered me that I'd cared so little for such a great sum as to leave it in the car like an old sweater. It was as if something had gone missing from my values.

As I changed into the clothes the steward had handed me, all of which—shorts, short-sleeve sports shirt, bathing suit, sandals, even sunglasses—fit perfectly, I could hear Roy and Davis yelling as they pounded along the deck above and whooped and spiraled into the water. Between the boys' yells I heard two other voices, hushed and taut. Debra's nasal twang rose with emotion. *You punished me plenty enough.* A man responded but I couldn't make out who it was, though I assumed it was B. I heard the word *apologize* and then a door open and close.

I left the room to lay on a chaise lounge in the shade with a pencil and pad of paper I'd found on the nightstand. I sketched the boys floating in the water, then the lake and hills, the steward busy in the kitchen. In sketching, I felt safe.

/ / /

The next I saw B was at dinner. The steward served trout fillets roasted in butter, potatoes cut into identical cubes, pared glazed carrots. Anchored trimly at the head of the table like a black-and-white movie star, Jim ate with fork in his left and knife in his right and asked me polite questions about my work, though from his flat affect and distraction I could tell he already knew about me or didn't care. He might have searched my name on the internet—no doubt the boys had told him who I was, if he didn't already know—and read the review, and seen the Wall Street mural with its OCCUPY, and maybe Woodby's bloody lip too. He gave no indication. He sustained a toothy smile from under a private-eye moustache etched to his upper lip. His and Debra's teenage boy and girl sat on either side of him, heads bent to their phones.

When I asked Jim about his own work, he blustered for several minutes about oil fields and the rigging his company sold to work them. *Don't mine the gold, supply the miners,* he quipped, before confessing that he'd inherited both his company and the modest patch of wells on which his grandfather had started the family fortune. In the twilight, oil seemed to seep from his words and blacken the sky as he spoke. Only when the quarter-moon lay itself on the eastern bluffs to spill its molten light across the lake did the spell break. My grandfather would have whipped this man with his tongue—*what did you build yourself?* asked my father, my brother. They saw men like Jim as placeholders, teeth on a gear rather than the builder of the machine. Only a person who didn't need wealth should inherit it; my father said this so often he seemed to damage himself with each telling, his wealth never having matched his own father's. He wanted, above all, to be known as a man who made money, but even I had made more money than my father ever had, and if he hadn't already died, that fact alone might kill him, to be outdone by his least promising son and an artist at that. It hadn't ever made sense to me. What was so wrong with a parent ensuring their child's security, if they had the means? Grandfather's entire philosophy, in its practical implications, centered on the moral dignity of wealth creation. Denying the legitimacy of inheritance seemed spiteful, and why was it okay for someone who didn't need money to inherit it? It seemed an even greater moral hazard to deny a less-able child the means to raise their own family. Would Jim's phone-addicted teenagers live their best lives by being given nothing of their family's wealth? Or would they waste it, and themselves, as Mama had told Roy and Davis they would do, given the chance? What might I have done with some portion of my family's wealth? I would still have painted, would always paint. I might have skipped building a company and the atrocious art it was made on, but who's to say if that's true, or if it would have been a good or better life? We inherit much more than money, after all, though family, strangely, was unessential to grandfather's worldview.

I said none of this to Jim, though he might have read grandfather's words himself. It seemed like everyone had, or at the least, everyone had an opinion about them. Just to be sure, or maybe to torture him, I would leave the copy of the Great Book.

///

After dinner I sat in the lounge across from Davis, who stared into the glow of his phone. Roy had left his cap with the squealing Pig on the coffee table, and I picked it up. The rendering was so crude it could have been done by a child, but somehow the grin and attitude of the face were unmistakably those of my Pigs. Who had examined the mural closely enough to find these Pigs and then coopted them to their own mysterious purposes? We were a long way from Wall Street, and as far as I understood at the time, the notoriety generated by the mural had been brief and loudest right there in New York. Of course I was wrong, at least to the extent that my Pig grinned at me from a baseball hat on a houseboat in the midlands.

Up to then Davis had mostly ignored me, except for the occasional scornful glance, and when he looked up from his phone and saw me holding the hat, I dropped it on the coffee table.

"I found it online," he said.

He showed me his phone's screen, but from across the table I could make out only some lettering in the bright glow.

The scorn in Davis's face whenever he'd looked at me had narrowed to suspicion, which I took as improvement. Scorn was for worthless people, after all, and to know someone's worth was to know them, at least in some fashion. Davis had scorned me as if he knew me, as if I wore a sign around my neck that revealed my worthlessness to him. He saw only my neat hair, clear skin, soft hands. He knew from B that I was a New York artist, a little bit famous, and fair-to-middling rich, and altogether this may have been enough for him. I revealed myself with every word, my posture, my obvious discomfort at being a traveler among natives whose traditions I didn't know. In fact I knew so little of his world that it was easy for me to assume the opposite, that I knew on paper, as it were, the impacts of economic and cultural movements and the lives they left behind, for which I probably had my own scorn. Children raised on Mountain Dew and daytime television, with the pride of poverty. But I'd met Mama. She fed them the food triangle and pushed them to fly from the nest. When Davis reached out to me with these small gestures, I nearly leapt at the chance to connect in some way, to diffuse his scorn and its implied threat, real or imagined. As long as I was there, I wanted to fit in.

I asked him what the Pigs meant to him.

He'd found them on social media, he explained, on a platform where people felt free to speak. A group of the like-minded, he said, gauging my reaction. One day, the de facto leader of the group had replaced his avatar with one of my grinning Pigs. Soon they were every-where. Roy had made his own with an iron-on patch and a marker.

"Strange you haven't seen them," said Davis.

He snatched a pair of binoculars from the table and handed them to me, pointing to a nearby houseboat. Through the lenses I spied a pole at the houseboat's stern, on it a flag lilting in the moonlight. A gust loosened the flag's folds, and there grinned a Pig, more carefully drawn, but the same image as on Roy's hat. My Pig.

I handed the binoculars back to Davis, who toyed with the strap.

"B says you're all about freedom," he said.

Was I all about something other than painting? I had left my life, so yes, I believed in the evident freedom to leave my life. My early work extolled freedom of capital, the freedom of man to think and create, freedom from government interference, freedom to use the resources and opportunities around us. I had freedom so long as the bag of money was safe in the Snowflake.

"I'm not sure I think about it like that," I replied, but Davis was staring over the black lake and its prisms of light.

When he turned back he spoke so quietly I had to lean forward to hear him. "You should come to a meeting. They should meet the Pig artist."

It was a VR social media site, he explained, rendered in three dimensions to lifelike perfection. There the Pigs met in secret to discuss the great evils of our day. The great evils, when I asked, were vaguer than I'd hoped but included government overreach and Leftist overreach and when he got down to it, socialism in whatever its forms. He closed with some unkind words for environmentalists. The group held frequent meetings in the virtual world. They were all about freedom, too, he told me.

Eager to defuse Davis's scorn, I agreed.

/ / /

The next meeting of the secret council of Pigs was the following night. After another dinner of roasted fish and buttered vegetables, Davis led me to Jim's office, where we sat at a curved desk under banks of monitors hung from the wall. He tapped an address into a browser window.

"It's way better with a VR headset, " he said, "but they cost like twenty truck payments."

I remembered Ming's visorless helmet over my ears and her diaphanous robes and lips so close to mine.

The screen faded to black, then cobalt blue. This was one of Ming's platforms; the same colors and font that had spelled *Welcome, Ming* now spelled *Welcome, Davis*. On the screen, an environment took shape that appeared familiar—land, sky, structures with doors and windows. Using a track ball and spinning it impatiently, the graphics stuttering to keep up, Davis steered us to a dome-shaped building among other, similar structures, all with thatched roofs. From the outside it appeared to be a modest hut, but inside opened to a vaulted great room with a fireplace sized for a hunting lodge. Davis navigated past the fireplace to a door in the corner, where he tapped on a numeric keypad to open a dialog box into which he typed a code. The door opened to a plain, rect-angular room. A vast circular table floated in its middle, surrounded by seated avatars. Most of the avatars had Pig faces, some squealing, others grinning lasciviously. Davis's avatar took the last open seat.

"This guy always starts us off," he said.

He hovered the pointer over a squealing pink face like all the oth-ers. A label appeared above it: TRBL73.

"If we wasn't on Jim's boat, I'd turn on the sound, but, you know. We have to read it instead."

The AI, he explained, converted text to speech for those with speakers or headphones, and speech to text for those without. Another of Ming's AI. Everything we said and did in this world would be known to her, if she chose to know it. Ming, who always knew.

The Pig leader waved its arms for attention. The black line of its mouth opened, but no sound came out. Davis cursed the boat's poor bandwidth and Jim's graphics card and his own lack of a headset. A moment later, words ran across the bottom of the screen.

Now is the time. Now is the only time, said TRBL73. He foresaw an imminent erosion of personal freedoms and a sharp break from our dearest values. He blamed the government, the elites, muddle-headed socialists, irrational jurists, malfeasant corporate actors. The speech itself was evidence of a freedom that the author would fight to keep. *Now is the time*, it concluded.

Exclamatory responses flooded the screen. A person with the handle RYooL-B wrote, *Pigs get slaughtered!*, sparking hoorays from the other Pigs.

"That's Roy. He's on my phone downstairs."

Seeing the words I'd painted cheered by strangers gave me a brief thrill. The appropriation didn't bother me; after all, none of it was really mine, aside from the brushstrokes and the colors. Rather it was the who and why that troubled me: Who had seen the mural, and what did they intend? The Pigs were still losers, but now to be pitied rather than pilloried for irrational greed. When I asked Davis who had inverted the Pig narrative, he stared at me. The source wasn't important—didn't I understand?—it was their narrative now. People with more money and time could ponder the ironies and transitions of history.

RYooL-B wrote, "WE GOT THE PIGS GUY!"

This confused everyone, but eventually someone posted a link to a photograph of the Wall Street mural, and after a few seconds, an image of the mural popped up over the conference table, my name hovering above it. I doubted anyone could read the words *Pigs get slaughtered* in the tiny image; you could barely read them standing at the mural. The words were lines of paint, rounded cheeks, an axe handle, spattered blood, but the Pigs themselves were clear as day, and the screen filled with exclamations and questions.

Several lines of *Pigs get slaughtered!!* scrolled up, like the answer to a question they'd never been asked. Someone started a call-and-response—*Who Pigs? We Pigs!*—that consumed the entire screen. When this swell subsided, LINKUP69 posted a second photo, a blow-up of the word OCCUPY from the bottom of the mural.

Davis muttered something.

With Chase's rationalizations in mind, I told him to type a response explaining that this word was buried like bones beneath the feet of the bull and the bear and the traders. He asked me to repeat this several times and tapped with two fingers, swearing at each typo, until I pushed him aside and typed for him.

"True dat," wrote AR39.

"Savage," said CLINDED16.

A second window opened over the virtual table, this one playing a grainy video. My spine tingled when I saw myself turn abruptly, take two steps and throw my fist at Woodby's jaw. Woodby crumpled and fell. In the video I reeled back and hit him again and again without pause. My hand throbbed as I watched.

Davis turned toward me.

"That's our guy," he said.

My fingers dug into the chair's arms. I was in Woodby country and didn't even know it. My ignorance astounded me. On the screen, several of the avatars stood from the table and left the room, their legs pumping awkwardly.

"He insulted my father," I said.

Davis studied me. I felt around behind my chair for something to defend myself with.

"You sucker punched him," he said.

"He deserved it. Ask B."

The computer emitted a chime.

"You've got a message," I said.

It was a DM from TRBL73, asking to meet with me and my "host," meaning Davis, if we happened to be in Oklahoma or the general North Texas or Panhandle regions. My fame had finally saved me from something.

This development caught Davis between emotions; he couldn't alienate me if he wanted to meet the leader of the Pigs.

Into the public chat, TRBL73 spun a two-sentence masterpiece on the paradoxically harmonious composition of the ancient violence embodied in the Wall Street mural. I assumed he did so to assuage the remaining avatars and turn their attention away from Woodby, to my benefit, and possibly his own. He used the word *liquidity* to describe traders with their hands full of cash. He was a finance guy, or had been; he'd seen the mural because he followed the markets. The Pigs he had stolen for his own purposes. A soft-fingered finance guy would not arrange a meeting like this to direct trouble at me. He wanted something.

TRBL73 messaged Davis an address and a time.

Davis hesitated, then replied yes. As soon as he pressed the return button, I left the office to look for B, perhaps to hide behind his bulk. I found him in the lounge, staring out into the dark. Roy sat across the coffee table, tapping at Davis's phone. He watched me as I passed, his mouth agape.

I sat next to B.

He adjusted his meaty shoulders under the polo Debra had pushed on him. "It's not that I'm not sorry sometimes for things I say, except when they're true and need to be said. Anyway, yelling and being sorry are fine when there's a house to hold them, but this ain't no house." He threw up his arms. "This a playhouse with play people and play time. Jim plays at work, oh, always workin all the time. Like he knows from work. What kind of house has a slide on it?"

Davis came down the stairs as B complained. He and Roy conferred in whispers that I tried to hear. Roy's face opened in wonder at the complex turn of events.

I tried to engage B.

"We should leave tomorrow," I said in a low voice.

The boys laughed at something on Davis's phone. Was it an AI video of Woodby punching me? Or of me being eaten by Pigs?

"We're going to meet the Pig leader," I said, louder, so that Roy and Davis could hear.

"What now?" asked B. He tugged at his polo's sleaves.

"He means TRBL73," said Davis. "From online?"

"You should come with us," said Roy, "unless you want to stay here and complain some more. Or yell at Jim like you did last time."

"You the damn reason I'm here complaining. Oh and by the way, yelling is no longer allowed on these here premises. Fucking boat. Boat's exactly where some yelling should be."

"We're going in the morning," said Davis. "We'll take this guy." He gestured toward me with a flick of his wrist.

B wasn't listening. "Jim don't abide yelling no more, don't you know? Instead we'll all just trim our mustaches an talk about daddy."

The boys giggled.

"He all mustache and teeth and daddy's money," said B.

He pulled off the polo and threw it over the side.

15

I slept fitfully and dreamed of Pigs, rampant in the streets. In the morning I left on the kitchen counter the copy of grandfather's book I'd brought with me, along with the sketches of the boys and the lake and hills.

We took the Snowflake, with the boys crammed in the back seat, complaining. The address TRBL73 had given us led to a diner in a town a two-hour drive west. Throughout the drive Davis picked at Roy over how he'd treated Davis's last girlfriend and how she'd left because of it, to which Roy enumerated Davis's many faults, which in no doubt pushed the woman into the arms of a Sherriff's Deputy one county over. They lapsed into a chill detente, then started again. By the time we reached the diner and settled into a booth, they'd grown weary and irritated and flung sugar packets at each other, until B reached across the table to intercept Davis's volley and put a stop to it. White paper packets littered the table.

Distracted by the boys' spat, we'd not noticed the approach of a bald, medium-sized man with olive skin and odd, elfin ears.

"Which of you is D-DOG04?"

"Right here sir," said Davis, stiff at attention. "And this here's my brother, he's RYooL-B."

"And this?"

"My body guard," I said.

B snorted.

"No offense," I said to the man, who I assumed was TRBL73.

He sat delicately next to B.

"None taken, none taken. You should be cautious."

His face was clean and evenly tan, and he wore sharply creased slacks and a short-sleeve shirt of fine cotton. I imagined him taking master-of-the-universe calls from his beach house.

"And I must ask, because you are known to me: You came to Oklahoma for the Pigs?"

"The Pigs found me," I said.

I recognized him as a breed of market evangelist, a self-satisfied, whip-smart devotee to the morality of capital. He was every creature from the Wall Street mural, except for the Pigs.

"You were in finance," I guessed.

"What gives me away?"

"Everything."

"I knew your brother a little. When he worked on the Street."

"If I were my brother, you would pay me to be here."

"If you were your brother, we wouldn't be talking at all. He's a vapor in the zeitgeist, a pure thing, elemental. He's not like you, with the . . ." He waved vaguely.

"Why are you in Oklahoma?" I asked. Meeting a market evangelist in a diner at the edge of the Plains was like seeing a friend from high school in a foreign land.

"Many reasons, friend."

He crossed his arms on the tabletop.

"Why my Pigs?" I asked.

"You wrote it: Pigs get slaughtered. It's true. Look around."

"They get slaughtered for being irrational."

"Pigs are slaughtered to be eaten," he corrected.

"They're my Pigs," I bluffed. "Money should change hands."

"Money changes everything," he agreed. "Now, why'd you hit Woodby?"

The boys watched me squirm as if I'd crawled from a swamp.

"He insulted my father," I said. "My father's passed, leave him alone." When no one spoke I added, "He might be a battering ram but he's still a tool."

TRBL73 looked at the boys, then around the diner. "That may be a true statement, friend, but it would make you unpopular here. Some of these people might have more than words for you."

I held still as a deer at the snap of a twig under the hunter's boot.

"Now, a painter of Pigs might get some respect."

"You've already got the Pigs," I said.

"I can copy and paste, but I don't paint. There's a movement just waiting for a flag. A spark."

"How many of your group know I'm that guy? You know, Woodby."

"Listen, you're lucky that no one around here knows who you are. You're lucky I found you first. You might consider rehabilitating your image." He brought his hands together in a soundless clap. "Now, I can help you, if you wish, and you can help me. To answer your question, only a few aside from us here know about you and Woodby. In fact, most of our online group are AI Presences. They started joining last year. I still don't know what motivates them, but they make our numbers grow so the algorithm sees us. It was the algorithm that spread the Pigs."

The algorithm chose our future? Or was it Ming?

"Your group isn't even real?" I asked.

"It's very real, in the important sense of being visible. How we get the numbers, who they represent, this doesn't matter. Having the numbers is what matters. With the numbers, the message becomes visible."

"You have numbers but you don't paint."

"You're getting it."

"I'm really not. I'm getting that you stole my Pigs, and now you're threatening me."

"Maybe a story will help," he said. He rubbed his hands together and leaned over the table. "Picture the common man," he began. "This man, he wakes with the dawn. He sleeps in pajamas, the full set, with the button-down top. His wife makes breakfast. The TV news is on. They watch the news between bites of toast. He drives to work, something agri-industrial, selling pesticides maybe, or managing a warehouse. He listens to talk radio while he drives. He changes his coat when he gets home, puts on slippers. These are the things he does, this man. After dinner, he and his wife watch TV, take their evening aspirin and antacids, go to bed. They've been married since high school. Sometimes he thinks about the news, or repeats what he's heard on the radio, but mostly the information passes through him, as if he's got a pipe in his head. News pours in, it pours out. He holds it for an instant, the way we hold our breath, then gone. What thought has he had of his own? I mean beyond the thoughts of the cow: need to piss, eat sweet grass, follow herd. He's not what you'd call an emotional man, but his breath quickened when he first kissed his wife, his heart swelled at his son's birth—like that. These are just the highlights, you understand. This man has felt his life as it flowed past him. At some point, he realizes he's made no mark on the world, however ordinary, and he's stunned by this fact, speechless, dumb. This ordinary, essentially common man. He's nameless he's so ordinary. When company comes, he sits on the couch with his wife and recounts the day he first asked her out—on the stairway, between classes, graduation on the horizon—and his wife pats his hand. This is it. He has the life people fight for, dream of, whether they know it or not. And yet, no one dreams of being a worker ant. We dream of freedom and after breakfast put on our shackles. We dream of flying and in waking choose chains. Act for this man. Paint the Pigs. It will seem as if gods have visited him, from his own mythic soul."

B nodded along, but I was lost. The boys and I exchanged a glance, our first of shared understanding, or in this case, not understanding. We shook our heads at TRBL73.

"Do you believe in freedom?" he asked me.

"Without it life is nothing," I said.

"Liberty or death, then?"

"Freedom or the fight for freedom," I replied.

"You do get it."

"No, I really don't."

I checked the boys to see if our mutual misunderstanding held. They shook their heads again, confused.

"Okay," said TRBL73. He raised his hands. "Let's try a Bible story instead. You know that parable where the swine run to the sea and drown?"

No, I told him.

"Government is the sea."

"So do I stop them? I don't understand."

"I know that story," said Davis.

We all turned to him.

He cleared his throat. "There's like a crazy guy. Jesus strikes him or something . . ." He trailed off.

Roy smacked him with his baseball hat.

"Word is you're close to Ming. Do you know about this bill in Congress? Your brother knows."

Global Collective something, Dag's obsession. Ming seemed unconcerned by the alleged powers of the government.

TRBL73 had a more nuanced perspective. Ming's VR platforms had redistributed the narrative of the nation, he explained, such that it was no longer controlled by the state. So of course the government was coming for her. They wanted that power only for themselves; it was the only true power they had.

They had the power of guns and money, I pointed out, to which he shook his head. These powers too existed only through narrative, he insisted.

"What they don't see is that to propose the question of control means that we are controlled," he continued. "And that's what offends me, being controlled like so many ants. It's time for the Pigs to have their say."

"Saying what? Who are they?"

I kept glancing at the boys, who wrinkled their faces.

"In that Bible story," said TRLB73, "when the Pigs are running, before they hit the water and drown? I see a whole life in that sprint."

He stood up and left.

The boys looked around, as if for a ghost. I got up to follow TRBL73 outside, but he'd disappeared. On the table, he'd left a folded sheet of paper, on it a list of addresses across the Midwest. *Paint the Pigs*, was all it said.

"Did that make any sense?" I asked. I was pushing my moment, forcing a beachhead of mutuality.

Roy frowned. Davis looked through me.

"Jesus like touches the guy or something," said Davis, "and then the swine go running."

"Bible stories," said B.

"Why paint Pigs?" I asked.

All art is propaganda, wrote Orwell, that infamous maker of pigs. But were my Pigs Orwell's more-equal-than-others fascists? Greedy and reckless investors? The disenfranchised? Or all of us ordinary Americans, living our lives dumbfounded on the couch?

"We eat the slops and then get slaughtered," said Roy.

"What did he mean?" I asked. "Are we supposed to save the Pigs from the government?"

"No dumb ass, we paint them on government buildings," said B.

"What's that going to do?"

"Piss them off," said Davis.

"Start something," said Roy.

Davis stared over the Formica table and the sugar packets scattered across it.

"How are we gonna get by?" he asked. "Just painting Pigs for nothing."

He'd surprised me with how quickly and easily he went along with TRBL73's directive—we would paint Pigs of course. Whatever his reasons were didn't matter, because I too had made a quick decision, one aimed at ensuring my safety and inclusion. I could pay our way, I offered. As long as the bag of cash lasted, we would cover the Midwest in Pigs.

All three boys stared at me.

When he recovered, Davis asked if they might have their own money, like an allowance for food or things they needed or wanted that didn't have to involve my saying yes or no like a parent. While his negotiating for my money raised my hackles, his suggestion made sense, and we agreed that I would cover transportation, supplies, and shelter, and give them each a weekly stipend for their individual needs. B twisted his lips in amusement or surprise.

My rehabilitation was in progress. New York was a stale trap, California a dream I couldn't grasp. In between was this vast canvas. Pigs romped and squealed in my mind.

10

I had hoped, foolishly, that as part of TRBL73's antigovernment cause, the boys would be more proficient in acts of disobedience, but IRL all they'd done was sit in the light of their devices. B, on the other hand, revealed a ken for planning and organization. We needed to practice, he insisted. He shepherded the boys through a Walmart to buy black T-shirts and cargo pants—not the head-to-toe camo the boys favored— and to a second big-box store in another town for cases of spray paint. Unable to find pink spray paint, he learned from videos he watched on Davis's phone to mix his own by sticking the nozzle of a can of white spray paint into that of a can of red, the white one upside down and chilled first in the motel room's minifridge to decrease its pressure, this according to B.

Thus prepared we prowled backroads, searching through the shifting green fields for somewhere to practice. We chose a dilapidated barn, brown as earth and marooned in the grain. We waited until nightfall. The barn's back side canted toward the ground, suggesting imminent collapse, an angled void in the night, until Davis figured out the gas lantern we'd bought. It was too bright, and instead we used camping headlamps that cast a pale, sterilized light. B set up a nifty extension ladder that folded small enough to fit in the Snowflake's hatchback, though it made no one happy. Every few minutes he reminded Roy and Davis to stop bickering and shut up. I painted a circle in matt black, its apex high as I could reach. The boys followed, filling it with white. Here they proved surprisingly adept, working with a can in each hand, four in all, while B and I watched. After the boys finished I shaped the cheeks in thin layers of fleshy pink. I'd played with spray paint in my building, but it was a new medium to me, and from the first can I learned that it did not mix like oil or layer like acrylic.

B made us wear disposable gloves to keep the evidence off our hands, and the gloves' fingers became clogged with paint and stuck to the cans' nozzles and had to be changed frequently, forming a pile of paint-smeared vinyl gloves in an open garbage bag that B had laid out. We'd started just after midnight, and pink streaked the east as we stood back to admire our work. The boys were giddy, possibly from paint fumes and lack of sleep, and jostled each other and giggled until one of them stepped on the other's toe and he squealed and B had to shut them up. The Pig's head was off center and the colors needed work, but to the little team, it was a triumph. Roy took pictures with Davis's phone, which B deleted. On each side of the Pig, I painted a question mark.

///

After replenishing our supplies, we made the daylong drive to the first address on TRBL73's list. The number matched a grand, pillared courthouse in the county seat, an orderly town organized around a wide central square lined with brick sidewalks and shops in two-story buildings that may once have housed factories. I knew at once it was impossible. The white stone courthouse rose from the center of the square, with lighted walkways and open garden areas on three sides and a loading and utility area on the fourth, all encircled by floodlights and cameras. Roy suggested we paint an area near the loading dock, but anyone could see us there, like insects under the lamps.

B pointed to the parking structure across the street, shaded by the pollarded trees that lined the sidewalk. Surely the judges and jurors and clerks and bailiffs and assistants parked their cars in that garage before crossing to the courthouse. Along one wall of the garage was an alley, into which the garage's staircase emptied. It seemed to have no cameras or lights, no dumpsters or trash cans, and was wide enough for a small car.

Just after midnight B backed the Snowflake into the alley. The hiss of spray cans and the boys' urgent whispers echoed in the narrow space. We waved our hands uselessly at the fumes that curdled around us. The cast of our headlamps was just wide enough to see one piece of the Pig at a time, the snout, the ears. The headlamps' light was blue and flattened all colors and depth. As I obsessed over the tone of the Pig's cheeks, a spray can fell past my head and clattered on the aluminum step ladder, echoing off the brick walls. No one breathed. A car rolled past the alley's entrance. A lone cricket creaked in the heat. Davis crept to the alley's end to peer out, and Roy crab-walked after him. They waved to B. I kept working, using a can in each hand to feather the shading below the Pig's pugnacious grin. There was still no hint of dawn as I finished the curlicue tail and question marks and stepped back to admire our first true graffiti. Though they were hard to see in the blue light, the colors looked better, the figure centered and crisp.

B and the boys beckoned to me. I joined them to watch a dark-clad figure behind the courthouse moving something metal—we could hear the faint clangs and screeches as whoever it was worked. The boys tiptoed like cartoon villains across the street to a row of hedges bordering the square. Worried they would attract attention, B and I threw our supplies into the Snowflake. I climbed in back and B pulled out from the alley, our headlights sweeping the sidewalk and catching the boys like racoons at a dumpster.

They tumbled in, Davis in back with me and Roy up front, while I watched the back of the courthouse. B wanted to leave the county immediately, but I insisted we investigate, as two acts of vandalism at the same spot on the same night seemed unlikely to be coincidence. As B turned the car, Davis yelped at some insult of Roy's and smacked Roy across the back of his head, to which Roy grabbed Davis's shirt, locking their forearms and fists. I saw the figure move its hands feverishly, then sprint across the courtyard, leap the hedge, and dart across the street into an alley between dark shops. B stomped the accelerator, throwing our heads back, and whipped a left turn just as a rusted Chevy pickup launched toward the intersection, jerked right, and raced up a two-lane road. B pursued, pushing the Snowflake until the engine cried, but the pickup rapidly outpaced us, and when it sped through a yellow light that turned red by the time we reached it, B gave up.

17

B refused to stop driving until midday. At an IHOP in the next county, the boys celebrated our first graffiti by shaping crude Pig shapes with their sausage links and remnants of pancakes. B snagged Davis's phone while Davis was distracted and after a quick search showed me a photograph from a newspaper's website. Centered in the photo of the courthouse courtyard was a gleaming golden dollar sign, bolted to the concrete walkway. It looked to be made of painted metal and was about the height of a mailbox. The accompanying article was short on reporting and noted only the dollar sign's sudden appearance and the obvious unanswered questions as to who, why, and how. TRBL73's involvement seemed certain to me, though his purposes remained inscrutable. There was no mention of our Pig, which must have gone unnoticed or been dismissed as the work of common vandals.

B suspected that TRBL73 had assigned the courthouse first to get us arrested ASAP, bringing media attention to the Pigs and putting the somewhat-famous younger brother of the Great One's heir in jail, where reporters circled. I agreed to choose the least risky targets from TRBL73's list of government buildings.

After two days of driving, we selected an unemployment office housed in a strip mall with poor outdoor lighting and no traffic on the road after midnight. We painted the Pig on the back of the building, between dumpsters and propane tanks, where few would see it.

Yet again the media did not report on the Pig but on a mysterious lead-colored dollar sign that appeared by the office's front door. It seemed a curious message, the reporters mused, a lead dollar sign the size of a mailbox, blocking the unemployment office. B snickered as he read the news reports, but the boys turned red and threw balled-up chip bags out the window as we turned north on the Interstate.

If this dollar-sign artist was following us, we either had to sit tight and outwait them, catch them, or elude them in some way, which seemed impossible given Roy's loud mouth and the Snowflake's clownish speed.

B suggested another way to beat our competition, even if they knew exactly where we'd be. If we painted faster, he said, we could do multiple Pigs in a night. Beating the competition, as he put it, seemed a convenient excuse, as he'd been complaining from the first that the Pigs took too long to paint. He'd been searching the internet at night using Davis's phone and recited to us the legal codes and penalties related to graffiti on government property. Painting a Pig on Federal building, he informed us, violated 18 U.S.C., section 1361, which prohibits the willful destruction or damage of government property. The penalties reached up to ten years in jail and a quarter-million dollars in fines.

The possibility of getting caught felt distant to me, until I remembered Woodby's threat, relayed by Dag, to have me arrested for assault, so I suggested to B that we make a stencil of the Pig and spray most of it in one pass. It would still take time to shape and color, but would cut the total time by hours. B nodded sagely. It was all very rational.

That evening, we scavenged sheets of cardboard from a row of dumpsters behind a Motel 6 and laid them out in the empty back lot. I outlined the Pig in white spray paint, while B followed behind me with a box cutter. In less than an hour we'd made basic stencils for the white circle on which we grounded the Pig and another for the Pig itself, ears poking up into the negative space. The boys celebrated our innovation with a 12-pack of Coors Light and several hours of UFC on the television.

The next night, with the stencils balanced over our heads, we drove to a small-town Post Office, and in just over an hour, painted a Pig and two question marks on the metal shutter covering the loading dock. Giddy with adrenaline, we left a second Pig on the side of an abandoned concrete factory just outside town. These stenciled Pigs were more uniform than our freehand Pigs and lacked the obvious marks of true painting, but what we lost in artistry we gained in speed. They became symbols, like the question marks around them, unadorned and common. We left fifth and sixth Pigs on a Social Security office and another Post Office in a neighboring state. No dollar signs followed us.

18

Whenever possible during our travels, I paid for two motel rooms, B always with me and the boys together down the hall. When only one room was available, we all heard Roy smack his lips for a full five minutes before finally settling down, and B emit a medically threatening snore of glottal gasps when he lay on his back. Davis, I discovered, would wander off some nights, his phone's light sometimes visible through the room's front window and sometimes not. I awoke often, as was my habit since leaving New York, and watched him slip out and slip back in smelling of tobacco or fresh mown grass or rain.

No one slept especially well on the nights when we shared one room. Roy used the bathroom like clockwork at 2 AM and managed each time to leave the bathroom light on and the door cracked open so that the light spilled out. When B started snoring, the whole room soured, and before long Davis or I would be trying to roll him onto his side. I took to stuffing pillows behind B's back to prevent him from turning over, which worked until he eventually reached around and flung the pillows onto the floor. When we finally roused, the room would stink of sweat and musk and grease and often alcohol, if the boys had celebrated or B had needed to blow off steam, which was at least weekly.

B and I shared the driving. He preferred being crammed behind the wheel to suffering in the back with one of the boys. Roy and Davis were impatient and aggressive drivers, so I drove when B didn't, partly for my own comfort and partly to ensure we kept to the speed limit to avoid the attention of law enforcement. On B's insistence, we changed the oil every few weeks, the tires once, and the timing belt, brake pads, and rotors outside Omaha. A mysterious wiring flaw caused the right rear back-up light to burn out every few days, such that B kept a box of replacements in the precious space of the hatchback, the packing of which B also took charge of. Cases of spray paint, trash bags, boxes of gloves, the stencils, the ladder that seemed bigger every time we closed it, food for the long road trips, clothing we accumulated from gas stations and roadside malls—tank tops and shorts for the boys and a few extra button-down shirts and jeans for me—all this had to fit into the hatchback every morning. B swore convulsively at the bag of books Dag had left in the car, and because I couldn't bring myself to throw them out, I gave them away whenever I could, much as Dag might have done, leaving copies on diner counters and park benches. Bored one day, Roy asked for a copy, and Davis, not to be outdone by his brother on matters of intellect, grabbed another from the bag. Over several weeks of roaming across the Midwest they pawed through the Great Book, lying on picnic table benches or the spotty grass of suburban parks. Reading quieted Davis, but for Roy it was a dull sport, and he swore as he read and flipped the pages impatiently.

"Did all this stuff really happen?" he asked.

I didn't know. Any person writing down a story would make decisions on what to include and what to emphasize and what might confuse or distract a reader. Even a man so convinced of reality as grandfather would have favored some details over others. The book had ceased to be a story to me; it was a text to live by, though how to separate the philosophy from the narrative was never clear.

"The people don't seem real," Roy complained.

It's not really about the people, I told him, though Dag would have smacked me for any critique of the Great Book. It was all and entire to him.

"How can a story not be about people?" asked Roy.

"It's about the people," said Davis. "They just don't feel like real people."

"I thought this was a true story. The people aren't real people? This thing is too long to be made up."

"I see it like an idea that came true," said Davis. He avoided looking at me, not wanting to know what I thought.

"It's the other way, Davis," said Roy. "It happened and this is the story of it."

Davis scratched his nose. "Yeah but we got the idea of the Pigs before we made them. Gotta have one before the other."

"Well did it happen or didn't it?"

I thought of my rooftop abstracts, of which I'd had no vision before they emerged on canvas. What difference to me, rooftop or its idea, idea or canvas?

"I kinda get what he's saying here. But Christ on a cracker it's long."

"I've forgot what's happening like two-hundred pages ago," said Roy. "And I'm not even at the middle. It's the same stuff over and over."

As the bag of books diminished, I hid one copy under the driver's seat, in which I recorded the dates and locations of our Pigs, filling the margins and the title pages and the extra pages at the back, where the reader could detach a perforated post card to send in for more information about the Great Book, the great man behind it, and his living philosophy. A mailbox that Cheryl checked daily.

19

We kept getting away with it, and slowly our Pigs garnered attention, as photographs of the Pigs appeared on Ming's social media platforms—and the *WANTED* pages of local police departments. B tracked both the growth of Pig fan clubs on social media—Oinkers, as they became known—and the disconnected queries of far-flung law enforcement offices, wanting information. All the police had to do was go online, B mused, but he touched the subject gently out of a superstitious fear that he might somehow draw their attention. Online, the two most common Oinker topics were the identity of the Pig artist and the meaning of the Pigs. We listened in rapt attention as B read that our Pigs were unclean and impure; intelligent and clever; greedy and undiscriminating; symbols of comfort, a simple country life; or worshiped and sacrificed. They were invaders, fleeing before God to the sea.

We were all Pigs, it seemed, whether clever or greedy, impure or bucolic, venerated or murdered. B found blogs claiming that the Pigs signified a coming apocalypse or civil war; still others decried the Pigs as symbols of white supremacy. My stomach turned as B read, but so far no one in the media had connected the Pigs to my mural, or suggested my involvement.

One afternoon, when the clouds mixed to an unearthly green and the boys joked that I needed to *get into a fraidy hole* when I nervously asked about tornadoes and other mythic Midwestern weather, they agreed to wait out the storm in a motel. I watched cable news while B and the boys spent hours trading Davis's phone between them. As night fell, B showed me an image on the phone's screen. It was an AI-generated painting from a company website showing the twin towers, haloed and shining in the light. The likeness to my own painting was undeniable. Somehow I'd lost my paintings by selling them, or the AI had scooped this painting's image from the CHARLES website. The image had been generated and refined by some prompt artist to create value for their corporate employer. The prompt artist had likely never even seen my painting and was probably unaware of its existence. Was it still my beautiful painting? Had it been consumed, cut into pieces? I imagined my paintings hanging over mantels or behind desks, filling their owners with feeling. Perhaps the wrong feelings, according to Dag. I should do a survey of the buyers of my beautiful paintings: What does my painting make you feel? Tell me they are beautiful.

Only once during these weeks did a dollar sign eclipse our Pig. It was a brilliant copper-colored balloon-like creation by an industrial park that housed the EPA's regional office. We had painted our Pig on the side wall of the building, near the parking lot and away from the entrances. The dollar sign artist's persistence perplexed and inspired me, but with that office, we had run out of suitable targets from TRBL73's list and from then on selected our own from the multitude of lesser government buildings that lurked amid the office centers and strip-mall outskirts of middling towns.

Each night B searched the internet for Oinkers. The Pigs had spread beyond social media and law enforcement *WANTED* pages. People posted photos of Pig tattoos, crude Pig graffiti scrawled on buses, printouts of Pigs stapled to telephone poles like ads for lost dogs. The thought that Ming watched his every online move amped up my own paranoia. Did she watch us paint and drive and drink in motel rooms? She watched all.

We looped through Indiana, southern Illinois, Missouri, up to Iowa, Nebraska, the Dakotas, south again to Tennessee, Arkansas. The Snowflake's AC labored at full volume to keep us from sweating, which was, outside of some air-conditioned space, a constant state. The insects changed, the accents changed, the corn grew taller and darker as we moved on. The heat was constant, air heavy as bathwater. Pigs trailed behind us, questioning all.

By late August, reviewing the Great Book in which I'd been secretly recording our Pigs, I saw that our next would be our fiftieth. Once we'd left it grinning from a motor vehicle department (a Federal target not available at the time), I bought the boys Drumsticks and caramel corn to celebrate and parked a quarter mile from the end of the regional airport's runway, where we lay on the grass, and the boys hollered and hooted at the great white bellies of commercial jets that screeched overhead.

Finally done with the Great Book, the boys discarded their copies in one of those little libraries that crop up in residential neighborhoods. They returned to watching video clips of hunting, drag racing, boat racing, hot dog eating, and other contests, which they streamed on Davis's phone during the late mornings and early afternoons, between sleeping and painting Pigs.

Before it seemed possible, it was time to paint our one-hundredth Pig. Afterwards we drank highballs from plastic cups and lounged on a bluff above the Mississippi, the river's breeze wet and thick with insects in the twilight.

It was this one-hundredth Pig, on a side wall of the Division of Workforce Services in Arkansas, that finally reached the national news. Instead of question marks, I had painted *Pigs Get Slaughtered* encircling the Pig, a new touch to commemorate our achievement, and the phrase goosed the newscasters' imaginations. Who were the Pigs? Who slaughtered them and why? The story passed with the news cycle, but a week or so later a journalist linked mentions of the Pigs in local papers to the phenomenon brewing in the corners of the internet. He penned a story of emergent anti-government sentiment, but having no hero and no real victim, this story too dissipated after a week. Finally my friend the Critic, observer that he was, wrote a column fingering me as the likely Pig artist of the greater Midwest. At the end was a photograph of our one-hundredth Pig and its slogan.

Feeling paranoid, I heard footsteps. *Omnibus dubitanda sunt*, Ming had lectured me: doubt everything. Convinced that my brother was stalking me and the police were close behind, I threw my flip phone into a river, then, feeling foolish, bought a new flip phone at a pharmacy and dialed Chase's number—my number—and had that disembodied experience of hearing my own voice on the voicemail. I managed to say only that I'd lost my phone and would call again.

/ / /

We stopped after the one-hundredth Pig. No one wanted the work of choosing and vetting our next target, or buying and mixing paint, or eluding cameras and police. We wandered along the small highways of farm country. One afternoon, hungry and tired and listless, we stopped at a road-side restaurant that sold only ham and cheese sandwiches or, if one preferred, the ingredients to make them. It was the only establishment for miles of endless rolling farmland. We sat at a picnic table in the shade of a tall spreading tree, chewing white bread with mayonnaise and thinly sliced honey ham and Swiss.

I'd been named, and anyone who'd read the Critic's column or had been told by someone who had might think that the once-great purveyor of consumer art, the Painter of Might, had run off like a drug addict to tag dumpsters and office parks. The Critic had pontificated on the meaning of the Pigs, or so I gleaned from B, who'd found the column and read it—of course I hadn't—and from what I could tell, had uncovered a dawning cultural moment of the Pig. The greedy among us ate like pigs, the thoughtless gambled, the clever schemed, the relentless pawed through the mud for treasure. And then we ate the Pigs. And there we were, calling Pigs to slops or slaughter.

Through a paste of half-chewed bread and ham, Davis said what we might all have been thinking: "What are we doing?"

We looked off across the highway and the grain, heavy headed in the humid air.

Roy answered first, with a confidence that said he'd been thinking on the topic. "Revolution," he said, still watching the fields.

"Just freedom," said B. "And a job with dignity."

"I wanna know what kind of job that is," said Roy. He flicked a toothpick at B, who swatted it away.

"Like, none of this did anything," said Davis.

Roy had given Davis his Pig hat, and Davis wore it square and low on his forehead.

"We are getting paid," Roy reminded him, "to be a part of something." He smirked at Davis, owning him, but his brow wrinkled when Davis ignored him. Roy reached across the table and knocked the hat brim sideways. The faded Pig winked at me.

"We're like jokers," said Davis. "Like those Saturday morning cartoons, the coyote and the road runner flipping each other off every show and nothing ever changes. They don't suddenly get a job like B wants and freedom, whatever that is, they just keep going at each other like they've got no choice. And we keep on painting Pigs, and what of it? We're small-timers making jokes on Post Offices and Unemployment Offices, and honestly neither of those places has ever harmed me."

Roy's mouth hung open in incomprehension. "Did you hear the part about getting paid?" he asked.

"He'll run out eventually," said Davis, meaning me.

Roy swatted at the air like he was shooing a fly. "We're part of something, Davis," he said. He slapped his thighs, the picnic table. Our plasticware and Solo cups of coleslaw jumped.

None of us knew what to do with this vigilante freedom we'd stumbled on. We had repeated these Pig signals without understanding why or whom we were signaling to. We had worked together, traveled together, housed together, ate and drank together for an entire summer. We knew each other's sleep habits, food preferences, and clothing, down to the underwear, but we'd not bothered to know each other. We had come together only within the constraints of the Pigs, a dead-simple routine of spray cans and cardboard templates. Outside this routine, only the flow of money had been established, from me to them.

After the first week I'd stopped feeling intimidated by Davis, and any urge I'd felt to know him or Roy better was eclipsed by a fear of what I might disturb. California remained an idea, like sobriety to an alcoholic. I had made no effort to find Ming or consider any next move. With the Pigs as exhausted as our spray cans, I was like the lost guiding the listless.

"He's like another daddy to you," said Davis. "You just want to follow someone and do what they say."

Roy slapped at a bug, which eluded him.

"You no different," said Roy.

"You just want Daddy back. That's all you ever wanted."

Roy's mouth tightened but he deflected Davis's barb. "Let's take it all back!" he bellowed.

"There is no back," said B. "Rivers and all that."

"He's telling you that Daddy's dead," said Davis. "Time to stop dragging his skeleton around."

Roy scowled. "I could hurt you right now."

Davis gazed unbothered over the gravel. "Remember what Daddy did when that opossum took up under the trailer? You remember?"

"Like you remember. You was four."

"Yeah, well, Mama said Daddy left a open jar of peanut butter in the yard and shot the big rat when it got hungry."

"Told me it tasted like a good night's sleep," said B.

"It didn't happen like that anyway," said Roy.

"Maybe that's what I mean," said Davis. "All those tales she tells—none of it real. You see? Daddy's just another of Mama's stories. We got to stop dragging him around."

"All kind of animals came for that peanut butter," said Roy.

"Home is just a bunch of stories."

"I miss home. And I miss Daddy," said Roy. He flayed another toothpick between his thumbnails. "I'm just saying it's not like it used to be. You know Daddy did alright before he passed."

"You can go roughneck if you're not too afraid," said Davis.

Roy scowled and bit at the inside of his cheek. He mumbled something about Walmart in a half-hearted dig at Davis, who knotted his paper napkin and flung it overhand toward Roy. It fell short and drifted into the gravel where it twitched in the breeze.

"You ain't competing sufficient," said B.

He too was distracted, watching the straight shimmering gray of the highway. After a moment he turned back. "I wonder if Jim sold your truck, left it there like we did."

The joke pricked the boil of anger building between the boys.

"Shiiiiit," clowned Davis. "I don't own it anyways."

The boys hooted.

I turned to ask B where he landed on the need for revolution, but he'd wandered off. I left the boys to their discontents and found B urinating on a thick tree behind the restaurant.

"A private moment too much to ask?" he said.

He tucked himself away.

"You want a revolution like Roy?" I asked.

He nodded to the clapboard building while he zipped his fly. "Looks to me like a restaurant with only one idea."

"Every choice is ham and cheese," I said.

B produced a cigarette and lit it. "Lady at the counter," he explained, meaning the cigarette.

Smoke sidled between us, the scent of my mother, always smoking.

We headed back up the slope. At the table, the boys sulked.

"So let's do something that matters," said Roy. "Or go home. Get a life on."

"Let's do a Walmarts," said Davis.

"How's that gonna matter?"

"The one I worked at."

The idea broke over Roy like a sunrise.

B sighed and picked at a callous on his palm.

"Everyone would see it there," said Roy.

"That's right," said Davis.

"They'd catch us for sure," said B.

"You ever stop bitching?" asked Roy.

"I have not yet begun."

20

We drove straight to Oklahoma and directly past the Walmart Davis had worked at, nestled in the bend of a viaduct over which the highway swooped southeast. It was a terrible idea, but somehow Davis won us over. For my part, I still feared saying no to Davis, though in retrospect it's hard for me to understand why, and anyway I had no other ideas besides California, which I continued to postpone. For Roy it was this Walmart or go home, and he wouldn't go home or much of anywhere else without his brother. B professed his misgivings in no uncertain terms, but he too seemed inspired by his cousin's zealous arguments for vindication and retribution and, above all, visibility.

At dinner that night, Davis outlined his plan. He would attract the attention of the night guard, attempt to gain access to the security office, then turn off the cameras and lights at the back of the building. The plan hinged on his ability to subdue, convince, or evade the guard.

We were dubious, but none of us could fault his courage or the advantages of accessing the security office. As we gathered paint and supplies in neighboring towns, I considered what I would say to Ming when I called from a jail payphone. She would already know. Her AI calculated probable next actions and outcomes. My call would serve only to discover what Ming had already done.

We surveilled the building's backside for a day and a night from a knob of dirt punctured by clumps of tall grasses. The viaduct of the highway passed directly overhead, offering curious drivers an unob-structed view of the tall wide rear wall we intended to paint. Even with the security guard distracted and the lights and cameras off, late-night travelers were sure to see our headlamps. And there was a design problem. The wall was so large that a Pig the size of our stencil would shrink to meaninglessness in the ocean of concrete. We decided to ditch the stencils and hand-paint a much larger Pig, which meant a taller ladder, cases more paint, and hours more time.

The next night, as we watched the building where nothing happened, B kept turning to peer into the shadows. Roy and Davis yanked at a pair of cheap binoculars we'd picked up at a roadside shop, until Roy won and squinted through the glasses with the strap sill around Davis's neck. Roy had been moved by his brother's courage and transformed into the keeper of our plan, which he recorded in laborious notes on a clipboard. Who knows what was in these notes, for the plan was simple and sure to fail: We waited for the lights to go off, we painted the Pig, then we ran.

"Someone's watching us," said B.

He nodded to an 80s sedan moored cockeyed by the curb below the overpass. Its windshield was dark, and I couldn't see anyone inside, but B stormed down the embankment with his fists balled only to stop short when a woman popped from behind the wheel. They faced off, but we couldn't hear them. Roy's breath was loud over my shoulder. Davis crouched behind a clump of grass. The woman followed B back up the hill to our position. When she got close, she smiled, her face the map of Ireland, rosy and Celtic.

"This is a professional courtesy," she said and held up her phone.

On its screen, my brother, in a white shirt and crisp slacks, midstride with a black bag slung over his shoulder. Behind him, the cheeky grin of a Pig leered from the Division of Workforce Services, framed by police cars. The inevitability of the moment crashed over me.

B stretched out on the ground.

Roy craned his neck to see the photo. "Who is it?" he asked.

"Who is she?" asked Davis.

"That's his brother," said B.

We watched the picture as if expecting it to speak.

"You're the dollar sign artist," I guessed. Who else would be following us, other than my brother and the police?

She smiled, revealing slight gaps between her front teeth.

"You owe your brother money or something?" asked Roy.

"I'm not sure what I owe him."

She sat with us among the grasses. Her name was Saoirse.

"Why you messing with us?" asked Davis.

"It's not about you," she said.

We all asked questions at once: What *is* it about? What kind of name is that? Why dollar signs?

"It's complicated," she replied. "Did Todd give you the money speech?" she asked me.

"Who's Todd?"

"You probably know him by as TRBL73."

"You know him?" I said, a tinge of accusation in my voice.

"Yes, I know him well. He loves to give the money speech."

I shook my head; he'd given us no speech about money, just two cryptic stories. "He said I needed to rehabilitate my image," I told her. "And something about Pigs drowning in government."

"They drown in the sea," said Davis, bitterly.

She appraised me, her irises hazel with flecks of gold. "Maybe you don't need the money speech."

I'd had enough of money speeches from Dag, this was true.

"I know who you are," she said.

By then I wasn't so sure who I was or whether it mattered to know. I insisted she explain herself. She had been evasive in the manner of someone without rational answers, and I began to suspect that she was an agent of chaos with no values beyond interference.

Instead she quoted my grandfather's book—*when men cease to use money as the tool of their trade, they become the tools of men*—getting the phrasing wrong but the message right. I found myself nodding in agreement.

"That used to make so much sense to me," she said, "but now I wonder if we got it backwards."

Well-worn family words spilled from my mouth: Without money, how could any society be free? Money was the product of our capacity for thought. Destroyers came for the money because it was our protection and moral base. Money was freedom from violence, not its enabler.

"I'm not saying money is evil, just asking: is it really right for us?"

Davis groaned.

"For example," she continued, "does money expand freedom or limit freedom? I thought I knew, now I'm not sure."

At this B sat up. "What's that now?"

"What's this about freedom?" asked Davis.

"I wonder if we know what real freedom is," she said.

B sighed and lay back down.

"It means do whatever we want," said Roy.

"That's not freedom, that's just being a asshole," said B.

"You an asshole. Whyn't you get you rich mama to pay back our Mama for raising you."

"I don't owe Mama nothing you don't owe Mama."

"Cover all those extra-large clothes she had to buy you."

"Mama didn't buy me clothes. We went to church rummage sales and took what they couldn't sell. You don't know because you always begged off church."

Roy giggled. "You remember those shirts so tight B looked like a sausage dog?"

"I got car sick on that road," said Davis.

"I got into trucks to have freedom from you all's nonsense," said B.

"I saw that Wall Street mural," said Saoirse to me. "You glorified the blood lust, the money lust, the Pigs—the whole capitalist fantasia. And under all that you buried OCCUPY. Who are you, painter?"

What could TRBL73 and this woman possibly have in common? TRBL73 was a paranoid market evangelist and Saoirse, apparently, some socialist agent of chaos. And then it clicked: Such opposites could only be held close in the magnetic field of a failed marriage.

"You were married," I accused her.

She grinned coldly.

"You're doing this to get back at him."

"It's more complicated than that," she huffed. "Anyway, I came here to warn you about your brother."

"How did you get along with TRBL73?" I asked, still confused.

"It's Todd, and you can probably guess."

She winked at Davis, who blushed.

"Without money we'd be reduced to barter," I said, while in my mind the Pigs leapt down from the slaughterhouse to dig up the bones of OCCUPY. "Anyway," I was growing irritated. "All art is propaganda."

"That barter thing is a myth," she said.

"How she gonna trade for gas?" asked Roy.

"It's not just money, it's the money economy," she said.

"What now?" asked B.

"It's like a child, the money economy. It runs hot and then crashes. It charms and enriches our lives, then makes us tear our hair out. And the constant worrying and pampering, all the expectations. I might have started these dollar signs because I was pissed at Todd, but then I started to wonder if there might be a way of living that's more dependable than a toddler and more human than dollars."

The boys dismissed her.

"What's your brother want?" Davis asked me, growing suspicious.

I wasn't sure anymore. The thought of Dag in pursuit thrilled and terrified me. We had to keep running.

Dag and Saoirse could easily have seen the photograph of our one-hundredth Pig on the news and followed it to Arkansas, but how had Saoirse tracked us to this Walmart, hundreds of miles away?

"That's a long story," she demurred.

Once I'd asked the question, I stopped listening. I was already running.

"If we're going to do this, we have to do it soon," I declared. "Tomorrow night, no later. We do it and we move on."

21

Saoirse said she couldn't stand to watch four men go so cluelessly to their fate without doing what she could to help, and though I entertained a passing paranoia that she planned to plant a giant ironic dollar sign while we labored on our Pig, she seemed as eager as the boys. Davis wanted her gone but relented when she complimented his plan and courage and his idea to paint the Pig where it could finally be appreciated. In the end he grudgingly accepted a kiss on the cheek. B tried to warn her off with a recitation of state laws regarding the defacement of private property and the likely number of lawyers at Walmart's disposal, but she just laughed. She'd done worse already, she replied.

After midnight we lugged our bags and boxes and ladders up the knoll and crouched amid the tall grasses while we waited for Davis to work up his courage. He sat cross-legged like a swamy between clumps of grass, taking deep breaths. Jail was the mostly likely outcome. I practiced what I'd tell Ming.

Davis took a final deep breath and jogged down the knoll and around to the building's front. An age passed before Saoirse asked how we'd know if he got caught. No one replied. The wind pressed down the grasses around us, swirling from low clouds that softened the harsh klieg lights with a woolen gray. A sedan circled the lot and left.

Saoirse grabbed my forearm. The lights were off.

I became aware of each of us breathing, a collective adrenal moment as we crouched in the grasses, ready to pounce on the mastodon and eat or die. Without a word we trotted down the hill, cans and bottles jangling in our giant Costco bags. The lot was a football field across, and we had to catch our breath when we reached the wall, leaning with our hands on our knees in the dark.

After a few minutes of agitated confusion, the routine of the Pig took over. A huge target formed as Roy and Saoirse filled a circle with white. I put the Pig right at its middle. Roy kept jogging to the corner, looking for Davis. In the plan, Davis would join us after turning off the lights, but we were to proceed with or without him. Saoirse proved adept with the spray cans as she built the Pig's flushed cheeks in pink and red and yellow. I feathered the colors, highlighted to three dimensions. It was a beauty, and big as a billboard. Davis still hadn't shown up as B hurriedly collected our trash and packed our bags. I got greedy and began to paint *Pigs Get Slaughtered* around the circle. I had to reach high from the step ladder for *GET* and painted *SLAUGH* before the ladder began to tip and I had to climb down and move it. Saoirse painted *PIGS* in letters swollen as over-filled balloons, and I got as far as *T E R* before the towering klieg lights came on, washing us in white.

We blinked in the sudden light.

B pushed a bag at me, and Saoirse and I broke for the building's far corner, where the dark was closest. Roy started after us, then turned back for the ladder, B hissing at him for help. We watched as Roy turned quickly to grab the ladder—too quickly, such that the bag slung over his shoulder flung itself with centripetal force against the ladder, knocking it into a slow descent. It clattered loud as shattering glass on the pavement. I sprinted back to help. Roy had the ladder wobbling under one arm as he started toward Saoirse like an errant knight. B had dropped his bags and was hopping around on one foot, cursing. I thought I heard voices behind us, the hard clacking of a policeman's belt. I got B under one arm and Saoirse dragged the bags behind her, and together we limped to the building's corner.

The loading docks at the back were empty save for two trailers abandoned at closed roll-up doors, and we huddled between the doubled tires of the trailers. B's shoeless foot was purple and already swollen. Roy nattered urgently about Davis and crouched as if ready to run, until B grabbed his wrist and pointed with the captive hand to the trash-strewn dirt beyond the sweep of lights.

"That way," he said.

Roy managed to loop two of the bags over the ladder, and with B between us, Saoirse and I dragged into the bright light. The back lot was narrow but interminable as we hustled across it. Anyone turning the building's corner would see us, as would anyone in the security office, if the cameras were working. The pavement crawled past. My own gasping deafened me. B grunted and grimaced as he swung between us and squeezed my shoulder so tight it was like being hugged by a drunken uncle. It was surely a miracle of fate or the security force's incompetence that we reached the dark of the grasses. We rested for a moment, watching the building. Nothing moved in the sterile light.

It took us a half-hour to circle back to the cars through the dark brush. We collapsed on the far side of the knoll. Roy got up on his hands and knees and crawled to the top. I followed to make sure he didn't do something stupid. The spinning lights of two police cars prowled the empty lot. Cops stood in pairs, hands on their belts, looking up at our Pig, grinning gloriously in the floodlights. I swelled with pride.

Three men turned the building's corner, two uniformed and one in dark clothes—Davis.

"He needs a distraction," said Roy. He bolted down the knoll.

I reached after him but grasped only his black sweatshirt, which came off, unzipped, in my hand.

B spat when I told him. "That's that," he said.

/ / /

We drove to a Waffle House on the far side of the next county and sat with three plates of waffles and eggs congealing before us and B's injured foot raised on the bench next to me, where I could watch it swell and blacken as I contemplated my food.

"Hospitals and doctors cannot be trusted," B was saying, repeating his protest whether we responded or not. "*And* they'll tell the police," he added.

I told him that his swollen foot, so close for my inspection, appeared ready to molt or fissure.

"Anyways I don't got money to pay for it," he said.

Only after assurances that I would pay for his care and several dire assessments of his status—"Your dead foot will come for you," threatened Saoirse—did B agree to go to the ER.

We found a hospital of last resort in a highway-strewn section of town. After several hours under the waiting area's flickering fluorescents we rolled B's wheelchair into a curtained bay. A series of nurses asked the same questions again and again—"Dropped a full cooler on it," repeated B—before a man with a red-brown complexion and a short white coat gave limited options. Surgery now, he said, or no surgery followed by chronic pain and disability. Immediate surgery would give B a good chance of walking normally. B, perhaps under the influence of the pain medication the nurses had given him, suggested that the doctor cut his foot off right there, insisting on his rights as a patient. The idea horrified the doctor and us, though I admitted it sounded cheaper than reconstructive surgery. Eventually B dozed off, and Saoirse and I left to find rooms at a hotel down the street.

I had just laid down on the bed covers when the phone rang.

"Channel 372," said Saoirse.

A news program showed an overhead shot of police cruisers with pulsing lights sweeping an empty lot and our Pig, bright as day, grinning stupidly from the wall. We watched together from our separate rooms. The newscasters assured us that the police had suspects in custody.

///

We collected B the next evening. While he and Saoirse sipped coffee in the hospital cafeteria, I spent an hour and nearly six figures in a back office, leaving with a pile of receipts and a much smaller pile of money. I thought, absently, to send the receipts to Chase, then dumped them in the trash. B wedged himself into the Snowflake's backseat with his leg up and cast elevated, per instruction.

Saoirse had spoken with Todd. The boys had been arrested, she told us. Dag had paid their bail.

I glanced at B in the rearview mirror.

"I know," he said. "We got to go."

Saoirse touched B's knee and smiled and disappeared past the smokers outside the ER.

Part 4

"We have granted you everything you demanded of us, we who had always been the givers, but have only now understood it. We have no demands to present to you, no terms to bargain about, no compromise to reach. You have nothing to offer us. *We do not need you.*"

—Atlas Shrugged

22

The Snowflake labored west into a stiff wind, while B snored and groaned in the backseat. The car shied from the gusts, and I strained to keep us steady as heavy pickups buffeted past, eating the miles of asphalt between distant ranches and low-slung towns. At Amarillo we stopped for gas and food. Empty cups and sandwich wrappers eddied in the corner of an Arby's lot where we ate meat and fried potatoes. My gut had long since entered a stunned constipation, and the less I ate the better, but the food was like oral therapy, and I crammed it into my mouth in big thoughtless bites.

With a moment alone, B off to the bathroom on his crutches, I swallowed my shame and called Chase. We'd not spoken in weeks.

"Are we still running a business?" she asked after a chill silence.

"Do we still have a building?"

We still had a building, she said, but could easily lose it, and cited as evidence a litany of unexpected expenses, unpaid taxes, uneven sales, impatient clients, media requests, and demands from building inspectors. Had that always been my life? And something odd was happening, she said, people were leaving. Charles had left his gallery to his long-time assistant. Dag's lieutenant Cheryl had closed their New York office. Ming's people had collected the portrait, finished or not, and headed west. Offices went unstaffed and phones rang unanswered.

"What about my brother?" I asked.

She considered for a moment. "You didn't tell me how good looking he is."

"He can be charming when he's not pissed," I replied, but I could tell he'd cast a spell over her.

"He's an extraordinary man."

"Where is he being extraordinary?"

"Oklahoma, I think." Her voice lowered, confidential. "The police are searching for someone."

"Which police?"

"It matters which police?"

"Some of them cross state lines."

"What are we talking about here?"

"Call me when you know," I said and hung up.

///

We continued west until the sun was an orange hole on the horizon from which the wind howled. In a small city on the edge of the Plains, I stopped at a Marriott. We sat by the windows of the top-floor lounge and watched a sliver of vermillion cling to the earth's rim. Cruciforous clouds encroached from the south.

B ordered a margarita, then a second, then switched to tequila shots, alternating with lite beer. Even through the plate-glass window we could hear the wind, and when B let out a long sighing whistle it was as if the wind had found its way in through him.

"Layers and layers," he started, as if to say more. Maybe he meant the shroud of atmosphere that kept us alive, or the layers of paint on my beautiful paintings. "It's never done between brothers," he said.

A waitress bounced to the table on ballistic legs. "Y'all thirsty!" she exclaimed.

Her downy face told me she'd barely left adolescence, despite the showy jewel on her left hand. I ordered a half-dozen dishes, ostensibly to keep B from poisoning himself with alcohol. Perhaps I was spending my money to see what freedom was like without it. And was I free anyway, pursued by Dag, the police, the Critic, Chase and our bills and clients?

"If I was younger," said B, watching the waitress bounce away.

Feeling ungenerous I replied that she was engaged or married, based on the big jewel she wore.

"That thing's glass," he replied. "She's got a cheap man, or a poor man, or she's keeping off men like me."

He finished plates of wings and fries and sipped beer. We discussed the likelihood that the boys would cave on questioning and tell the police about the Snowflake and their cousin B and this painter guy they met from New York City who started the whole thing. B felt it was all but certain that the authorities were looking for us by then, and though I had to agree, I harbored a hope that the boys would keep their mouths shut. It was fantasy, not hope; Davis, already taciturn, could hold his own, but Roy was a loudmouth, and, so far as I could see, they had little to gain by taking blame for the whole Pig enterprise.

With no boys to wrangle and no Pigs to paint and therefore no purpose, I was adrift. Instead of trying to calm my anxiety, I turned my frustrations on B.

"Why did you intrude on my studio?" I asked.

"*Intrude on,*" he mocked me.

"I'm serious."

"I dug your paintings."

"You invaded my home. You had no right."

"What's a right? Anyways, I'd say we about even on all counts."

"You will never pay back what I just spent," I said.

His cast, already graying and fraying at its edges, sat propped on the chair next to me.

"Money's just one way of adding it up," he replied. He crossed his arms behind his head and belched.

This was the intruder I'd found on my couch, drinking lite beer and smoking.

"You've hardly smoked in weeks," I said.

"Only a asshole reminds a person they haven't smoked."

"Why were you in that alley that day, outside the hotel? When I first saw you."

"Tried to sneak in," he said.

"Sneak in—to my brother's event?"

"He got things to say. They wouldn't even let me use the bathroom. Then I saw you and I thought you was him."

"But not at as good looking."

"Anyways, I figured it out. I'd seen your paintings through the window at that gallery. That one of the twin towers," he wagged his head heavily. "It all started there, seems like. Or ended, I don't know."

His praise soothed me. "Symbols of commerce," I said.

"Paper towers." He smiled, amused, drunk.

"If they're just office buildings then why did you care?"

"The shadows," he said.

I had painted the towers as if they were angels, he explained, the clouds above suffused by holy light, but below, the buildings' long shadows lay across the land.

"Paper towers with halos over their heads near enough," he slurred. "You know, that Critic was right. There's plenty in your paintings you don't see."

I repeated what I'd told the Critic at my opening: Capitalism catches the light because it's the tallest thing around.

"And people like me in the shadow of it—you don't see that?"

"I thought you were inspired by them," I lamented.

"You in the shadows too. You'd know it if you ever looked up."

"There's no shadow on me."

"You talk to your brother like that—not listening?"

"More the other way around," I admitted.

"Then you ought a know the feeling."

///

Rain slapped the windows all night, and I slept poorly. At dawn, I went down to the lobby café. I filled a plate with pastries and sat at a table where I could watch the morning news on a television hung on the wall. My stomach knotted at the first bite of a bear claw, and I switched to oatmeal. Urgency burbled in my gut. I was vacillating between finding the lobby bathroom and risking the long trip to my room when mugshots of Roy and Davis appeared on the screen, followed by the Walmart Pig. The male newscaster's set mouth softened, as if Roy and Davis were good ol' boys after all and acting like boys will act, except they had a message. Dimples creased the woman newscaster's cheeks as she took the lead. The screen cluttered with images of T-shirts, bumper stickers, canvas tote bags, mugs, all bearing Pigs. The dimples deepened. A shot of the boys, this time waving to the camera as they exited a courthouse.

When the news went to commercial, I hustled to the elevator and up to my room to sit on the toilet. Afterwards, I lay face down on the bathroom floor, the tiles cold through my shirt. I traced my finger along the grout lines. Dag was collecting the pieces of my life, erasing me.

I dialed his number. My gut clenched again when I heard his voice.

"What took you so long?" he asked.

"Why are you following me? Why are you stealing from me?"

"I'm not stealing, I'm cleaning up behind you. Not only did I save your friends—when you ran away—but now they're heroes. They confessed to everything. The concept, the planning, painting, everything. Our lawyers successfully argued that their actions were protected political discourse. And now they've licensed the Pigs to Walmart!

"It was their followers that did it. They packed the courtroom in their trucker hats and T-shirts with Pigs on them. Terribly tacky, but the judge fell for the Americana, you know, the sap of it. He got Walmart to drop the charges in exchange for licensing the Pigs from the boys. And now the boys have the many thousands of followers who were once yours, and many thousands of dollars for their intellectual property."

Property that had twice been mine. Each time the Pigs had wriggled through my fingers, only to be captured on hats and bumper stickers.

"Why do you always run away?" he taunted me.

"I wasn't, you would have—"

Just stop, Tag, stop talking.

He chuckled.

"You can still come back," he said.

I shook my head and said nothing. Incredibly, some part of me still longed to be his little brother. But why would he want me back when he had the boys, my followers, and the Pig narrative in hand? Did Woodby still want my endorsement, even after my crime spree? Did Dag want to be friends again?

"What is it?" I pleaded. "What is it you want?"

Then I remembered Ming.

"One doesn't walk up to the richest woman in the world and propose that she leave behind all she's built," he said.

"I'm not helping you do that," I replied, realizing that he meant to go on strike, as grandfather had.

"It's the only thing you can do," he said.

What could I say to convince Ming to follow Dag, when she could do anything she wished? The answer was clear to Dag: She would agree because he was right.

"Once she understands she's enabling her own oppressors, she will join us," he said.

"Ming has no oppressors. And that's what you want from me, to enable my oppressor."

"She will understand the logic," he said, implying that I did not.

If Ming withdrew, what would happen to me? I would have to go on strike with them, or wander alone. Woodby would be there. Cheryl. My brother, their prophet. I pictured them congratulating themselves in flourishes of dull language, then insulting the waitstaff. Or would they serve their own drinks and canapes? They'd forgotten how or never knew.

"You know what's right," Dag continued. "I know you—you're my brother."

I forced myself to hang up. The phone I snapped in half and dropped in the trash.

23

Again we headed west. From the depths of a hangover, B only grunted when I told him about the boys.

We traded plains and grasses for tumbleweeds and stone. Outside Albuquerque, in another moment of sudden inevitability, the Snowflake began to shudder, and its engine seized up just as I rolled down an offramp and up to a service station on the outskirts of town. The mechanic frowned at the engine and gestured up the road to a "suitable" hotel and told us to call tomorrow.

B refused my offer to hail a taxi and instead swung his wounded leg between his crutches down the sidewalk. It was a good half-mile past lots lined with tractor trailers, under the highway, and through a neighborhood of adobe ranch houses to two hotels separated by wide parking lots. We aimed for the closer of the two, a Quality Inn. B wiped the sweat from his face. At the reception desk, he asked for the bar. A tan teenage boy in an oversized gold vest replied that the only bar around was in the hotel next door.

"There's a better place next door," said B.

Having choices was what it was all about, even so simple a choice as which of the sad roadside hotels to sleep in. The bar next door consisted of three stools and a waitress station in the corner of a fluorescent-lit restaurant by the lobby. An age-lined woman with lank, curly hair sitting at the faux-wood bar looked B up and down as we entered. He swung his cast around the stool to her.

I sat at a table and watched the mute televisions above the bar. The news was on but had forgotten Roy and Davis. A rainstorm in the Gulf, wildfires in California. After a thirty-minute news program, mostly ads for medications, B and the woman at the bar headed together for the door. As he left B pointed at me, the wallet.

The restaurant, with its paper-covered tables, was so white and so lonely a scene, awaiting color and vibrance, that I missed my studio. How lucky I'd been, though of course we in our family did not believe in luck, only volition. Man was order in a random universe. After eating I took the pen the waitress had left with the bill for my Cobb salad and sketched the restaurant on the paper table covering. Scattered among the two-dozen two-tops with heavy metal pedestals and white paper covers were a red-faced couple with soft middles and four men, each alone before a laptop. I forced the perspective to dramatic effect. It was technically good and terribly dull, so I slipped over to the next table, which had not yet been set and had only the blank paper on it, and this time drew the Pig. I took my time, shading it into three dimensions, and wrote *Roy and Davis* in the giant bubble letters Saoirse had used to paint "PIGS" on the Walmart mural.

When she came for the bill the waitress studied the drawing of the restaurant, then the scene I'd sketched, then me, at the next table, drawing again.

"You an artist?" she asked.

Yes, I told her, and I hadn't had a chance to paint for a while. I apologized for drawing all over her tables.

She looked over at the Pig and the balloon-lettered *Roy and Davis*. "It's good they let those boys go," she said. "Just speaking their minds, don't you think?" She pulled my salad plate and utensils onto a tray. "Hey that's not bad. Just like the ones the boys did." She raised the tray to her shoulder and walked away.

///

Over a week passed before I saw B again, and another before the Snowflake was ready. After breakfast every morning, I walked loops through the surrounding neighborhoods of adobe houses and gravel lawns before the heat became intolerable. I took a siesta after lunch and walked again in the evenings. The walking, much like the fast food and cross-country driving, I did to stop my thoughts, but walking, it turned out, made thoughts flow, and after a day or two I gave in and let my mind wander. My studio, Chase, my beautiful paintings; Mama and the boys; TRBL73 and Saoirse and the Pigs; the endless Midwestern highways, grain everywhere, cows in crowds; then spare rangeland and stone. All of these thoughts rose and fell like bowling pins in a juggler's hands, but none had the same substance and gravity as thoughts of Dag. The bagels I bought from a café along my route were dry and flavorless and made me miss New York, and any thought of New York conjured Dag. The children tumbling down slides and floating on swings on the playground I passed made me wonder about Dag's children, who were young and playful when I last saw them. Passing a gallery on a shop-lined boulevard, I paused to study the Southwest-style art in the windows—dignified Native Americans in feathered headdresses, cowboys on horseback, pastel stones, azure skies—and heard Dag's voice decrying its sentimentality. But even with his voice inside my head, did I really know Dag? Who was he to himself? I had only his words and actions to judge by, and though these compose the entire objective world of human affairs, they are but arrangements of the stars, tea leaves through which we seek each other's truths.

Passing the playground one morning, I saw a father lecturing his son over some infraction. The man was my size and unremarkable. He shook his finger over the boy, who was maybe four years old, wearing a tiny red sports jersey and sweatpants painted with sand. Under his father's finger, the boy's pink cheeks held a quivering pout. My heart opened to him. I became the boy, and Dag the father. Then Dag the boy, and our dad the father. I saw Dag as a child, trembling proudly upright, as he'd been taught to stand, using his every power to hold back tears as father loomed over him, flashcards in hand, finger wagging, face stern and distant; on the flashcards, words for Dag to memorize: reason, non-contradiction, self. Dag nodding sharply, yes sir, his hands twisting one in the other.

Oh Dag. I may not know you, but I see now that you are a product, as we all are, of implacable forces. I sat on a bench with the plasticine bagel and like the boy tried not to cry.

Enough running, enough hiding.

///

A few days later, I was sitting in the hotel lobby reading a brochure for Taos when B hobbled through the door, his hair matted and beard mussed. He fell into the seat beside me. He raised a crutch and waved it toward the restaurant.

"Beware women you meet at that bar," he said. He breathed heavily for a minute. "The boys ain't in Oklahoma anymore."

He explained that, between pugilistic bouts of coitus, he and the woman from the bar had consumed hours of cable news. The story of the Pigs, it turned out, had not dwindled after the Pigs had been sold to Walmart, but had been picked up by the host of a late-night news-and-opinion show. The host had linked the Pig graffiti and the nascent movement of so-called Oinkers to a screed of dissatisfactions with the deteriorating economic, political, and moral core of our nation. B imitated the host, stretching his mouth in indignant emphasis. We'd heard this all before, I reminded him. Sure, he said, but according to this host, the boys and Dag had left for Colorado after the trial.

It made sense. In our family, Colorado was a land where silver spilled from the hills, oil bubbled in the shale, and our grandfather had rekindled the world—or so the story went. Dag would seek out the Gulch, the high, remote valley where grandfather had gone on strike—but what did Dag want with the boys? He had used them for their Oinkers, our erstwhile followers, but beyond their marketing value, the boys were of little use to him. I doubted they could paint more than a crude Pig without the templates, which we'd cut up and crammed in a dumpster, and if they did paint more Pigs, it would now be copyright infringement, a crime that Walmart's lawyers would leap to prosecute, not merely the defacing a private building. Maybe Dag brought them up on stage for impromptu endorsements: Pig artists for Woodby! Or he'd mounted them on the hood of his car like prize elk.

I stuffed the flyer for Taos back into its plastic display. Running had kept me free of Dag and the police but changed nothing. Dag had New York, he'd taken my Pigs, the boys. Ming would be next. Was I really so powerless as to let him pluck off parts of my life like wings from a fly? If I ran to Ming, he would follow, unless Ming had already joined him, in which case I would run to an empty promise. And what of the boys?

I informed B that we were going to Colorado to find Dag and the boys, but he was past caring.

"Alright, let's go take away this excitement they're having," he said. "And you can make a ass of yourself with your brother. Anyways, they got legal weed."

24

The location of grandfather's Gulch had long been a secret. The few historians who still cared about the legend located the Gulch in one of the alpine valleys that dotted the state's mountainous southwestern corner, where towns and small cities had since taken root, burying or destroying what remained from the brief civilization built by the strikers. In the family we had always doubted these guesses. All the clues we needed could be found in the Great Book, we believed, and so I scoured its lengthy text for symbols and signs. For example, according to the Book, there had been a train line that at one time ran from the Gulch down into the Panhandle, and though it was now gone, traces would remain amid the geography through which it had run. The populated valleys the historians favored were too accessible, too easily found to satisfy grandfather's obsessive need for secrecy and control. His valley would be remote and forbidding. On the gas station map I found only two such high valleys that could have allowed a trainline, and only one of these had a paved road.

As we bent over the map, B kept glancing at the copy of the Great Book in which I'd recorded the details of all our Pigs. He could see what I'd written in the margins and end pages, and I understood that his admonishing look asked how soon I would dispose of this evidence. The journal of our crimes suggested that the boys had perjured themselves, and with their ruling invalidated, a judge might reconsider the acceptability of painting graffiti Pigs, along with our having fled the scene of a crime and destroyed evidence.

When we finally picked up the Snowflake, the mechanic spun a lengthy story of gaskets and boots and valves, as if I'd paid him by the word, and gave me several shoulds and mights along with the bill. When I told him where we were going, his head wobbled on its stem. With a grimace he asked if we had any tools (none, I told him). He disappeared into his shop and returned with a grease-smeared canvas bag sagging with battered sockets, a dull screwdriver, bits of wire and hose.

"Good luck," he said.

For hours we skimmed between accidental buttes in the pan-flat landscape, the ground first red, then yellow, then brown as we looped east, then north, and climbed gradually toward the mountains. No building in the towns we passed had heard of stairs; second floors were a rumor from three-dimensional lands. We were ants again, crawling over warped planes, the world too big for us to see. Heat lines rose from the road like sprites and shimmered.

As soon as we crossed into Colorado and reached a town with more than one stoplight, B directed me off the highway to an address he'd seen advertised in green letters on a black billboard. Afterwards he smoked a joint the size and shape of a humpback whale. I expected him to pass out, but instead he took a scatological interest in everything we passed, Quonset huts, parched grasslands, buttes like retaining walls along the road. He searched the sky for chemtrails. The unmarked Quonset huts in rows might house alien remains, he pontificated, and the black rectangles of solar panels certainly implied nefarious government intent. The chemtrails, of course, spoke for themselves; chemicals dispersed overhead for mass control. After an hour of excited paranoia, he lapsed into a ponderous silence.

Straight, straight went the road. Cattle appeared and disappeared. High noon on the high prairie, the light buttery with early autumn. We stopped at a Mexican restaurant and spread the map across the table.

I located the valley to the north and west of us, a long, difficult drive through mountain passes on twisting two-lane roads.

We slept at roadside motels with Western styling and faux-wood paneling in the rooms. B ate microwave popcorn and drank vodka rocks from a plastic cup and watched his new favorite talking head on the cable news.

///

After noon on the third day, we crossed a bridge over a knife-cut canyon. The bridge curved between buttresses of stone protruding from the canyon walls, and its long, flared pillars reached hundreds of feet from blasted talus to float the roadway on their tips with a lithe Deco strength that I recognized immediately as grandfather's design.

Past a grove of pines, we rolled over an abandoned railroad track that had subsided into clay, then past a shaggy meadow where the posts of a decayed structure poked from between fallen timbers. A fire had swept the valley at some point; scorches marked the bark of the larger trees, and jagged spikes of heartwood veined with charcoal spotted the meadows like the columns of a Greek ruin. I sensed ghosts in the pockets of shade, the husks of trees.

The Snowflake coughed as we forded a dry creek bed, and when the engine sputtered and died, I braked into a gravel pullout littered with pine needles. B poked around under the hood with his crutches propped under his armpits, his face sour.

"Can't get in there like this," he said. He swung himself to a boulder at the pullout's edge and sat down.

I bent over the engine, seeing wires, tubes, fans.

It would be a cold autumn night at elevation, with only the bubble of the Snowflake to keep us warm. I grabbed a bottle of water and a box of cheese-and-crackers and followed B as he crutched toward an over-grown dirt road I'd not noticed. The trees around the road were tall and slender. No doubt grandfather and his strikers had felled the ancient trees they encountered on migrating here, and used the wood for their cabins and bridges and fenceposts and warming fires.

We came to a small clearing, slowly giving itself to the encroaching forest. A dilapidated husk of cabin, burned on one side, its beams fallen and rotting into the earth, offered evidence that no one lived in this valley anymore, only the ghosts. It was hard to believe anyone ever had, at over eight thousand feet and with so little flat land. It was far too small for the nascent industry and culture of grandfather's stories.

His stories were absurd, taken literally. Who weeded the fields in the summer heat and harvested wheat in the fall? Who graded the roads, or built the grader to grade the roads? How did they replace the worn-out parts of their cars? What happened if the farmer, facing so much difficulty growing in a short season at altitude, had to raise her prices, and as the only farmer in the valley, could raise them however she chose? Which professional among them would forego their profession to compete on the limited land good for farming? They would raise the prices on their own goods or starve. This was a child's diorama of an economy without complication.

Dag didn't see it that way. To him, the valley was the birthplace and cradle of our nation, and grandfather's stories were truths on which to meditate. He would certainly have come here.

We wandered among the meadow grasses. I kicked a few rusted bolts and pieces of steel from the dirt. B sat on a rock and scratched his beard. He pointed to a set of tracks sharp in the dusty soil, made by new tires and recently.

"He's been here already," he said.

We nibbled at the cheese-and-crackers. We followed the sound of a creek through a stand of thin trees with trembling leaves—aspens, said B—and lay like boys with our feet in the water, B's cast propped on a rock. The aspen leaves quivered and clapped, voices in them, a murmuring.

"Should have brought more cheese-and-crackers," said B.

"People lived here once," I said.

"More than once."

He was right; indigenous peoples had lived there first. They had gathered plants and speared trout and trapped rabbits, perhaps by this very stream. Perhaps it was their voices I heard in the aspens' leaves.

"Think I could live here?" asked B. "I got my clothes, a jar of weed, and a pocketknife. Bet there's fish in there." He sat up to light a joint. "I ain't afraid of hard work, long as it meets my needs and don't humiliate me. Dying might be a alright alternative to success, which, staying here, would be the two options I think."

While B watched the clouds I went back to the car and returned with the Great Book I'd used as a journal and a short-handled spade I'd purchased at a roadside hardware store. With more effort than I expected, the earth being rocky and webbed with roots like rebar, I dug a two-foot hole in the bank of the stream, where in the spring the water would flood and soak the Great Book, dissolving its wordy message. B watched me struggle.

"A pointed shovel is best for that kind of digging," he said.

I was sweaty and grimy by the time I tamped soil over the book. Downstream, around a brief bend, I found a shallow pool in the creek and draped my clothes over shrubs and sat in the icy water, my parts shrinking inside me. I lay back, water running over my neck, my hair, only my nose and mouth above. The river stones as they slid in the current and the water burbling over them spoke tongues in my ears.

When I started to shiver, I dried myself and returned to B, who lay on the bank dozing. He got up drowsy and we headed toward the car.

As we got close, I saw a shape by the hood. My mind, consumed with spirits, imagined Sasquatch or the ghosts of Indigenous peoples or Dag. When we got closer, we saw a man in a dirty red shirt with a knapsack on his back, leaning into the engine compartment. B and I shared a look of surprise and suspicion.

The man lifted a long, stubbled face. "I was hiking," he said. "There's a ledge up there."

I didn't know how to respond.

"Saw your car. Hood was up."

We stood watching each other. In a quiet voice B told me to start the engine, and the stranger looked back and forth between us until I climbed into the driver's seat and turned the key. The engine coughed, then wheezed mortally. The man told me to shut it off and asked if we had tools. It was all too clever, the mechanic's gift of old sockets, this stranger happening by in an abandoned valley. I grew paranoid, but for no good reason. The kindness of strangers was foreign to me, but then I'd never needed it.

The man picked through the canvas bag. As he worked he talked about belts and torque and airflow and fuel mixtures. B nodded along. After a half-hour, the man signaled for me to start the engine. It whined for a moment before settling into a rough idle. He shut the hood and handed me the bag of tools.

"My name's Paul," he said. "I get a ride?"

In our lengthy travels, B had expressed a native suspicion of hitch-hikers and refused even to slow when we saw someone on the roadside with their thumb out, but we could hardly refuse a ride to the man who'd fixed our car. Without him, we would all be hitching, or gathering wild lettuces. The man named Paul climbed into the backseat.

"Pretty decent steakhouse over the pass," he said.

None of us spoke as we left the valley and began the long climb to the pass. Spirits followed on the wind as it rose alongside us. The hitchhiker stared out the window, deep in some complexity of thought. I asked if he'd seen any mine shafts or tailings while he was hiking, as fabled in my father's retelling of grandfather's stories, but he shook his head and said no.

He had a small knapsack, which might at one time have held food and water, but now sat deflated in his lap. What, I asked him, had brought him to such a remote valley, with no car and no plan for getting out? Hiking, he replied. After a moment he explained that he'd come to the valley years ago on a rock-climbing trip, during which he'd discovered a wide ledge of granite at the base of the cliff from which one could observe the valley and the higher peaks to the north. There was something about the elevation, he said, the expansive view, the way the sun fanned from right to left, casting the valley in the relief of shifting shadows, that opened his mind to new, fluid thoughts. He'd returned to the ledge to grapple with a theory of how the physical world formed itself in our minds.

I glanced at B, who returned a smug what-did-you-expect look.

"I got stuck up there," Paul continued. "A good ways up. It's all talus. You have to scramble, and some of the rocks are unstable. I was thinking about this stochastic uncertainty, which rock would move, which would not, when a boulder shifted under me and trapped my foot. It was rough there for a while. I thought I might have to cut off my foot to get out."

"You got two feet I guess," said B.

"I contemplated the puzzle of my foot under the rock. The mass of the boulder and the mass of the earth, attracting each other. My foot was just in the way. Einstein's theory uses the curvature of spacetime to explain gravity. Like pool balls on a thick blanket, mass deforms space. That's for big objects, like planets. The interaction between closed strings may explain the relative weakness of gravity compared to other forces at close ranges."

"Weak my ass," said B. "Trapped you."

"It made me think in quantum terms," said Paul. "String theory."

Strings, he explained to our silence, were a mathematical concept that had been theorized to underly all of reality.

I could tell from the way B shifted in his seat and leaned over to examine the instrument panel that he wanted me to stop and give the Snowflake a rest, so I watched for a pullout as we weaved up the canyon.

The hitchhiker, once he'd started talking, couldn't stop. Despite our silence and ignorance he grew excited. He was interested in thoughts, he explained, how they reflected the reality they modeled, and how we communicated them between us.

"How'd you get out from the boulder?" asked B.

"Oh, I untied my boot."

"You thought of that after you spent how long pickin' your nose at the universe?"

"Have you ever considered what a thought is? What a thought looks like?"

B stuck another joint between his lips. Paul watched him suspiciously.

"Thoughts have a shape," he continued.

Where the road lifted steeply, the shoulder widened into a bulb of gravel and I pulled over. We sat on the boulders that lined the edge of the cliff. There was nothing here, at least not in the way my family believed. It was a lonesome, freeing knowledge.

B bent down to pick up rocks, which he tossed over the cliff's edge, counting the seconds until they clattered. The stranger joined in, and they laughed when one of them hit a pine tree, causing a branch to drop a pinecone into the shade below. They kept at it, hooting and whistling. Softened up by the rock tossing or bored by the silence, B asked the man what he'd meant about thoughts.

"What I'm proposing is that discrete thoughts can be represented mathematically and visualized as a shape. And a shape is determined by its limits. You understand. Where I end is where I no longer am. No, no, I can explain. A finite line is only a line if it connects at least two points—its limits."

B stopped throwing stones and instead picked up a stick and drew lines in the dirt.

Many people, Paul continued, believed that the shape of a thought might be like the shape of the network of neurons that formed it. His theory differed in that the shape was quantum. A mathematical shape in complex space.

"So for example, when I try to tell you about this idea I had, you take these symbols—I mean the words I'm saying—and reconstruct the thought in your own minds."

He was silent for a moment. B lit the joint.

"You're the first people I've seen," said Paul. "When we try to communicate a thought, like I'm doing right now—so I have a thought in my mind and it has a specific shape, and I'm trying to communicate that thought's shape to you—that information takes a shape in your brain. And the more I tell you about this thought, the better I describe it, the closer those shapes are, the one in my head, let's call that the original, and the one in yours, which would be a copy. An inexact copy. And that's the thing. No matter how hard we try, the thoughts are never perfect mirrors, right? They can't be, because it's a quantum shape. This is complicated. In string theory there are certain values, certain limits. It's M-theory really. It requires the Calabi-Yau manifold of eleven-dimensional space."

B exhaled blue smoke, looking into the sky.

After a moment the man started again.

"The thing about thought from a quantum perspective is its imperfection. That rock there"—he pointed to the rock in B's hand—"we all see it. It exists. But what does it mean that it exists? What can we know about it?"

B stared at the rock in his hand. He looked confused. "If it hit you, you'd know for sure," he said.

The man flinched. The rock, he continued more cautiously, has a weight, a texture, a particular mass. All of these qualities became language when communicated to another person, but they also became language when we ourselves attempted to comprehend the rock; we told ourselves about it. In this way, he claimed, language became the world.

B flung rocks in rapid succession and watched their parabolic arcs over the treetops. The man seemed brilliant or unhinged. He ignored the chalky dust that billowed up around him when gusts of air rushed up the cliff's face and tousled our hair, as if the substance of the world was itself words and not a crystalline dirt that stung our eyes and the linings of our nostrils. The man's conception grew shadowy and tentacular as I reflected that our knowledge of the world and each other would become a hall of mirrors if he was right; like a game of whispers, our words distorted infinitely.

"Now, now, see here," said B.

He looked around with his arms out in exasperation, as if the dust, the wind, the rocks that he hucked over the cliff's edge, these were the world. We touched, breathed, saw, heard them, even the invisible wind as it buffeted our ears and stirred the sandy soil.

"I don't like what you're saying," B concluded.

"It's not that reality doesn't exist," the man persisted. "It's just more complex—there's always more information than we can take in, or that our brains can model as a thought. So you see what I mean—realism is a false premise."

"Tell me if he says something about chemtrails," B mumbled.

"Oh, chemtrails are real," said Paul.

B's head snapped around.

"So they are controlling us," he gasped.

"Oh, no, that's not what chemtrails do."

B whipped a rock in a line that eventually bent to gravity. "What the hell. They is or they ain't."

"Not with chemtrails."

The muscles of B's face twitched. "Maybe some other way," he grunted.

Paul pondered this. The desire to believe that others control us is an interesting paradox, he said. We desire freedom, but there's a sense of safety in being controlled, and agency and identity in reacting against it. Blaming others helps us maintain a belief in the promise of freedom without the uncertainties of freedom itself.

Whether he understood the man or not, B was not pleased.

"Goddammit!" He banged his crutches on the ground with a ringing hollow clang. "You tell me I can't touch what's real and now I don't want freedom because the government controls us and the media covers it up!"

B sounded crazy. I wasn't much help. The man's paradoxical attack on what I'd always believed to be the substance of life, which I touched and heard and tasted, etc., made bile rise in my throat.

Paul was unperturbed. "The government has all kinds of secrets," he said.

"That's damn right. They controlling us," said B.

"Not with chemtrails. There are easier ways. Laws, for example, and their selective enforcement. Also, what story do they tell us?

That story lives inside us, imperfectly, I argue. It takes a shape in our minds. Why do we wave the flag, for instance?"

B erupted, red-faced. "YOU GOT A PROBLEM WITH THE FLAG?"

"Not if we consider why we wave it," Paul said, placating with his hands. "It's a symbol, like words. It makes different thoughts in different heads."

"It means America, goddammit."

America too was an idea, the man responded.

"Damn good idea," spat B.

I agreed silently.

"My point is that these are all shapes in our minds, and they differ from mind to mind, even when the emotions they spur are similar."

"Anyone can't agree on freedom can lick my ass," said B.

"This has implications for how government is structured. How we organize. Maybe it could be different. Maybe there could be more freedom."

"So government is the problem."

"That's a reasonable hypothesis," said Paul. "If our perceptions of reality differ," he continued, "then how is a leader supposed to understand our thoughts—unless they put the thoughts there themselves."

"The media," said B.

Paul scratched his neck. Given the right incentives, he suggested, the media could shape thoughts toward reality as we perceived it, or away, or toward whatever story the incentives promoted. The thought shapes were agnostic to truth; their formation was only mimicry. We were like parrots who learned to repeat words they didn't understand. This mimicry, he concluded, could only exist if it conveyed an evolutionary advantage. Mimicry, not truth, advanced our species.

B shook his head and spat. "Why you care about any of this nonsense crap?" he asked.

"Oh, it's because AI is limited by the networks we build it with," Paul explained. "Humans can intuit answers to problems, but AI can't, not yet. It's doesn't shape thoughts like we do."

"So are thoughts things or are things thoughts?" asked B. "Like, does a thing change when we think about it?"

"The moon might be light, or it might be time," said Paul, staring into the pale sky. "Or a flower, decoration for a table or sustenance for a bee."

B threw one more rock over the cliff and wiped the dirt off his hands and pulled himself upright.

"The question is whether a thought affects its object or if the object is only ever thought," said Paul. "That's very close to what I'm—"

He paced in a circle, muttering.

"I've had enough," said B. He swung his crutches toward the Snowflake. "You want a ride you better get in now."

///

When we reached the town over the pass, Paul pointed out the steak house's plastic sign, and I pulled into the lot. Paul jumped out and hitched a ride on a propane truck headed north.

B and I sat before plates of iceberg lettuce and runny blue cheese. I saw runny, but maybe B saw gourmet. He ate hungrily while I nibbled.

Something in the runny cheese or a reality beyond my apprehension or an AI that might exceed me in thought caused my gut to clench. I excused myself to the bathroom, where I sat on a broken toilet seat with my elbows on my knees and my head in my hands and missed my brother. The certainty of being with him, the righteousness of knowing the world was as we saw it to be. The strength of this belief, our heritage, was our bulwark against destructive or frivolous change.

Gas expanded in my gut, my abdomen taut as bowling-ball bag. How could cells so small produce so much gas so quickly? I heard the clump-swish of crutches and the squeal of the bathroom door's hinges and B's baritone asking if I was okay in there, just as I released a resounding belch that echoed off the tiles. I allowed a moment of gratitude for freedom from the bloating.

As I washed my hands, B watched me with something between alarm and concern.

"Waitress says three guys came through here a couple days ago. One of them looked like you."

"She said that?"

"Said the tall one looked a little like your friend, but more Clint Eastwood."

"I see."

"I believe she meant he had movie-star qualities."

"Say where they were headed?"

"Only the one highway through town."

/ / /

We spent the night at a roadside motel with dirty orange plaid carpet that might have been laid in the 60s. In the morning, we followed a sporadic stream of Subarus and RVs and pickups north along the two-lane blacktop as it meandered between thinly treed hills and low cliffs fringed with browning brush. The day passed like a flip book of hills rising and shrinking. Where the highway met a narrow river, a town cropped up, not much more than a Dollar General and a pizza place between scattered cabins and trailers. We passed a rental shop stacked with fluorescent kayaks, a ski lodge shuttered for the season, more churches than a town that small could possibly support. B spotted a new-looking brew pub and directed me to stop.

I watched pints disappear beneath his moustache while we waited for the kitchen to open for dinner. B became jolly and joked with the waitress, and I excused myself to the bathroom. B and the woman were still bent in laughter when I pushed out the tavern-style doors, so I detoured out the front.

The air was cool at elevation, and I leaned back against the building to warm my face in the sunlight, when a rhythmic pulsing vibrated the air, rousing me; a helicopter rose over the flaking cliffs to the west and pounded north. In the light it turned cobalt blue. Ming.

Back at the table, B was tipping a slice of pizza into his mouth. Sausage, peppers, onions. My gut recoiled. When the waitress passed, she smiled at B.

"She seen a man looks like me but better-looking?" I asked.

"No, but she says there's something going on up the canyon."

///

We continued north to an intersection at a river, where we turned west. The road followed overgrown railroad tracks that ran along the riverbed into a valley that narrowed between scabby hills to our left and brittle cliffs to our right. Around a sweeping bend in the road, a town came into sight. The highway lost its yellow ribbons where it became the town's main street. A dog panted across before us. A dark liquor store, blank storefronts hung with real estate signs, an empty café, garages and sheds with rusted metal roofs. No people. The road meandered past small cabins and marooned trailers, then bent to the right through a quaint downtown of red brick and dark-stained wood. Beyond the buildings, sheer cliffs rose on both sides, narrowing as if to enfold us. A canal sluiced rusty water along the roadside where the pavement gave way to gravel, then dirt.

"Anything going on around here has got to be behind us," said B.

He was probably right, but something clawing like a nervous animal in my chest made me want to drive the Snowflake until the road ended, and then to keep climbing into the canyon until it too ended. Ming was somewhere ahead. So was Dag.

A sign boasted of an Underground Mining Museum, and we agreed that it would be destination enough for us, and that we would turn around once we had seen it. I parked past two wooden shacks and a row of black SUVs.

Like tourists, we stretched our legs and looked about. Tailings feathered the rocks below the cliffs, the abandoned mines black slots above them. The air vibrated again, and another helicopter, or the same bird I'd seen before, rose beyond the shacks and headed west.

I was losing my steam and ready to give up when B pointed to a shack that served as the museum's ticket booth. To my surprise, a prim age-lined woman with round glasses sat behind the partition, awaiting business. She frowned at me and scrutinized B's tank top and facial hair.

"You are here for the meeting," she said to me.

I nodded, a vacuum forming in my chest.

She assessed B with clinical detachment.

"He's with me," I said, then added, "an associate of my brother's."

"Like him but better-looking," said B.

She pushed two paper tickets across the counter. "You're quite late," she said.

Under the lintel of the mining museum's entrance, a pimpled boy in a martial uniform tore our tickets in half and waved us into the shaft, where awkwardly posed mining equipment lined the rock walls, and faceless mannequins in blue overalls paused in postures of work, picks overhead. Steel ventilation ductwork snaked along the ceiling, stirring the fungal air. I stumbled forward, my pupils adjusting to the dim light, past a mannequin pushing an ore cart with no rails to run on.

B sneezed volubly.

We passed hewn walls, an empty gift shop, more mannequins, and came to an oak and iron door opened for us by a large man dressed in black.

25

We entered a domed room, hollowed from glittering earth. Swirling green dazzled us, Dag's disciples in their money-colored capes twirling amidst men and women in tailored suits and long dresses who crowded the ovoid space and raised a din of chatter that echoed off the walls. By some invisible cue, the disciples stopped twirling and mingled among the crowd. Laughter, polite smiles, champagne flutes. This was no strike.

"It's a cocktail party in a mine shaft," I said to B, but he'd wandered away.

"It's called a vug," replied a resonant voice.

I saw a red tie under a dark suit, an American flag pin in the lapel. Woodby.

"This was all silver telluride," he purred.

I felt my hands clenching into fists and stuffed them in my pockets.

"One of the largest silver strikes in history." He squinted at me like a hunter sighting his rifle. "I could have you put away, you know."

I pushed past him, searching for Dag. Across the chamber I saw Cheryl close a paneled oak door and stomp into the crowd. I made for the door, sliding my way between clusters of partiers, but before I could get close, two black-suited guards took positions blocking the entrance. Cheryl returned and spoke to them, pointing at me. She puffed her cheeks and shook her head. In case I wasn't sure, she also raised her index finger and wagged it like a metronome. No admittance for me.

Woodby had followed through the crowd and now blocked my way.

"Thanks to your brother—" he said, then stopped, distracted by something behind me.

I turned to see B loitering by a table laid with galvanized tubs of ice and drinks, chatting with an older woman in a floor-length black gown. He had a bottle of gin by the neck and gestured wildly with it, sending globules of liquor glimmering into the air. The woman threw her head back and laughed, touching B's forearm.

"Get that man away from my wife," Woodby growled.

The scene transfixed me, B in his flip-flop and cast and tank top, the woman a generation older and accoutered like the chamber itself in dark velvet that glittered among its folds. She had her fingertips on his forearm, her throat naked. At that moment I appreciated B more than any person on earth.

"Careful," I told Woodby, "the man flirting with your wife is also your voter base."

Woodby shot me a look of contempt and horror and brushed past me to collect his wife.

A flash of green caught my attention, Cheryl in her cape. She stalked over to me.

"The only reason you're not in handcuffs is because your brother wills it," she said.

Handcuffs or banishment, which was it?

She pulled the collar of her cape tight around her throat.

"He let those boys go," she added.

Over her shoulder I watched B cup a joint between his hands to light it. A guard stopped him, moving in close enough to kiss his cheek. B tilted his head and nodded agreeably and slipped the lighter and joint into his pocket, then leaned toward the guard's ear and said something that made the man almost smile. Seeing this, Woodby stepped in and jabbed a finger at the guard's chest, his words drowned in the echoing chamber.

"Something's always ruining everything," Cheryl pouted. Her face purpled as if she were holding her breath. "It should be so simple."

Woodby now yelled at a second guard who moved to corner B against the wall. The tiny enameled American flag pin on Woodby's lapel had spun sideways, as if in a stiff breeze. I left Cheryl and weaved between clusters of men in dark suits.

"He's with me," I called to the guards, who turned impassive faces on me.

"Sir, please," said the second guard, his skin pale against the dark wall. He was maybe a supervisor, I guessed.

"This man is my coworker," I said.

B snickered.

"We've been instructed," said the supervisor.

"He's not elected yet," I replied, which confused the guards. "My family built this country," I boasted, pressing my advantage. "This whole world."

The supervisor's head lurched back on his neck.

"And he's with me," I repeated, taking B by the arm and leading him away.

The supervisor spoke into his sleeve as we retreated to a passageway opposite the entrance.

"That guy wants me out of here," said B.

"Maybe don't flirt with his wife."

B's eyebrows squirmed. "That was all her. She's alright though. I could sit a piece with her."

He stuffed a chocolate mint he'd lifted from the food table into his mouth and offered one to me. I unwrapped it automatically and told him the boys weren't there.

"Yeah, I know," he said and sighed. "But that girl of yours is here. Little one from your studio? In there with your brother." He pointed to the oak door.

Chase. Of course she was with Dag now. How did B know Chase?

"I can see," he said.

I peeked into the chamber, where Woodby was lecturing a half-circle of guards. The mint oozed a chemical joy over my tongue, a contrast to every other feeling in me. I tried to crumple the wrapper, but it resisted, so I stuffed it in my pocket and left my hand there to prevent me from hitting Woodby again.

B leaned over to see what I was looking at. "I still might vote for him, given the options."

The thought of confronting Dag wearied me, and having to do so in front of Chase felt like too much to bear. The boys were free, according to Cheryl. There was nothing to save.

"Let's go," I said.

I hauled B by the elbow like a swimmer tugging a boat, he was so much bigger than me.

"You go on see your brother," he said.

"The boys are gone."

I started again toward the door, but B wouldn't budge.

"It's now or never, and never won't do for you."

He had found a cane somewhere and thrust it like a spike at the stone floor.

"Fine," I said.

"And see to it that you hurry. I got a feeling my freedom here is about to be limited."

He slipped down the hallway away from me, and I slipped away from the murmuring crowd.

Cheryl and the guards had disappeared. I took a breath and opened the oak door.

Inside was a smaller chamber hewn from the same black rock and spanned by a table of dark wood. When the heavy door closed behind me, the noise of the crowd silenced, and I heard only the clicking of keyboards fingered by Dag, Chase, and three others in green capes. Chase didn't look up from her laptop when I entered; this final indignity was either malice or, worse, disregard.

Dag rose and took me aside.

If I'd had fantasies of closure, whatever that is, or somehow getting even, or that Dag deserved one last chance, or that we might depart unsatisfied in our separate goals but enriched with a nascent mutual understanding, I'd have been disappointed. Dag's irises were circles of blue flame. Stand aside or be immolated, they told me, though his posture—upper back slightly bent, shoulders perceptibly forward—showed the strain of the weight he carried.

"If you're here for the boys—"

He left the sentence unfinished.

I stuffed my hands in my pockets again and felt the crumpled mint wrapper, which in my nervous state I couldn't help but play with and so rather than be seen playing with something in my pocket, I pulled it out and threw it toward Chase. It uncrumpled itself mid-flight and fluttered to the floor like a maple seed. Dag watched me with amusement, as if observing a child caught in imaginary play.

"They're in Federal court now," he said.

Adrenaline shot through my chest. "What?" I asked.

"They settled with Walmart," he replied, pleased with himself, "but when they confessed to painting the Pigs, the Feds nabbed them for all the graffiti you left on U.S. government buildings."

"And you just let them go," I said, aghast.

"You're the one that did the crime. Anyway, there's new evidence. Did you know about Davis?" he asked, almost coquettish in his contempt.

I shook my head. The adrenaline had passed, leaving a cold feeling.

Dag smirked. "All along he was posting to the dark web. He left details anyone could follow: GPS coordinates, the weather the day you painted, how you mixed your colors." He smiled at my shock. "And his opinions, did you know about his opinions? He had lots of opinions. Dangerous opinions. Opinions that would curl your hair."

Like a man hit on the head from behind, I felt stunned before I realized what had happened. All those nights Davis had snuck out with his phone. I shivered, wondering what dangerous opinions he might have promoted, all while leading Dag right to us. I imagined racist rants, hate-filled diatribes, warlike words, or worse—what was worse? I didn't want to know.

"We followed you for weeks before your Walmart Waterloo. Knowing you, you had no idea, did you? Did you know that Pigs would capture the zeitgeist? That you'd create a movement? You just make these things without knowing. You're like an idiot savant."

"You always make it so fun to see you," I mumbled.

I waved my arms at Chase, who remained stone-faced at her laptop.

Dag caught my arms and pinned them to my sides. He said, not unkindly, his tone that of an overworked clerk tasked with managing the ignorant public, "Stop distracting yourself. Tell me what you want."

What did I want? To be free from the guilt and alarm I felt on hearing that the boys were on trial for my crimes—and that Davis had been spreading hair-curling opinions. I wished I hadn't come, that Dag's face wasn't inches from mine, while Chase ignored me without so much as a hair flip.

"If it helps, the boys seem to have forgotten you," he said. He let go of my arms. "And no one knows you were involved. No one suspected that the mastermind was an idiot savant. Now all your Oinkers run to Woodby, because he understands, he has a plan. You're like a fairy-tale Pig that leaves golden shits."

What could I do but change the subject.

"We went to the valley," I said. "The Gulch."

He examined me. "So you know."

"Yeah, nothing there."

"Nothing—it's everything. You don't see that?"

"It was just a story."

Dag's face seethed and he called me a *cheap little hypocrite*, one of grandfather's epithets. My paintings he called *unfit for human consumption*, an odd and sinister phrase. Had he seen my show? Or did he mean the rooftop abstracts, or the mural, or the Pigs?

"You're no artist," he concluded. He wiped spittle from his lips.

I watched Chase, still huddled over her screen.

Dag typically calmed after his outbursts, and though he rarely apologized in any meaningful way, he would often relax enough to allow some common ground. Instead he got a second wind.

"You used to paint the glory that is rational man. I've seen what you've done since. Garbage, confusion. Amateur graffiti," he said, chin lifted, his face radiant with mockery. "The muddy middle. At least be honest with yourself. Pick a side."

More dichotomies. I craved the color and movement of oils. It had been so long. I felt a brush's handle in my hand.

"You don't know what you're doing," he said.

B had been saying this to me daily for weeks now, and I couldn't disagree. To B this meant I was following a hunch, one he might not follow himself, but something he admitted he might do from time to time. To my brother, it defied logic.

"You built a movement," he scoffed, "by accident." The bliss of contempt softened his features.

I recalled the blue helicopter coming and going.

"You still need me because you still need Ming."

He blinked several times, then sneered and said, "It's just like you to choose swine."

"Brother must mean nothing to you."

His brow furrowed. It was like watching a statue frown and roused my compassion.

"It means we have the same name," he said.

I'd come to confront Dag, but without a plan. I had only grievances, mostly ancient and irreparable.

"I'm sorry dad was so hard on you," I said.

He stared blankly at me.

"I forgive you," I said, "for how you were to me."

The words hung in the air between us.

"Give me Ming," he said, his voice flat.

"There's nothing in that valley," I insisted. "The Gulch was just a story."

What had once been, could now never be. The lesson we keep learning.

"And I can't help you with Ming," I told him. "I don't know where she is."

We stared at each other like toddlers meeting for the first time.

"I'm going," I said.

///

Out in the hallway, I gathered myself. I half expected Dag to burst out through the door, and it was not without some disappointment that I waited there, alone.

Up the hallway, Cheryl leaned against the wall like the unpopular girl at a dance.

I joined her.

"I see you got in," she said.

"He's my brother."

She shrugged.

"What is this, anyway?" I asked. My skin felt cool and clammy.

"Not what it was supposed to be. This was the beginning of something, and now it's this foolish party. It's free booze and snacks. These people are just stupid animals."

"Is this the strike?" I asked.

She pulled at the collar of her cape.

"They're making too much money to go on strike. They'll only go on strike if Ming goes too. I had so much hope."

A shift in the timbre of voices signaled a slow drifting of bodies into factions along the walls. B appeared at my side with the bottle of gin.

"Time to go," he said thickly.

///

We were making our way out of the museum, past the mannequins frozen in their fruitless labor, when B stretched his neck left and right like a hound on a scent. The odor was faint but acrid, then intensified as we passed the gift shop. I heard crackling and a siren. It occurred to me that someone might have set fire to the mine to smoke out the billionaires and representatives and their functionaries, and so I hurried, crouching below the smoke I imagined gathering above me. When we reached the entrance we saw, across the dirt road from the ticket booth, a ten-foot-tall dollar sign ringed with orange flames. Pillowy black smoke trailed east, embers streamed against the wood-plank shacks. A dozen security agents stood around the fire, arms crossed. Down the road, two firemen dragged limp hoses from an engine, then stood with the nozzles on their shoulders and watched. *Fire, fire,* whispered the guards into their sleeves.

No one noticed us scurry to the Snowflake. B took a last swig of gin and left the bottle on the bumper of an SUV and belched. In the tight cabin of the car, he reeked of alcohol.

"There's a lady in here," he said.

Coiled tight in the back seat was Saoirse, a finger to her lips. Her hair was cut short and dyed black. In the rearview I saw the guards backing away from the fire as it ballooned in the wind.

"Any time, painter," she whispered.

I eased the Snowflake onto the dirt road and skirted the security guards and the firemen standing by their engine, all too distracted to peer into the Snowflake's backseat. In the rearview, blue-orange flames fondled a black metal skeleton. Flocks of ash fluttered on the waves of heat. On the firemen's lips, *water, water, water.*

Part 5

"Who pays for the orgy?"
—Atlas Shrugged

26

We slept for a few hours in a pullout.

I awoke before dawn and relieved myself in the bushes. Unable to sleep, I sat on a graffiti-graven picnic table with my feet on the bench and watched the stars to the east slowly occlude with light. And what now? We were running again, this time with an arsonist. Dag would follow me until he got what he wanted—Ming, ostensibly, though maybe he needed me, too, needed my beliefs to align with his own. How else could he be unequivocally right? I was left with the fraught choice of leading Dag to Ming or walking off into the wilderness.

B groaned himself awake while I wrestled with this non-choice—how could I choose other than Ming? He limped on his cane into the bushes to make water. Afterwards, he sat beside me on the table, then lay down.

"Where'd your crutches go?" I asked.

"See what I heard there was they my crutches, so I did what I wanted with them."

B's voice was rough with mucous. He rubbed his head.

"You concerned about your investment?" he asked, voice drifting toward sleep.

"Did you know about Davis?" I asked.

"Yeah they been arrested again," he said. "That bossy little lady of your brother's told me."

"No, I mean Davis. He was betraying us."

"What now?"

I told him what Dag had told me about Davis's posts, the GPS coordinates, and his vile opinions, whatever they were.

B was quiet for a such a long spell that I thought he'd fallen asleep, and maybe he had for a moment, but just as I was about to prod him, he responded.

"I keep learning not to trust the quiet ones," he said.

After a long moment, B added, "You know their story won't hold up against the Feds."

"What story?" I asked.

"That they did all the Pigs themselves. Walmart just wanted the Pigs so they could use them to sell stuff—they maybe didn't care so much about who did what. But government lawyers only care about winning."

"You think they're looking for us now?"

"Hard to understand why anyone cares so much about some paint, but the boys was in the news, so yeah, the Marshals or some such will need to track us down."

"Where should we go, B?"

He yawned. "Since when you ask me?"

"We can't stay here," I pointed out.

"Ask the lady. Maybe you'll listen to her."

Saoirse, when she awoke and joined us, thought about this question as she combed her hair with her fingers. There was a place, she said, where no one would find us. It was a place of nothing, she warned, and a long drive to get there.

Under the sharp morning light, we glided off the ridge onto a viaduct that spanned a flat, parched valley. A ring of white rime showed a high-water mark; it was a reservoir, or had been. A scar of river cracked across its flats. Beyond the basin, the road folded into canyons of exfoliating red, then unfolded into a salt-white sheet. A scribble of mountains or dark clouds on the horizon, far, far off. We drove as if standing still, the land unchanging.

As B dozed in the back I told Saoirse about Woodby and Dag and having to leave New York.

"It's your brother you wanted to punch," she said.

Who hasn't wanted to punch their brother?

"No, no," I denied. "Woodby deserved it."

"You keep saying that."

"Because it's true."

"It's so obviously your brother."

I asked if she had known about Davis and his opinions.

Yes and no, she said. She had come across the GPS coordinates of the Pigs online and used them to track us. Then one day she saw us coming out of a Kroger's. "The boys were fighting over something," she reminisced. "You were like a little family." From then on, she simply followed the Snowflake and didn't bother looking for information online. She hadn't come across Davis's opinions, whatever they were.

My skin tingled like I'd been dipped in wastewater when I wondered what these opinions could be, and how I'd traveled with the man for an entire summer without hearing them. We'd developed what I'd thought was a mutual reliance, at least around matters of security, and I had trusted him, perhaps with a measure of performance—that is, wanting him to see my trust to show him that I too was okay—and as a result was blind to the reality that he had betrayed us every night. Saoirse asked me what I would have done differently if I had known, and I wasn't sure. It was just freedom I'd been after, from Dag and from what people expected me to be, to believe, to paint. Maybe the voices of the internet were right, and the Pigs were manifestations of ancient hatreds that seethed below the skin of America, waiting to erupt.

I asked Saoirse her opinion of the Pigs. She had first tried to thwart us with her attention-grabbing dollar signs, then helped us paint the most glorious Pig of all.

The light reflecting off the salt flats turned her skin white as paper, and she rubbed at her cheek, her nose, as if cleaning them of invisible marks.

Her feelings were difficult to explain, she said. To her, the Pigs had eventually become symbols of freedom, but their story was complex. At first, she'd seen the Pigs as symbols of Todd's capitalist vendetta, and she troubled them with her dollar signs. Then, as they spread across the land, the Pigs somehow slipped free from ideology. In fact, the Pigs with their question marks painted on the buildings of what she considered the country's father figure—the government—suggested to her a questioning of the traditions that bound them. It was only a choice, after all, and not a law, that women should favor reproduction over ego. When this choice became codified and defended as if it were the land itself, any act that wasn't resistance was an act of compliance and complicity. In this way, she said, each Pig became an act and symbol of freedom.

In the end, though, the Pigs were eaten by Walmart. Any reference suggested by the Pigs now spiraled in upon itself. The Pigs had become no different from a peace sign or a Valentine's heart. Their mystery had been dissolved, their story done.

27

So flat was the land that nothing past the highway could be seen. Signs told of invisible towns. The soil over-exposed, bleached. The air tasted of ash.

Over hours of this placelessness, the scribble on the horizon had swelled to a woolen cloud that cast a muslin light over the flatness. B sniffed at the air, but we all smelled the smoke. As we neared California, where the mountains lay bare and wrinkled as a dead man, we joined a crawling mass of cars on the Interstate, a shock after so long alone in the salt flats.

The fire had closed the Interstate heading west, and Saoirse produced a phone from her bag to find an alternative route using its map app. We turned south and flanked the mountains on a two-lane highway that wandered little from straight. B borrowed Saoirse's phone and tapped away in the back seat. The traffic thinned through a series of interchanges, and the Snowflake hummed along in a line of cars like beads on a string. As we crossed into California, I wanted to whoop or make some small celebration, but before I could, B pointed up into the mountains where orange swallowed the tree line, smeared with black and streaming downwind onto the mountain's shoulders. Red and white lights pulsed in the distance, planes circled overhead. The fire was still in sight when we a crossed another highway headed west, my way to Ming, but it too was closed.

"More trouble," said B.

I nodded, thinking he meant the closed highway, but he pointed to Saoirse's phone and passed it back to her.

"*Arson fire burns mining museum,*" she read.

According to the article, the embers from Saoirse's dollar sign had ignited the wooden shacks we'd passed, and then the surrounding brush, and then two of the black SUVs and the timbers of the museum entrance. No injuries were reported, and there was no mention of the powerbrokers gathered inside. The fire's spread had been stopped before it escaped the canyon. The arsonist was still at large.

"I'm sorry," said Saoirse. She twisted her hands together. "I imagine they're looking for this car."

B sighed and lay back down. I focused on the road, and on how close I must be to Ming, though I still didn't know where she was.

An hour later, we stopped for gas in a frontier town fringed with arid wooden facades. The place Saoirse led us to was off in the dryness. A place where we would be left alone appealed to me, but B kept peering up the street toward the town center as I pumped gas.

"Just as soon bunk here," he said. He started hobbling up the sidewalk with his cane.

I called after him. He tossed back some words I couldn't hear and kept going.

It was dark when we turned onto a cracked asphalt strip, running straight as a ruler for miles before turning to dirt. The headlights' beams swept over the carcasses of cars rotting on the roadside. I parked beside the last skeletal car.

We followed a trail of stones in the faint starlight up to a knob of rock with a wide flat top from which we could see the distant lights of town, the only lights to be seen in the broad dark. Saoirse produced a blanket from her knapsack, and we lay down on it. The Milky Way cast its veil across the sky, torn to the north by the voids of smoke and mountains.

How could I paint such a vision of black on black, sprinkled with star dust? Only the darkest blues, tubes of flat black, purple of an old bruise.

Would I paint us too? A man and woman, prostrate before a dead land, an anti-life, breathing air that ate the bones of cars. Warmth streamed over us, the winds adjusting to night. Was this a vision of freedom, a rock bed in an empty land? Cavemen at least had caves, and fires to keep away the night and marauding beasts.

My brother would lash me. My father would lecture me. My mother would tell me that my only freedom, my only choice was to think or not to think. To choose not to think was to choose death, no choice at all. Was there any freedom from unwanted thoughts? I could never explain to my brother how during that night all I wanted was the peace—the false death—of thoughtlessness. To be freed for a few hours, even a moment, of time clocking overhead. So much had happened, I'd become one thing and then another—objectivist, painter, owner, recluse, chimera, pugilist, vandal, leader of unseen followers, forgiving brother, fugitive—now what, what next?

Dawn might never come. And without dawn, no life choice to be made, no brother or law to run from or to. And no painting—and would this not be hell, to be forever immobile under heaven, unable to hold a brush? My brother rose flesh-and-blood in my mind. I could walk a thousand miles in this desert, and he'd match me step for step, reminding me of my responsibilities and faults. I could never paint the absolute; I could only stab at its outlines.

Overhead the grindstone of stars turned in the shape of a thought.

/ / /

I must have dozed because the next thing I remember was Saoirse sitting up in the silver light, smoothing tangles from her hair. She gave me her cheeky gap-toothed Celtic grin, guileless. We stood and stretched and followed a dirt path to a cluster of boulders that overlooked the dozen scattered trailers and buildings below, some little more than sunken rafters, others with lit windows. A green Subaru had joined the Snowflake.

"That's Pema," said Saoirse. "She'll have coffee."

We descended to a grid of dirt streets blurred by the wind. We passed a narrow building with a grand, wooden façade, hung with a small unlettered marquis. Below the marquis was a hand-painted sign for the U.S. Post Office, but the building was empty.

At the next corner, a lithe woman in a loose ochre dress and matching wide-brimmed woven hat came to the doorway of a shack, its rusted sheet metal door the color of the surrounding dirt. She greeted Saoirse.

"Pema, this is painter," said Saoirse.

Pema took my hand.

"What is this place?" I asked.

"Refuge or exile. Depends on your mood."

"Refuge," I said and smiled weakly at Saoirse.

She smiled ruefully. "Let's go to the circle," she said.

I followed the women past the faded trailers and the husk of a burned-out cabin built into the earth. Up a small rise stood a canopy of brown fabric with a gentle peak. Around its perimeter, a circle of black person-sized stones flashed with crystals, each carved on one side in geometric patterns. From the tops of the stones rose metal posts that supported tubes of rust-patinaed steel that joined at the tent's peak like the spokes of wheel. Over these spokes stretched the fabric roof. Pema poured coffee into the cup-top of a thermos and we passed it around. Small sculptures and found objects—bottle caps, railroad spikes, keys of every shape—decorated the spaces between the rocks, peeked from holes in the stones. In the distance I heard the crackle of a welder.

"Rose is up early," said Saoirse.

As the light slipped down the waxed fabric of the tent it filled the space with an earthen glow. I expected the tent to capture the heat and stultify, but vents along its top sluiced hot air upward, channeling a warm breeze around us.

I asked who had built the tent and carved the stones.

"This was a gift from a son to a father," Pema told me.

"A memorial," said Saoirse.

"I know who you are," said Pema.

"That makes one of us," I replied. The parched air sucked the moisture from my skin. "Why are you here?" I asked.

"Same reason as you, I'd guess."

Arriving in the night with the veil of stars for light, this desert had felt like refuge, but in the brightness and heat, I saw the desolation of the land. This was exile.

We sat among the stones and listened to the flutter of fabric in the wind. I was hungry but it didn't matter. I felt nothing. Maybe it was the empty landscape I felt, devoid of colors beyond brown, or plants beyond yucca, or animals of any kind. A few oxidized buildings and trailers.

"What's here?" I asked.

The Shoshone had lived there, she told me; their stone carvings could still be found among the canyons and boulders. Then, a century ago, miners had come for veins of silver and lead. The miners killed the Shoshone or drove them off, and after they pulled all the minerals from the earth, killed each other or left. All that remained was this history of prodigious lawlessness, a graveyard, and a few artists and outcasts.

When she asked what had brought me there, I had trouble explaining how I'd ended up on the edge of nothing. My brother, Woodby, the boys and the Pigs. A stream of words flowed out. How might my life have been different if I'd not hit Woodby, if I'd just walked away?

"You should have hit your brother," said Pema.

Saoirse grinned, satisfied.

"Like punching a steel girder," I replied. And he wouldn't have fallen as Woodby had.

When Pema asked about the Pigs, I tried to explain how government was the sea and the Pigs a kind of freedom, but in my fatigue I stumbled over the words. Instead I told her a simpler truth, that something about seeing them in the world had pleased me.

"The now is about visibility," I concluded, repeating Ming's words. They felt hollow on my tongue.

"People confuse being seen with being in the world," said Pema.

When I asked what she meant, she took a deep breath. "Would you mind a story?" she asked. "Nothing else will capture it."

I leaned against one of the carved stones to listen.

Long ago, she had lived in a city, she began, amid the thousands of others, who were always everywhere, as in any city. It was a city well suited to walking, and she walked wherever she could, including her doctor's office, which was housed in a cast-concrete commercial development at the top of a long, gentle hill that steepened near its summit. Down this hill, late at night, teenage boys would slalom on skateboards, their boards' trucks complaining shriek-like as they absorbed the rider's momentum in wide, hard turns, giving them (the riders) at least the illusion of control as they shot-gunned through the dark four-way stops to the hill's bottom. Up this hill she climbed on her way to a follow-up appointment. Steam rose from the sidewalks and pavements as the sun returned after a brief rain. She weaved around the people coming down, headed to work or breakfast or shopping or exercise. They were like traffic cones, she thought, a sort of game to distract her from the mild worry she always felt on going to the doctor. The doctor she knew to have a rushed, friendly, business-like manner, and it was in this no-nonsense voice that she (the doctor) told her without any change in intonation that imaging had revealed a deep flaw in Pema's body. The doctor called it an incidental finding, but to Pema it felt intimate and pointed. It wasn't a cancer, or some grave organ dysfunction that would sallow her skin, but a malformation in her body's circulatory system. It was like a crack in a foundation that might remain unchanged and without consequence, or, if the right conditions conspired, collapse her life to rubble. The doctor reassured her while encouraging caution, but she could see in the doctor's face a knife's edge of uncertainty.

This new fact of her mortality was no different, Pema told herself, as she pushed open the building's heavy out-swing door into the moist summer air, from any other day of her life. Still, the granite curbstone step dividing the building's entrance from the sidewalk might as well have been a cliff for the way her bowels floated up within her. She reminded herself as she reached down to the sidewalk with one foot into the dapples of light that evaded the sidewalk's trees, blinding her momentarily when the breeze fluttered through the canopy, this is life. She sucked in the humid air with its odors of diesel and ground coffee, burnt-grease from a taqueria, the shit and piss from the corner where tough-looking shrubs hid their own secrets. She inhaled so fully that no death could interrupt—how could it? This was life, so long as this breath lasted, and the next.

Breath by breath, then, each possibly her last but not, not yet, she fell footfall by footfall down the hill's grade. She stopped at each intersection, panting like she'd been running uphill. She breathed so obsessively, so mindfully, and without pause between breaths, that her vision thinned and she became lightheaded. And so she breathed to the count of her leg's rotations—lift, extend, drop, step—counting one, two, three, four on inhale and exhale, with four counts between each breath, sixteen beats per cycle. She felt for her inner flaw, a twisted and threatening knot of black she'd seen on her doctor's computer's screen, but could feel only her machine-like heart pumping. This was life. By then the pavements had dried of the morning's rain. In the sun, she began to sweat as if an inner dam had released its water in telltale dark stains on the tank-top below her breasts and, she imagined, the shirt's back, where it clung to the muscles along her spine. She wiped surreptitiously at her forehead, her upper lip, acutely self-conscious that the others on the sidewalk (a new mother with a baby carriage, a blue-shirted delivery man hauling a loaded pallet jack from the curb) were staring and wondering, judgingly, about her uncontrolled sweating, and what must be wrong in her life to lead her to such a public spectacle. When she mounted the courage to glance up from her shoes, she found no one looking at her. She was relieved, then disappointed. She had reached the hill's bottom, where stores lined the sidewalks and people strutted, rolled, shuffled, limped, staggered, jogged, pulled dogs on short leashes and otherwise enacted their day's plans, none of them aware of her distress at the flaw that she felt must gape like a shotgun wound from her chest. This was life, she told herself, and every person she saw hid their own suffering, their own certain death. What weakens your heart? she asked a tall heavy man with gray stubbled cheeks and a carbuncular drinker's nose, who glanced sidelong at the women and children standing in line at a froyo store. What torments do you suffer? she asked a flaxen-haired woman who tugged subtly at her salmon pants' waist button as it strained against the flesh beneath. She asked each person she saw, the scores out on that once cool-and-damp and now sultry late morning, each of them stone-faced and penetrable, for though not one person returned her look or answered her silent question, she knew that they too suffered like her and would die. She wanted to touch, to heal them; there was freedom in this desire, a freedom from her own suffering. With a great beating, her heart floated out from her chest and sparkled with blood. This was life, this was love.

In time, of course, the rawness of her sudden kinship with death scabbed over, and the immediacy of her silent connections with strangers waned, leaving only the feeling's residue and her memory of its radicality. She became both anxious and numb, something she hadn't realized she'd felt before the doctor's visit. She felt responsible for everything and in control of nothing.

To keep the awareness of suffering and death alive, as it were, she began in her spare time before work and on Sundays to craft small creatures from wire coat hangers and objects she found on her walks through the city: bottle caps crushed in half, the waffly paper sleeves for coffee cups, broken plastic straps from a child's toy watch, a lanyard with nothing clipped to it, empty soup cans, advertising circulars, random shards of black plastic, corroded nails, a balloon's ribbon with only the rubbery umbilicus of balloon still tied to it. The creatures were small enough to fit in a shopping bag and large enough to guard the tilt-lid of a mailbox. Inside each, she secured with a fine wire a bundle of found objects, which became each creature's wounded heart. Into a raccoon she planted a broken luggage lock, an eggshell, and three torn-off can pull-tabs. A monkey hid in its chest a discarded syringe, the needle snipped carefully into the trash. A crow, two black plastic zip ties wrapped in an Easter basket's lurid green grass. The creatures multiplied into dozens. They perched on her dresser and nosed from beneath the bed. Eventually she brought her newest creations, for which no space remained in her tiny bedroom and shared bath, out into the city, where they might remind others of the language of suffering that all creatures know. She left a kitten on a street tree's lowest limb, a frog peeking from a storm drain, a squirrel behind a succulent in a neighbor's garden. In the days that followed, she counted the missing and damaged—all of them. The frog was in the sewer, the kitten rescued or captured from its tree, the squirrel flattened by a heavy vehicle and left decomposing in the street.

At this time, she was caught in a wave of layoffs and found herself unemployed. Rather than find a new job, she decided to leave the city. She drove for days, camping as she went, until she wove her way to the coast, where bluffs crumbled into the ocean, and in that confluence of sea and mountains, felt at home for the first time. She hugged the coast, staying in trailers, a shed, then finally, a small cabin that became her home. She waited tables for money.

She breathed air scented with sage and juniper and wild grasses. When she made new animals, their hearts filled with objects of nature: feathers, dried rattlesnake rattles, shed fur and skins, owl pellets, rodents' bones, dried grasses. Into each she placed a chip of jade she gathered from the beaches.

Her creatures' little faces greeted her as she fussed about her kitchen and tiny garden. She found joy in their wiry courage, but she worried about them. The animals' parts had come from the world, but so long as she kept them around her cabin, they were no longer in-the-world.

The newest animals watched with eyes of shale as she gathered them into her Subaru and drove them down the ridge, trailing clouds of yellow dust. Along the highway, atop the ridge roads, in secret gardens, she hid them, often in pairs or small families so they would not be alone in the world.

Soon all down the coast one might glimpse a wire boar poking its face from the ivy, or a fox from the reeds, or a piglet from the wild mustard, the yellow spring bloom dusting its face. The animals-in-the-world delighted her. Some disappeared from their hiding spots, reappearing by a driveway or a front door. A few wandered off, not to be seen by her again. Every week, she released more, always with the same mix of joy and anxiety, loss and wonder at the world's capacity for beauty.

One day, as she hid an opossum of soda cans with a heart of turkey feather, rattlesnake rattle, and jade, she spied a man further south along the bluff, rummaging amid the brush. As she watched, he snared a family of wire javelina and dropped them one by one into a cardboard box, which he pushed along the ground before him as he moved further down the roadside.

It upset her, as one might imagine, that this man was harvesting what she had sown—but then, as she reminded herself every time she drove down the ridge, the animals were in-the-world now, with their own meanings to fulfill. Still, their independent lives were her great curiosity, and so she followed the man, keeping her distance and hiding behind brush as he filled his box and shambled to a wide flat rock that protruded from the bluff. There he sat and took the animals one by one from the box and opened their caged chests and pulled out their hearts. The carcasses he tossed off the cliff into the void.

She gasped. In her mind, two hearts held no more magic than one; the hearts were symbols, and once they had summoned the symbolized, had no further power. More charms did not make for greater magic.

She stomped after him. When he saw her red-faced and high-stepping it through the tall grass, her skirt in her fists, he scurried to the highway, threw his box into a white sedan, and tore off south. She determined on the spot to keep her animals safe, by her home.

Weeks later, in town for flour and eggs, she noticed one of her heart-charms threaded onto a hemp cord around the neck of the grocery store cashier. She had to admit that it was attractive, and despite her resentment, complimented the cashier's taste. The cashier blushed with pride. She'd bought it at the jewelry store by the pier, she told Pema, the narrow one with the long glass counter.

The store was easy to find, and there on the counter was one of those small metal displays like little trees that spun on its base to display all its wares equally, this one heavy with her animals' hearts. The buyer said that a man he didn't know had brought a box full of them, made into necklaces, brooches, bracelets, hatbands, and bolo ties. He frowned sadly at her.

When she got home that evening, she piled all the animals she had sequestered in her cabin into her Subaru and drove into the hills, where she released them along the roadside. Then she turned around and left the coast for good.

28

Her story confused me, not least for its implied dismissal of selling art, which seemed like a potentially happy solution to the problems of overcrowding of creatures and the men who took what was free, rather than priced. When I asked her what was wrong with selling art, she replied, "Nothing," and suggested that a wise artist in that world should do her best to sell as much art to as many people as she could. The animals, however, hadn't been made to be sold.

I asked her if she really had left her place of bliss just because some man repurposed her art.

Pema shrugged her narrow shoulders. She'd had a disastrous relationship, she conceded, that ended with her own heart torn out. And soon after that, a new neighbor had moved to the ridge, one of the monstrously wealthy who had discovered the coast, and this neighbor arrived daily in a deafening helicopter. She and the others on the ridge complained until the person bought a somewhat quieter helicopter, which exchanged a high whining sound for the bass thumps of the previous craft, but was still too loud to allow for sleep, or thought, or conversation.

"It was just time to go," she said.

///

As she led us back to her shack, where she offered us scones and butter and water bitter with minerals, I recalled Ming's story of having to buy a quieter helicopter to appease the neighbors at her coastal retreat. My mouth went dry and I had to finish my glass of water before

I could ask her where Pema had seen it.

She pursed her lips.

"They'll be looking for that car," warned Saoirse.

We all knew I would leave as soon as Pema told me.

///

I found B curled on a bench in front of a bustling café. His cast was gone, and he wore a new pair of flip flops. He crawled into the passenger seat, dragging his cane.

"That's one whole lotta woman," he groaned.

I didn't know what new woman he'd found and didn't care. I told him we were going to the coast, posthaste.

B grunted. He had a waxy pink smear on one cheek and had lost his sunglasses. He pointed north with the cane. "They opened the pass," he said.

I steered the Snowflake north, scanning for police cars.

We turned west onto a two-lane highway that traversed the brown plain into the mountains. Ash dusted the trees and eddied on the roadside. After a steep section, the road plateaued by a river that looped through a valley of tall heavy pines, where a pack station stood empty, closed for the season or because of the fire. Just past the station's small corral, and stretching for miles up and along the ridge, the forest turned to cinder, a cracked charcoal of limbless trees.

I parked by a riverbed to let the Snowflake cool. B got out and loosed a luminous arc of urine into the dust. To the north, a dirty cloud, bulbous as a thunderhead, streamed as far as I could see to the east. The air smelled like an ashtray. All sounds of the forest were silent.

Head west, Pema had told me, *over the mountains. Then southwest through the valley, then west again. More mountains, salt on the air.*

Past the wide hazy valley lined with fields and prowled by colossal machinery, we climbed through hills round as a baby's bottom to another pass, below which a wide basin stretched, another empty reservoir, a residue of water evaporating from its floor. I feared for the Snowflake's health as its motor whined higher and higher, a tight emphysemic wheeze. As we neared the pass, wind ripped over us, shuddering the car. Towering eucalyptus bent and rattled. Then fields on either side, rolling in ordered lines over shallow hills, artichokes, broccoli, cabbage, vanishing into a mist that glistened in the autumn light.

A line of blue, miraculous, under a wall of clouds hugging the ocean. Salt on the air, but also smoke. It seemed impossible, so much moisture, after weeks in the parched interior.

We stopped for gas amid towering dunes and bought bags of chips, two hats, and two sweatshirts branded with the town's name. I left half my remaining cash, keeping the hat low on my forehead and my face down so as not to be seen.

The road contorted to the coastline, rising and falling between dark waters and fog. A mobile road sign flashed: WILFIRE AHEAD. Fog gave way to night.

Pema had described a post office and deli, a series of turns and pullouts, a mile marker, none of which we'd seen. Our headlights showed fog like a wall before us, ever receding. After an hour B needed to piss again, so I stopped in a long pullout lined with boulders.

The Snowflake hissed as it idled, a new sound. I turned off the engine and lights. When B opened his door, the sonorous wash of waves rolled from the darkness. The fog hovered over us. B startled when a sea lion's bark reached up from below. He swore under his breath and rearranged his shorts, then peered over the cliff's edge, as if to find a way down. He limped back along the line of boulders toward the road.

I wondered what I would say to Ming. Would we kiss in her capsule to the moon?

Deep in thought I'd lost sight of B and panicked that he'd gone over the edge. I got out and peeked down a slope too steep to climb. I followed the boulders back toward the road the way B had gone, peering over, seeing nothing. I called out, but my words died in the fog. When I reached the road, nearing full panic, I noticed a thin trail that fell aside the concrete abutment where the pullout met the highway. Swallowing my fear I eased myself down the trail in a crouch, one hand on the smooth concrete abutment, the other on the rocky soil. The sudden crack of waves below revealed a sheer drop to my left. A ghostly white slab appeared before me like the seal of a tomb—a ledge formed by the abutment's concrete footing, B sitting Buddha-like in its middle.

"Let's get back in the car," I said.

B shook his head.

"Being up there doesn't feel right," he said.

"It's freezing here," I complained.

A spectral light appeared on the hillside to our right, sweeping above us. Moments later, a car rumbled overhead and disappeared around the next turn. The concrete was cold, and I sat on my hands and pressed myself against the wall to still my vertigo.

More headlights poked toy-like in the mist, and a vehicle slowed above us and ground into the pullout. The fog alit with a fire of swirling red and blue. A radio crackled. A searchlight swept the pullout like the beam of a lighthouse, making a wall of the fog. We had committed so many offenses I had no idea which they would arrest us for. B pulled my arm and we slid further down the footing, up against the narrow gully's far wall. A flashlight swept along the bluff above, moving closer. It flashed down at us, meeting the fog. A moment later the light went out, and the car pulled away.

"We should go," I said.

"We should stay," said B. "He's not going to forget that car."

I was horrified when B stretched out on the ledge, wedged against the concrete wall. He meant to stay there, exposed, for the night. We wore the sweatshirts and caps we'd bought, but B had only shorts and flip-flops; I at least had on slacks and tennis shoes and socks. When I lay down on the footing, the stone sucked away my heat.

The dark became a bottomless well. I shivered and stewed in anxious wonderment at how far I'd come. Having not slept well for days, I managed a few unconscious minutes, awaking each time with a start, terrified that I was rolling off the ledge. I curled my legs up under my sweatshirt like a teenage girl and pulled the hood so tight only my mouth and nose stuck out and still I shivered. B made no sound. Convinced at one point late in the edgeless black that he had rolled off or walked away, I leaned over and jabbed him with a finger. I envied his gift for sleep. As I cleaved to the concrete, I heard voices in the dark, not just the barks of the sea lions but faint quavers and murmurations. The air itself lived there, how terrifying.

At last the world took shape around us. In the morning light, I could see the gully's walls were near cliffs, falling two hundred feet or more to a dark crescent of beach, pebbled with sea lions, where the swell seethed against massive rocks.

B rose slowly, blinking and rubbing his face, as he always did in the mornings. The Snowflake was where we'd left it, a sheen of dew covering its skin. A sodden ticket stuck to the windshield tore in half when I lifted it away. B watched as I tried to start the engine, but it just clicked and clicked until that too stopped. We sat on a boulder and shared our last bottle of water. Overhead the fog receded, revealing a paper-white sky fringed with blue.

"We shouldn't take that car anyways," he said.

We argued over which way to walk, north or south, in the end flipping a coin. We headed north, the way we'd come, and clung to the guardrail when we heard a car approaching. B switched his cane from left to right and back and labored up the steep outside turns that availed a vast blue-water view, the fog a line on the horizon. The inside turns were worse, as the increasing flow of cars, mostly rented sedans with occasional luxury EVs and ancient gas roadsters, cheated into the skinny breakdown lane, which was only a few feet at widest.

It was terribly public walking on the narrow highway. Out of anxiety I found myself examining each driver heading south toward us, assessing their potential for manslaughter or, conversely, if they were a law enforcement officer of some stripe. When we heard the fading whine of a down-shifted engine, we glanced around for a place to hide, but there was none. A purple pickup ground to a stop in a pullout ahead of us. The truck was dusty and old, a breed of Toyota so slight it hardly seemed to exist. A Hispanic man's weathered face peaked out the driver's window, wise as dried fruit. He asked if we needed a ride.

B without hesitation swung himself up to the passenger's door and hauled himself in. He shook the man's hand as I climbed in beside him. We had to hunch our shoulders to fit on the narrow bench.

"You go to town?" the man asked.

"We got car trouble," said B.

The man nodded and put the truck in gear and coaxed it north onto the highway.

"No phones," he said and shook his head.

"No phones," I agreed, then realized he'd probably meant that cell phones didn't work here, and so I added a smile and nodded encouragingly.

"I take you to a phone," he said. He waved as if that settled the matter.

I asked him if he'd seen a helicopter and he nodded. "Always heli-copter," he said. He made a helicopter of his hand and moved it from the southwest. "Always come like this, low. So loud. They come over the ocean."

After reigning the truck through a series of tight swoops over bridges like scimitars, he downshifted into a parking lot aside a weath-ered plank building that might once have been a barn.

"They call for you," he said.

Instinctively, I surveyed the property for police cars and places to hide. A half-dozen cars filled narrow spaces along the building, none of them law enforcement. A few cabins trailed away from the former barn into a canyon, like chicks following a hen. Water tinkled in an unseen creek. The hillsides rose sharply behind the plank buildings, trapping them against the highway, then folded into the narrow can-yon. Towering, thick-trunked redwoods, unmistakable even to me, cast the canyon into cool shadow. Above the cabins, manicured gardens of flowering shrubs and bushes hung down the slopes.

As the man had predicted, the pulse of helicopter blades approached from the south, the helicopter itself hidden behind a protrusion of hillside that pushed the highway into a tight curve.

The man called out the window as he pulled away, "Very good breakfast." He pointed to the barnlike building and gave us the thumbs up.

We sat at a wooden counter and watched servers spin through the kitchen door with trays of plates on their shoulders. B engaged in a semaphore of smiles with the tiny young woman who poured our coffee and water. A waitress with page-boy hair brought us plates laden with country bread, eggs, home fries.

A man with pitted, sunburned cheeks sat next to me, a local I guessed from the way he chatted with the staff as they came and went.

"I've been hearing a helicopter," I said to him.

He turned incoherent eyes with lowered lids that might never have risen all the way up.

"It's the fire," he said in a voice like water over sand. "They scoop water from the cattle ponds."

"Any other helicopters?" I asked.

A shade passed over his features. He shook his head and turned back to his coffee.

I excused myself to use the bathroom, and when I returned, having only washed my face and put my fingers through my hair, B and the waitress had their elbows on the bar and their faces close. Rather than interrupt B's game, I examined a display of postcards, then went outside and sat on the flagstone steps. The wind had shifted and smelled of campfire. B came out and pointed north.

"She says there's a blue helicopter lands over the next ridge from time to time. Said to take a dirt road a half mile north up the highway."

30

We had crossed the narrow parking lot to the edge of the highway when a pair of black SUVs rolled by, heading south. We were hidden from them by a protrusion of hillside that sloped steeply to the road beside us, and I watched the square-jawed drivers from a few feet away as they passed unaware. A State Police cruiser followed close behind.

We pressed against the hillside. The SUVs and cruiser glided across a short bridge and through the S-turn of the highway and disappeared around a bend. I held my breath as we waited. A few civilian vehicles passed—an old minivan, a green pickup with a surfboard on its lumber rack. We looked questioningly at each other, but neither of us moved. After a long minute, another cruiser passed, heading south. This one pulled off the road and parked by the bridge. Its lights swirled, washing the trees in red and blue. Before we could react, several more vehicles—two large white pickups, an older SUV, a jeep streaked with mud—stopped behind the cruiser. Men in jeans and black T-shirts got out of the vehicles and called to each other. A second SUV pulled over in front of us, just a few yards from where we were hiding. The driver climbed down and joined the other men on the highway. We retreated behind a boulder that stuck out from the hillside. A third police car rolled slowly south, lights flashing. It passed through the S-turn and out of sight.

We were now hidden by the boulder and the SUV that had stopped in front of us, but would be discovered as soon as the men decided to search the area. B was looking back toward the restaurant, planning our move. The nearby SUV was a two-tone Lincoln Navigator, its red and brown so faded and sheen-less that they appeared like dried blood.

On its back was a black whip antenna on which hung two flags: a coiled rattlesnake on one, my Pig on the other.

The men wandered around the highway, lifting their phones to the sky, looking for signal. Finding none, the driver of the Navigator opened the car's door and leaned in, his jeans riding up over heavy boots. I heard the static of a radio.

"We need to go," B whispered.

He suggested we walk casually, one by one, back along the hillside to the bathroom, which was located down a short path behind the restaurant and away from the men. We would have to cross through the kitchen, he figured, to reach the far side of the building, where the men could only see us if they peered carefully through the shrubs that divided the property from the road.

I was only half-listening. I wanted my Pig flag.

B tapped my shoulder, telling me to go. I slipped from behind the boulder, but instead of walking casually left toward the bathroom, I crept to the Navigator's rear. B hissed at me. The driver had climbed into the car and now leaned over the radio to handle its controls, and from this position, couldn't see the rearview or sideview mirrors, or me as I approached. The antenna was long and attached to the left side of the tailgate, and I had to reach up and bend it toward me to access the flags. When I grabbed the antenna, my body must have acted to boost the signal, because the voice on the radio blared. Through the rear windows I saw the man sit up in surprise.

"We found the car," I heard him say. A word that might have been "copy" crackled back to him. "If they went inland, we expect the fire to drive them down to the highway when the wind shifts." More static, a long question with attached information that I couldn't discern.

B hissed again, this time from my side, where down on one knee he held up his pocketknife. I took the knife and cut the tough cord holding the flags to the antenna and let the antenna straighten before letting go, at which the signal must have faded again, because the man groaned and leaned over to adjust the device.

B was already behind the restaurant when I turned to follow him. I fought the urge to look back as I feigned a calm stroll along the hillside.

Two small men in kitchen aprons stopped working when we opened the door and indicated with hand gestures that we'd like to walk through to the opposite side. They nodded confusedly and whispered to each other in Spanish, but no one stopped us. I dropped my last five-dollar bill on the prep counter as I passed through. The only cash remaining from my stash from the safe was a twenty I'd kept for emergencies in the coin pocket of my trousers. It had been there for months. All the rest had gone for Pigs. I stuffed the two flags in my back pocket.

B hobbled across the inn's courtyard. I followed him past the reception office and the cabins and up a dirt road that switch-backed between redwoods into the canyon. The static of radios faded, and the pulsing lights lost their gleam though the foliage and distance.

Since we couldn't use the highway without being seen, we would have to traverse the hills and canyons to reach the road to Ming's. A bird could cross the distance in a few minutes, but for us the thick understory looked impenetrable, and the hillsides we would have to climb were steep and covered in loose rocks and soil. I would have thought it impossible, except that no other route occurred to us, and so it became the only possibility.

We passed shacks in the woods, a gathering of yurts, older pickups tucked into the road's edge. The dirt road ended at a foot trail, which we followed as it snaked along the canyon where it steepened and narrowed. Water clattered and burped among the rocks. On steeper parts, where the trail turned up the canyon wall to skirt a waterfall or a raft of fallen logs, B had to scramble up on his side, pushing with his good foot and his cane, then totter down the other side like a jalopy with weak brakes. When the trail leveled out, B leaned over his cane and breathed hard. He pointed to the creek bed where two large black plastic pots had wedged themselves under boulders. Water splashed around them.

"Saw two more below," he said.

He squinted up the canyon, but it was all sky, the trail just a hint among ferns and grasses. We clung to these plants, holding the stems low near the ground, then using the clump as a foothold to push our-selves up. It would get easier, I thought, as we neared the top, but the top eluded us, and we twisted upward through the loose dirt like snakes, pulling on the grasses, resting on the rare tree root exposed from the eroding dirt. B climbed using his one good foot and his cane as a sort of pickaxe, with his other hand clutching at vegetation. His feet were black and scraped and bleeding. At last we came to a twin-trunked oak that made a flat spot of dirt between its roots where we lay down. I fell asleep.

B sat propped against the trunk when I awoke. He advised me not to look down.

"There's a clearing up there I think," he said.

He showed me a piece of plastic tubing he'd picked up. It was from a garden, he thought, like the plastic tubs we'd seen.

"Must have got loose during a storm or something," he said. "There are certain people we don't want to surprise."

"You're worried about a gardener?" I asked.

"Depends what they're growing," he replied. "Like flowers, for example, the kind you smoke. Could be worth an awful lot."

"Isn't it legal here?" I asked.

"Doesn't mean *they're* legal. And even if they are, we sure ain't."

I couldn't see any reasonable option but to continue up the canyon wall to the clearing and then cross it as respectfully as we could on our way to wherever Ming's helicopter landed. B expressed his displeasure with me and the situations I got us into with a resigned, *Fuck you.* We resumed our halting ascent until the slope flattened and the canopy thinned. B grabbed my arm before I plunged through a thicket of tall shrubs.

"Poison something-or-other," he said, pointing to a vine with shiny oakish leaves.

We slipped around the thicket and into the clearing, where behind a tall wire fence, large black tubs formed a grid across the dirt and weeds, irrigation tubing strung between them. I saw tomatoes and cucumbers and squash, and beyond them, a jungly dense foliage. My feet crunched over something plastic pressed partway into the dirt—spent shotgun shells. I turned to point these out to B, but he lagged behind, peering through the fence.

"For shooting at ground squirrels or some varmint," he said when I mentioned the spent shells. "You can see the holes in there."

I peeked toward the fence but crept on. Shotguns didn't know one varmint from another.

"You got any money?" asked B.

I had only the twenty I'd kept in the change pocket for emergencies. I asked what he wanted it for, but he just held his hand out and didn't respond. I pulled out the bill, and we looked at it, limp and gray between its sharp folds. B took it and yanked open a wobbly door in the fence, while I continued through the clearing toward an embankment that blocked the view north. B limped to join me with his cane under one arm. I half expected gunfire but heard only the wind and the screech of a distant hawk. At the top of the embankment was a dense copse of small oaks and bramble, and between the trunks I spied a grassy hillside, and beyond that, a dirt road. B grunted up behind me. His pockets bulged and he smelled like a lawnmower that hit a skunk.

"Probably more than twenty bucks' worth, but I saved them trimming time," he said.

We scanned the hillside.

"Too easy?" I asked, half joking.

B watched the grasses flatten in the wind.

"No cover."

"Maybe don't steal like Peter Rabbit."

"I paid," he said, indignant. "Anyways, I'm not worried about them."

The grass shushed against our knees as we started across the hillside. Beneath the grasses, the ground was rutted with gopher holes and mounds and required attention to keep from twisting an ankle. B swore as he hobbled behind me. He thrust his cane down, looking for solid earth.

We picked our way over a split-rail fence that had been stiffened with barbed wire and slid down the berm beyond onto a driveway or fire road. The road widened as it sloped downhill, and we followed it until it intersected a wider road of packed gravel that curved up into the hills.

After a half mile on the gravel road, we reached a stand of oaks and sat in their shade and scanned the ocean. So vast it seemed, as it jutted away from the rutted earth. A light breeze dried our clothes. I stretched out, my muscles sore. For several moments, lulled by the faint heartbeat of distant waves, I couldn't tell reality from dream. I sat up and blinked in the brightness.

Far below, a short length of highway was visible between the rounded hillsides, and as I watched, a pod of black vehicles passed like a line of motorized ants. Last in line was a police car. A hawk turned circles below us. Another line of cars passed, this one a menagerie of pickups and SUVs and sedans with flags stuck to their antennae and signs taped to the windows. Only one sign was large enough to see, a golden dollar sign.

We shuffled along the dirt road, kicking up dust, and paused in the shade of the occasional trees that spotted the hillside. When we crested the ridge, a black shroud bloomed over the mountains, streaming northeast, orange flickering where it met the ground.

B whistled.

With the wind pushing hard at our backs, we hadn't smelled or seen the smoke of the fire that engulfed ridges to the horizon. Two aircraft flitted along the fire's edges like finches, leaving pink clouds behind that settled through the wind to paint the trees' limbs. We watched for a long while, sitting above the road.

The sudden grinding of tires on gravel brought us both to our feet. Two black SUVs hurtled over the crest of the road and skidded to a halt. Men in black tactical gear leapt out and approached us as if cornering bears.

"You're trespassing on private land," one of them said.

"We didn't know," I replied, but they hadn't come to turn us away.

The men secured our hands behind our backs with zip ties and bundled us into one of the vehicles. B gave me a flat *now-what* kind of look.

The road headed inland, then turned south around a steep ravine, which based on how far we'd driven, must have been the top of the canyon B and I had spent the morning crawling up, placing us somewhere high above the restaurant where we'd had breakfast. We passed through a park-like forest of evenly spaced trees, not the oaks we'd seen but some type of idealized evergreen with trunks black as coal. Past the trees, the ocean comprised the entire earth, so wide was the view. Another gate, more hillside falling to the water. A planar castle of iron beams and glass burst from the earth, a cobalt helicopter resting on a pad below. Ming.

31

The men in black vests pulled us into an elevator.

"I need my cane to get around," said B.

The men said nothing.

"Got a smoke?" he asked.

When the elevator door opened, a man in a black polo took our photos with a blinding flash. He watched his phone as he stood there, waiting, then nodded, at which the men behind us cut the zip ties and handed B his cane and walked away.

The black polo led us to a suite of rooms overlooking the knobby cliff and locked us inside. Modern-style furniture filled the space. B stretched out on an angular couch with his arms behind his head.

"This typical of how she treats you?" he asked.

An hour passed, then another. Even the billion-dollar view became a prison. B opened every door and drawer in the suite, revealing a bedroom and en suite bath, a full bar, a galley kitchen without food. He emerged from the bathroom in a terrycloth robe and hotel slippers.

"You take me to the nicest places," he said. He sipped bourbon from a rocks glass half-filled with ice cubes.

Just as I was dozing off on a divan below the windows, a woman in a lavender tunic opened the door and beckoned to us. We followed her through cool hallways and up a set of stairs that ended at a hangar-sized space, the exterior wall all glass.

Ming floated lotus-like over a wicker platform set with pillows, the cliffs and ocean arrayed behind her.

"Your brother is here," she said.

I looked around, expecting Dag's contemptuous smirk; he'd won again. Instead I saw the top of his head on a large video screen, one of several mounted to the wall behind me. He was standing on the road with his hands by his chest, as if giving a speech.

"He has brought quite an assemblage," Ming said.

On the other screens I saw the tops of black SUVs, a desert-painted Humvee, the motley trucks and cars with the signs in the windows that we'd seen from the ridge road. Around the parked cars people sat in lawn chairs, lifting plastic cups to their lips.

"This is the breakdown of their mode," she said. "And yours, if you choose to stay."

Unsure how to respond, I watched the monitors. My brother talked and gestured with a closed hand, as if tapping an invisible drum. A policeman leaned against a nearby cruiser with his thumbs in his belt.

"Your building has been seized," she said.

I couldn't turn away from the screens.

"We understand you are a fugitive."

"What is all this?" I asked.

"The only true freedom in this mode is through power," she replied. "And power curves to the infinite." She touched her ear and a section of window swiveled open, admitting the scent of sage and pops of gunfire. "These people understand simple power, but not the infinite."

"You not worried about the forest fire?" asked B. He put his half-empty rocks glass on a shelf and sat in a wide plush chair.

When she said nothing, I repeated his question.

"Not a variable at this time," she replied.

She touched her ear and one of the screens showed the forest fire's plume, boiling in the wind. I heard a loud crack like fireworks and watched on another screen as puffs of smoke rose from the pavement, a man in pink shorts and topsiders dancing around, holding an assault weapon aloft in one hand.

"And we have the helicopter," she said.

The helicopter we'd taken from Manhattan to the feast of the landed gentry might have fit six or eight passengers, and we'd seen at least a dozen polo shirts since arriving, never mind the men in tactical gear.

"The compound is firesafe," she said, as if reading my thoughts. "And the trees," she added, and touched her ear again.

A moment later a door opened, and two purple polos carried between them a large plastic pot with a sapling in it.

"Hey, it's the party dudes!" said B.

He pointed to a screen showing a fleet of boats as motley as the highway caravan, laboring south over the swell. Pudgy men in Hawaiian shirts waved from the rails. On the lead boat, a man in a blue suit stepped out onto the deck—Woodby. A flag fluttered on the stern, my Pig.

"These are smart trees," said Ming, extending a hand to stroke the sapling's needles. "More precisely, Tree Emulation Devices, or TEDs."

Her face softened into the incandescence that had so enraptured me in my studio. I wanted to kiss her again.

"Like Earth trees they absorb carbon and release oxygen and water vapor. Unlike Earth trees they do not burn. When they sense fire they spray moisture in a fine mist. You see, it is not so hard to improve on nature."

An explosion echoed up the canyon. On the screens, people crouched and scattered. Many produced weapons and pointed them in every direction, then stood and lifted the guns over their heads. The spectators in the lawn chairs raised their plastic cups in salute. From one of the boats, a canon's muzzle flashed, followed by a puff of smoke and another echoing boom. The assemblage clapped and cheered.

"We are safely surrounded by a forest of TEDs," said Ming.

The polos hauled the TED away. Music lilted in through the window.

"Margaritaville," said B, nodding in time.

"Ming," I pleaded, "I want a future—all that down there . . ."

A helicopter rattled over the ridge and onto the screens. It lowered a large bucket into a roadside pond. More cracks resonated, then a fusillade. Smoke drifted from the guns of the flotilla. The crowd on the highway pumped bullets into the water bucket as it lifted from the pond, water streaming from scores of holes as the helicopter turned inland. The crowd exchanged high fives.

A voice boomed over a megaphone, causing the revelers to assume defensive postures behind car doors and trees.

"There's nothing for me down there," I said.

"You demonstrated your abilities with the Pigs," she replied. "This was a fine test of the utility of your skills."

"A test?" I asked.

"Remember, we have the island. We will be as free there as it is possible to be on this planet. And we have the rocket. The moon awaits."

A woman entered bearing a silver tray with a glass of blue liquid and a ceramic bowl on it and offered them to B. He balanced the bowl on his thigh and ate popcorn and sniffed at the blue liquid.

"We will be the most alive of all," said Ming.

B chuckled. "I do believe they mean to fight."

"We all go, including B?" I asked, but she was whispering commands.

B looked up as I said his name.

"Per noctum ad astra," she replied.

"I don't understand."

Gun shots erupted as the helicopter returned for more water. Muzzle flashes flickered on the screens until the water bucket crashed to the pavement, and the citizen soldiers had to jog away to avoid the torrent cascading down the roadway. Outside, Ming's helicopter buzzed to life.

B rubbed his temples and sniffed at the glass he'd been given.

"What was in that drink?" I asked Ming.

"Mostly water. Please use the restroom before we go."

"That's a quick shitty hangover," B said and lay down on the floor.

Ming floated from her wicker platform.

Two polos strained to pull B to his feet. He grabbed his cane and the half-filled rocks glass of bourbon from the counter as they shouldered him out.

I followed Ming down a flight of stairs, out through a steel door, then down an embankment toward the helicopter, which sat on a clearing fifty yards away. The wind had shifted and stank of burning plastic. Above, on the gravel drive, a dozen polos carried padded shields before them as they advanced slowly on B, who cinched his bathrobe tight and shook a fist, his cane pinned between elbow and chest, the rocks glass in his other hand. A single polo approached him, head down and hands raised in submission. From a safe distance he said something to B, who listened with his fist on his hip, the cane jutting at a jaunty angle, before limping away. The man jogged after him and handed him a plastic water bottle, which B hoisted over the phalanx of polos in a gorgeous spiral that exploded on the windshield of an SUV. The SUV retreated further down the driveway.

I yelled to B to come with us, but he didn't hear over the distance and with the roar of the helicopter behind me. When I started across the grass to convince B to come along, the polo escorting me seized my elbow with surprising strength and pointed to the helicopter. I had to pry their fingers from my arm and then sprint over the grass, up the bank, and across the gravel drive.

B was muttering when I caught up with him.

"No, I am not getting in that vehicle," he shouted. "I'd rather die by choice than live without one. Cocksuckers! I ain't a goddamned dog."

Something on the wind tickled his nose, and he sneezed twice.

"Goddamn." He wiped his nose and mouth on the bathrobe's sleeve.

Ming's personnel scurried from her castle toward the half dozen SUVs, now parked by the gate. Several of the polos stopped halfway between us and the vehicles and gestured emphatically at the sky over the ocean, where the contrails of two long-since passed jets expanded in puffs of white fringed with lavender.

"Chemtrails," shouted B.

"Chemtrails," they shouted back.

"It's just water vapor," I said.

"You all saying that because the media's covering it up!" B shouted.

"Media," shouted the polos. "Media, media."

B stared at them with wonder and confusion, as if they'd started singing a lullaby that his own mother had made up to hush him to sleep as a child.

"WHO ARE YOU PEOPLE?" he screamed. "You believe anything you say? You think you're special 'cause you wear stupid polos? Y'all look like Crayons from the reject box. What color is that—puce? The hell is puce? Y'all sheepil. I know you ain't no different, you just *think* you think different. Y'all think some law of nature or man has changed so's you can be who you think you are."

He seemed to get lost in the syntax and rather than figure it out, turned and limp-marched uphill toward the forest. He still had the rocks glass half-filled with bourbon, and the ice cubes clacked merrily as he hustled it over the stubble toward the tree line. I followed and called at him to stop, ducking instinctively at a volley of gunfire.

Glancing back, I saw polos waving urgently to me.

B turned and planted his slippered feet in the mineral dust.

"Y'all won't listen but I'm going to say my piece!" he bellowed.

A dozen polos formed a line and took tentative steps toward us.

B rubbed his forehead with the back of his hand. When I caught up to him he jabbed a finger at my chest.

"What was that blue shit?"

"Mostly water," I told him.

He finished the bourbon in one long gulp and hurled the rocks glass toward the polos, who scattered under the arcs of ice cubes. The SUVs raced across the hillside. Smoke billowed overhead. Ash like paper snow wobbled on the breeze. The polos reformed a cordon and resumed their advance. Behind them, Ming's helicopter rose and tilted toward the ocean. I reached out my hand, as if to bring it back. It disappeared to the southwest.

With no other escape, we turned inland and entered a forest of black trunks, rows of TEDs, taller and more mature than the one we'd been shown, their branches touching overhead to shield us from the smoke.

B whirled on me.

"You might understand you need me and anyways I'm here by my own choices leastwise, but you no different than those people down there. You never stopped looking down on me and the boys. We were just comedy that made you feel better about yourself. Oh, I can laugh at those dumb people 'cause at least I'm not them. Now with the finger on Davis you probably feel justified. All this time you just slummin' it with us 'cause you can't figure out your own life."

I concentrated on the muscles of my face so as not to show that he'd hurt me. The boys had been like nephews, at least before Dag had pulled the curtain back on Davis, and still I felt a sort of filial responsibility for Davis's hair-curling opinions, whatever they were. As for B, he'd become my only friend.

"We get caught up in our stories and it's confusing," I lamented.

"Yeah I get that but all that running and hiding—and man I broke my damn foot in twelve places—and you end us up here? Where exactly one person is free?" He raised his fists over his head. "WE WANT OUR FREEDOM FOR THE WORLD!" he shouted.

"Thank you for coming with me," I said.

This mollified B and the feeling confused him and he snatched up clods of dirt to huck toward the line of polos still advancing up the grade. They'd discarded their foam shields for some reason and raised their hands over their heads to fend off the falling dirt. It wasn't clear what they wanted with us. The tactical units had sped away, the polos in SUVs behind them; Ming's helicopter beat southward over the ocean.

B yelled between flurries of dirt.

"And you people, what are you doing? You been left here. In a forest fire. By your boss. Y'all firefighters? Those polos spray water when they smell smoke? Y'all are the worst. I guess you did all your thinking getting where you are now. And this must be where you really want to be. Left in a forest fire by a lady got a island of Legos or some shit. How many of you add up to one rocket ship to the moon? Are you lizard people?"

He shook his arms as he yelled, appealing to the sky beyond the fake limbs.

The polos were near enough that I could see the customer service smiles stuck to their faces. Several of them had sweated dark patches from their armpits and bellies. They glanced furtively around. "Lizard, lizard," they said.

"You all stop doing what you're doing, man, this whole joke will collapse like a tent with cut poles. You believe that techno-future crap?

Well this is it, right here. You walking into a forest fire wearing a fancy shirt for a lady don't know your names to do something you don't understand because it don't make no sense. Anything y'all've done, you did it for a few bucks. Maybe you got looked up to by someone, ooo, you're working for Ming! Here I am following you around, oh oh!"

He danced a little one-foot jig and stirred up the dirt until the knot in the bathrobe's belt loosened and the robe fell open, showing his hairy belly hanging over the waistband of his boxers.

"Do you drink that shit she hands out?"

He turned to me as he asked this, and I recalled my headache evaporating and Ming floating into my arms in her U-Verse.

More of the polos had fallen behind, but an ardent few soldiered up the slope under B's spittle and sporadic volleys of dirt. I backed into the TEDs, intending to run. The polos looked knackered, and I figured they would tire before me. But B couldn't run.

"WE WANT OUR FREEDOM FOR THE WORLD!" B hollered again. He swelled with breath, arms raised like Moses on the Mount.

The last few polos stopped and cowered.

B worked his lips.

I called him, softly, then tugged at his sleeve.

He turned, hopping on his good foot, then cinched his bathrobe closed, stuck his chin in the air, and limped into the TEDs beside me.

32

With the fire to our northeast, we tacked south and up a steep slope where the TEDs were shorter and fewer. B cursed his slippers, which came off with every uphill step and forced him to shuffle and claw through the dirt. I saw a gap in the canopy and headed for it, then stopped when I heard voices. We crouched behind the trunks of TEDs, watching for polos. When I brushed a TED with my shoulder, a mechanical voice warned me to *STAY CLEAR*.

The crunch of footsteps came from behind us. I turned, expecting polos, but instead saw the man from the purple pickup who'd given us a ride, alongside the waitress from the restaurant. They climbed straight past us to a clearing.

As B and I huddled, uncertain what to do, a distant explosion shook the ground. It echoed in the canyons, followed by cracks and shudders, as of large blocks breaking off and hitting the earth.

My every decision had led us into this chaos. Like the polos, I'd chosen to run toward a forest fire after a man in a bathrobe. B was of the opinion that additional running and hiding were no longer profitable, and that finding shelter, food, and other support was indicated, and since there were no motels or restaurants in the forest and we were out of money anyway, we would be reliant on others, at least for the short-term, and the waitress and the man from the purple pickup had already demonstrated their generosity. I hesitated, paralyzed by guilt, nearly panicking, but B was done listening to me, and before I could come up with a reasonable excuse, he shuffled up the slope. I scrambled to catch up with him.

The man and woman started when we emerged from the TEDs

to a chorus of *STAY CLEAR*. They stared unabashed at us, B in the plush bathrobe cinched tightly around his girth, me with my shirt torn and dotted with blood. Dirt filled our every pore and stitch. My legs and back were sore from days of driving, the night's restless sleep on the ledge, the morning's climb, and I leaned over to steady myself as I slipped in the loose grit of the steep, packed dirt. B edged up the hillside sideways, leaning on his cane so as not to fall out of his slippers.

"You got yourself a bathrobe," said the waitress to B as he collapsed on a boulder next to her. "Bathrobe Boy!"

"You can call him painter," said B as I joined them.

Theirs names were Cruz and Erin.

From the knoll we had a clear view of the fire, several miles away, swirling like a cauldron as the wind shifted.

"What was that explosion?" I asked.

"Bridge," said Cruz.

"Don't know what else it could have been," said Erin.

I asked if they knew what was going on below.

"National Guard closed the highway," said Erin.

"Shooting," said Cruz. He mimed a rifle with his hands.

"What's south of here?"

Landslides, Erin told me. Even the roads across the mountains were shut.

"We're an island," she said. "It's okay, we're used to it. It happens most winters."

I heard movement below, and three others emerged from the TEDs to scramble up the hillside toward us.

"It's the Steves!" said Erin. "And Marcelle!"

Two trim middle-aged men and an older woman in gardening gloves and a wide-brimmed hat joined us among the boulders. One of the men slipped a rifle from his shoulder and leaned it against a rock.

"Only one of them is really named Steve," Erin whispered to me.

The five of them shared bits of news and gossip. It was the long bridge a dozen miles north, dynamited. The National Guard was on the other side of the bridge for now; they'd closed the highway just south of town. The inns and restaurants had been pillaged, likely by locals, who were now spread out in the forest or at properties high on the ridges.

"What do we do?" I asked, but no one answered.

A snarling in the air to the west caught our attention. It was a drone hovering fifty or so yards away.

B gestured to the Steve with the rifle. "That shoot true?"

The man nodded tentatively. "Like hitting a fly in a windstorm," he said, but handed B the rifle and a box of rounds.

B's first shot missed as the drone bounced in the renewed wind off the fog. A long brass casing sprung from the chamber with a little gasp of smoke. High overhead two military jets streaked like filaments, trailing thunder. The rifle cracked again, and this time the drone listed to one side and buzzed erratically before slashing into the treetops.

Everyone cheered.

"Boy can shoot."

"What can you do?" Erin asked me.

"Paint," I said. "And get around Manhattan. Not much else."

Marcelle stood and adjusted her gloves. She said something in French and the Steves said goodbye and followed her into the TEDs.

We listened to spats of gunfire. The wind shifted, frigid off the water, pushing the smoke northeast away from us. The air turned silver with western light.

"Where do we go?" I asked.

"We have a few shacks," said Erin.

She and Cruz led us into the TEDs.

"The first fakes they planted made the fires worse," she said.

Cruz nodded.

"They made too much oxygen is how Steve put it. That's why they made the foggers."

"Safe," said Cruz, pointing at the soil beneath his feet. "Nothing grows."

"You all live here in the fakes?" asked B.

I glimpsed shadows in the distance, people moving among the TEDs.

"Nothing lives here," said Erin. "Not even mushrooms. Birds can't nest because the bark makes them sick. They spread underground, the fakes I mean, and kill the oaks and bays and redwoods. But they don't burn. They even eat the smoke."

We came to a small clearing with a black structure in its middle.

"Take off the leaves," said Cruz, "and they fall down."

It was a cabin of felled TEDs. Inside was a single room draped in harlequin fabrics, patterned in reds and oranges and swirled purple paisley. The underside of the corrugated steel roof was painted with uneven strokes of blue.

Cruz had continued on, leaving us with Erin.

"Is this Ming's land?" I asked her.

"Some people think she started the fire to make the fakes look good, so she could take all the forest. We made these huts for fun. You know, bring some life back to the fakes. Then some people moved into them. The Steves and some others, they been here for a while. Unless you're rich, it's too expensive to live around here."

B and I sat on the rough black floor as Erin served us a cold cucumber-and-squash soup from glass jars she pulled from a cooler that doubled as the cabin's table.

I slurped it down in a minute and curled up against the wall like a dog and slept.

33

I awoke to bars of light bright between the fake logs. Erin was cleaning our mugs, singing to herself.

"Bathrobe Boy went down to the creek for water," she said.

I sat in the hut's doorway and wondered about my brother. I doubted a bullet could penetrate his shell. He was like the fire, consuming all around. He would survive all this somehow and return to his life unaltered.

B limped up the path, sloshing water in a pail. He wore new white sneakers with no socks.

"Met some people. Lady gave me these treads." He lifted one foot to show off the white tennis shoe.

We ate dry cereal and drank water from the bucket. Afterwards Erin walked into the TEDs with a roll of toilet paper, whistling.

"We need a plan," I said.

We slouched on the cabin's threshold like boys with our knees up by our chins.

B said nothing.

"I'm scared," I admitted.

"You ever not been scared?" he asked.

I stood up and paced. It didn't help the anxiety. How would this ever work? My feet started walking away from the hut, down the canyon, all the way to the highway, to find Dag. He would tell me what to do.

"Where you goin'?" asked B.

I kicked at the duff of shorn TED leaves. Nowhere, I thought, like always.

"I thought I might—build a Pig," I said.

B snorted as if I'd said something funny.

"You are a glutton, ain't you?" he said.

I headed for the hilltop where we'd met Erin and Cruz. Its north-facing slope was free of trees and brush. A few redwood limbs lay at the edge of the clearing, and I pulled them into the form of a neat porcine chin. Two smaller boulders needed only a short roll to make the eyes; I painted black pupils with charcoal from an old campfire.

B leaned over his cane and watched. People streamed up the slope from the canyon, arriving in pairs and small groups. A couple with three towheaded children, four middle-aged men in work pants, a stoop-shouldered woman with gray hair, arm-in-arm with another woman who looked to be her daughter.

B introduced himself as they passed.

"I'm Bertrand," he said, "but you can call me B."

Kyle, Bob, Hillary, Jim, Jacob; Tito, Ruben, Clara, Sasha; Tyler, a trio of Michaels, Mathew, two Melissas, Janelle; Pamela and Craig; Elizabeth, Carolyn, Dennis. As they passed, they asked what I was doing. A few stopped to watch. Two women gathered rocks and tree limbs and pinecones and filled out the Pig's ears and snout, its grin. Children in two groups, shepherded by three women, swept over the Pig like a wave, leaving a sediment of rocks behind. Jean, Laura, Charles, Ben; B greeted them all. They laughed and argued as they built the Pig. A couple aglow with youth drifted up the hillside as if on a cloud, holding a swaddled infant. Maggie, Sarah, Roger, Logan, Tom. Phil and Tawny. Mark and Marc. A man in overalls with sagging jowls helped me drag a heavy limb onto the Pig's jawline. Rene, Mateo, Francisco. Children with the names of birds and explorers. Biblical names, unpronounceable names. Andrei, Heather, Michelle, Alan. Tara and Tracy, Emily and Emil. Jack and Jacque.

Throughout, two people stopped short of B and hovered at the edge of the clearing, a couple in later middle-age. Afterwards, back by the shacks, I asked Erin about them. She didn't know them personally, she told me, but had heard rumors that their son was down on the highway. Whether he'd joined the crazies or been captured by them wasn't clear. When the couple went to find out, they were hounded into the hills.

/ / /

In the afternoon, we carried water and gathered broken branches from the TEDs and made a mud of the clay soil to plaster the chinks between the logs of the cabin's walls. With my muddied hand, I left a single ochre handprint on the black wall.

We weeded ramshackle gardens by a stream. We pushed over TEDs from which all the leaves had been plucked—*STAY CLEAR*—and broke off the limbs with a sledgehammer. The logs we rolled into a clearing to stack into new cabins.

We cleaned ourselves in a pool formed by a ring of rocks in a bend of the creek and ate stale bread and cheese. Afterwards we lounged under redwoods beyond the edge of the fake forest. A woman named Ruby saw my tattered shirt, which I'd attempted to wash in the creek, and offered to patch it together into a new one. I handed her the stained, ripped button-down along with the flags I'd stolen from the Navigator, figuring she might need more fabric, and what good were they anyway.

I sat shirtless while B shared a cigarette with Cruz. We laughed as three school-age children—Phoenix, Layla, Jasper—did cartwheels and shoved each other and chased through the trees. In the early evening, as people began climbing back up to the boulders, Ruby returned with a new shirt for me. It had no sleeves to speak of, but she'd somehow patterned the two flags into a snug-fitting tank top, using strips from my white shirt along with pieces of faded denim. The front showed off my glorious Pig in a kaleidoscopic red, white, and blue. The snake flag she'd turned on end for the shirt's back, so that the snake sat coiled on its tail with its head aimed skyward like one of Ming's rockets. She accepted a hug in return.

Together with Erin and Cruz, we climbed to the boulders.

The wildfire still burned, but its smoke had tempered and no longer choked the sky to the east. To the west the ocean spread like a corduroy sheet, the fog a pillow on the horizon. Two dozen people gathered around a pair of campfires. Occasional gunshots popped in the distance.

We passed around roasted tomatoes and some sort of savory crepe or chewy tortilla that two women toasted on a cast-iron pan. Where would flour come from, or iron, or the wine that made its way hand-by-hand around the fire?

As the sky darkened, a brilliant peach blossomed over the ocean, striking a mathematical arc into the heavens. Ming, in her rocket.

"Good riddance," said someone.

Marcelle said something in French and the Steves laughed.

I felt an ache in my chest, watching the rocket carve into the sky.

"I could be with her," I said.

"You knew Ming?" asked Erin, incredulous.

"She kissed like a lizard."

"Where's she going?"

"To the moon."

"She'll be back. She's gonna need people for things."

I watched the curve of peach as it faded to gray and began to loosen and drift. A fishing boat bobbed on the swell below it like a cork in a vast basin, lit by a point of light on its deck. All that ocean, one little boat.

None of it seemed real: the rocket, the endless ocean, the community building around the fires, the voices, the Pigs, party dudes with guns. Maybe they were all parts of me, flotsam on my ocean of self. If I imagined the entirety of my being filling the ocean basin, was my ego like that boat, tiny, bobbing cork-like?

A long silence, peppered by gunshots. B had his bath-robed arm around a woman I'd not seen arrive.

"We brought venison sausage and flatbread," said Steve.

"I got goat cheese."

"Stole a case of wine from the cellar. Don't tell."

"Anyone down there?"

"Kitchen door was off its hinges. Pillow feathers all over the parking lot."

"I hear they broke the gates on the ridge roads."

"Yeah, they're about everywhere you could get to on four tires. Everyone's out in the woods like us."

"What do they want?"

"They're all stuck here."

"I bet they're drinking John's whiskey stash."

"I don't care what kind of lock he put on that cellar."

"We're gonna need more tools, even if it's just a for a while."

"We could get Mahoney's tractor and drive it up that dirt road on the ridge. Take about five hours and twenty gallons of diesel."

"No, I don't know plant medicine. I only know the kind they sell at the pharmacy. I brought what I could. Delia brought what she could."

"Least we can do is get his four-by-four and use it to bring some tools. He's got landscaping tools, stonework, construction, you name it."

"The Texaco by the river. We filled every can we could find when we saw that caravan come through."

"The creek's fine to drink. The Forest Service tested it a few years back."

"It's in my genes, is what I mean."

"Said it was fine. Better than fine."

"Not just your genes."

"No not just mine. I didn't mean that."

"Paulson said he shot at a boar up that canyon."

"Yeah they're still up here. Might have to fence the garden somehow."

"I guess it depends how long we live like this."

"It ran away, never saw it again."

"You'd think they'd get bored."

"Or run out of ammunition. They're already siphoning gas."

B and his lady giggled by the fire. The evening star blazed over the horizon.

Steve pointed to the north. Small fires like beacons dotted a line along the ridge. Our new Pig winked back at them.

The sad-looking couple who'd lost their son to the highway caravans loitered at the edge of the fires' warmth.

"I'm wanted," I told Erin. "I punched a politician. Painted graffiti all over. Harbored an arsonist."

"Arson is spicy," she said.

"She burned a big dollar sign."

"Right on."

"We came looking for Ming, but I didn't—" I stopped and swallowed. "I think what's going on down there, all those people, I think they followed me here. I think this is my fault."

In the fire, sausages spit juniper and grease. A long moment passed when the only sounds were the wind rubbing over our shoulders and the fires snapping.

"Something had to happen," said one of the men.

"It was bound to happen."

"It was always happening."

A rat-a-tat burst of gunfire, then a response. A siren quailed feebly.

"Where were you going anyway?" asked a voice.

"New universes. The moon."

"We got all this," said Erin, lifting her arms to the winking stars.

"This is hard," I said.

Everyone laughed.

"We don't know how hard it really is yet."

"I remember mama's stories. They lived a lot like this."

"And they were drunk half the time."

More laughter.

"I never seen a place like this," said B.

"It calls to people who keep going until they run out of land," said the other Steve.

He cut the cooked sausage with a hunting knife and passed around the cutting board with the sausage wiggling in its purpled juices. I took a piece as it passed my way. Rosemary, juniper, gamey and sinus filling. I wanted to take more, but I'd brought nothing.

B had thought ahead. From the pockets of his robe he pulled the mangled branches he'd taken from the hilltop farm, heavy with flower. Erin squealed when she saw it. We pressed closer in the cooling air.

"Many of these women are painters," said Erin.

I wanted to paint more than to eat, but where would paint and canvas come from, I wondered.

"Who would buy the paintings?"

"Is that why you paint?" she asked.

Why did I paint?

Somewhere among the white dots in the encompassing black

floated Ming's capsule, weightless and cold as a ghost. The campfire softened to embers, voices low. The mountains lightless silhouettes against the sky. My brother quiet below.

"People don't realize that we choose what is," said Erin.

"Choice is all we have," I agreed, generations of belief in five words.

The couple with the lost son still stood off by themselves. I waved to them, then to the flat rocks around me: come, sit, warm yourself. They hesitated, then joined us.

"I think we have something in common," I said to them.

They watched me from sealed faces, uncomprehending.

"My brother is down there, on the highway," I explained. "I understand you've lost someone there, too?"

They looked at each other.

"Sorry," said the woman. "English no so good."

Embarrassed, I reached my hands out to them. The woman looked at my hand as if it were a tool she didn't recognize, then took it firmly in hers. The man took my left hand with his left hand, a grip both familiar and odd.

I heard B whistle, then snicker. A woman sang softly in Spanish, joined by another. Between breaths of wind, the far-off hush of surf.

"Me llamo María," said the woman.

"José," said the man.

I gripped their hands, so as not to float into the dark.

"I'm John Taggart Galt."